MARK TWAIN was born Samuel Langhorne Clemens in Florida, Missouri, in 1835, and died at Redding, Connecticut, in 1910. In his person and in his pursuits he was a man of extraordinary contrasts. Although he left school at twelve when his father died, he was eventually awarded honorary degrees from Yale University, the University of Missouri, and Oxford University. His career encompassed such varied occupations as printer, Mississippi riverboat pilot, journalist, travel writer, and publisher. He made fortunes from his writing but toward the end of his life he had to resort to lecture tours to pay his debts. He was hot-tempered, profane, and sentimental—and also pessimistic, cynical, and tortured by self-doubt. His nostalgia for the past helped produce some of his best books. He lives in American letters as a great artist, the writer whom William Dean Howells called "the Lincoln of our literature."

MARK TWAIN

THE PRINCE AND THE PAUPER

A Tale for Young People of All Ages

With an Afterword by
Kenneth S. Lynn

REVISED AND UPDATED BIBLIOGRAPHY

A SIGNET CLASSIC

SIGNET CLASSIC
Published by the Penguin Group
Penguin Books USA Inc., 375 Hudson Street,
New York, New York 10014, U.S.A.
Penguin Books Ltd, 27 Wrights Lane,
London W8 5TZ, England
Penguin Books Australia Ltd, Ringwood,
Victoria, Australia
Penguin Books Canada Ltd, 10 Alcorn Avenue,
Toronto, Ontario, Canada M4V 3B2
Penguin Books (N.Z.) Ltd, 182–190 Wairau Road,
Auckland 10, New Zealand

Penguin Books Ltd, Registered Offices:
Harmondsworth, Middlesex, England

Published by Signet Classic, an imprint of Dutton Signet,
a division of Penguin Books USA Inc.
A hardcover edition of the text is published by
Harper & Row, Publishers, Inc.

First Signet Classic Printing, May, 1964
40 39 38 37 36 35 34 33

𝒸 REGISTERED TRADEMARK—MARCA REGISTRADA

Printed in the United States of America

To
those good-mannered and agreeable children
Susie and Clara Clemens
this book
is affectionately inscribed
by their father.

The quality of mercy . . .
                     is twice bless'd;
It blesseth him that gives, and him that takes;
'Tis mightiest in the mightiest; it becomes
The thronèd monarch better than his crown.

Merchant of Venice

HUGH LATIMER, *Bishop of Worcester, to* LORD CROMWELL, *on the birth of the* PRINCE OF WALES *(afterward* EDWARD VI)

FROM THE NATIONAL MANUSCRIPTS PRESERVED BY
THE BRITISH GOVERNMENT

Ryght honorable, *Salutem in Christo Jesu,* and Syr here ys no lesse joynge and rejossynge in thes partees for the byrth of our prynce, hoom we hungurde for so longe, then ther was (I trow), *inter vicinos* att the byrth of S. I. Baptyste, as thys berer, Master Erance, can telle you. Gode gyffe us alle grace, to yelde dew thankes to our Lorde Gode, Gode of Inglonde, for verely He hathe shoyd Hym selff Gode of Inglonde, or rather an Inglyssh Gode, yf we consydyr and pondyr welle alle Hys procedynges with us from tyme to tyme. He hath overcumme alle our yllnesse with Hys excedynge goodnesse, so that we ar now moor then compellyd to serve Hym, seke Hys glory, promott Hys wurde, yf the Devylle of alle Devylles be natt in us. We have now the stooppe of vayne trustes ande the stey of vayne expectations; lett us alle pray for hys preservatione. Ande I for my partt wylle wyssh that hys Grace allways have, and evyn now from the begynynge, Governares, Instructores and offyceres of ryght jugmente, *ne optimum ingenium non optimâ educatione depravetur.*

Butt whatt a grett fowlle am I! So, whatt devotione shoyth many tymys butt lytelle dyscretione! Ande thus the Gode of Inglonde be ever with you in alle your procedynges.

The 19 of October.

Youres, H.L.B. of Wurcestere, now att Hartlebury.

Yf you wolde excytt thys berere to be moore hartye ayen the abuse of ymagry or mor forwarde to promote the veryte, ytt myght doo goode. Natt that ytt came of me, butt of your selffe, &c.

(*Addressed*) To the Ryght Honorable Loorde P. Sealle hys synguler gode Lorde.

Contents

Preface

I will set down a tale as it was told to me by one who had it of his father, which latter had it of *his* father, this last having in like manner had it of *his* father, and so on, back and still back, three hundred years and more, the fathers transmitting it to the sons and so preserving it. It may be history, it may be only a legend, a tradition. It may have happened, it may not have happened; but it *could* have happened. It may be that the wise and the learned believed it in the old days; it may be that only the unlearned and the simple loved it and credited it.

FROM THE NATIONAL MANUSCRIPTS PRESERVED BY THE BRITISH GOVERNMENT

1

The Birth of the Prince and the Pauper

In the ancient city of London, on a certain autumn day in the second quarter of the sixteenth century, a boy was born to a poor family of the name of Canty, who did not want him. On the same day another English child was born to a rich family of the name of Tudor, who did want him. All England wanted him too. England had so longed for him, and hoped for him, and prayed God for him that now that he was really come, the people went nearly mad for joy. Mere acquaintances hugged and kissed each other and cried. Everybody took a holiday, and high and low, rich and poor, feasted and danced and sang, and got very mellow; and they kept this up for days and nights together. By day London was a sight to see, with gay banners waving from every balcony and housetop and splendid pageants marching along. By night it was again a sight to see, with its great bonfires at every corner and its troops of revelers making merry around them. There was no talk in all of England but of the new baby, Edward Tudor, Prince of Wales, who lay lapped in silks and satins, unconscious of all this fuss, and not knowing that great lords and ladies were tending him and watching over him—and not caring either. But there was no talk about the other baby, Tom Canty, lapped in his poor rags, except among the family of paupers whom he had just come to trouble with his presence.

Tom's Early Life

Let us skip a number of years.

London was fifteen hundred years old, and was a great town—for that day. It had a hundred thousand inhabitants—some think double as many. The streets were very narrow, and crooked, and dirty, especially in that part where Tom Canty lived, which was not far from London Bridge. The houses were of wood, with the second story projecting over the first, and the third sticking its elbows out beyond the second. The higher the houses grew, the broader they grew. They were skeletons of strong crisscross beams, with solid material between coated with plaster. The beams were painted red or blue or black, according to the owner's taste, and this gave the houses a very picturesque look. The windows were small, glazed with little diamond-shaped panes, and they opened outward on hinges like doors.

The house which Tom's father lived in was up a foul little pocket called Offal Court, out of Pudding Lane. It was small, decayed, and rickety, but it was packed full of wretchedly poor families. Canty's tribe occupied a room on the third floor. The mother and father had a sort of bedstead in the corner; but Tom, his grandmother, and his two sisters, Bet and Nan, were not restricted—they had all the floor to themselves and might sleep where they chose. There were the remains of a blanket or two and some bundles of ancient and dirty straw, but these could not rightly be called beds, for they were not organized; they were kicked into a general pile mornings, and selections made from the mass at night for service.

Bet and Nan were fifteen years old—twins. They were goodhearted girls, unclean, clothed in rags, and profoundly ignorant. Their mother was like them. But the father and the grandmother were a couple of fiends. They got drunk whenever they could; then they fought each other or any-body else who came in the way; they cursed and swore always, drunk or sober; John Canty was a thief, and his mother a beggar. They made beggars of the children but failed to make thieves of them. Among, but not of, the dreadful rabble that inhabited the house was a good old priest whom the king had turned out of house and home with a pension of a few farthings, and he used to get the children aside and teach them right ways secretly. Father Andrew also taught Tom a little Latin and how to read and write, and would have done the same with the girls, but they were afraid of the jeers of their friends, who could not have endured such a queer accomplishment in them.

All Offal Court was just such another hive as Canty's house. Drunkenness, riot, and brawling were the order there every night and nearly all night long. Broken heads were as common as hunger in that place. Yet little Tom was not unhappy. He had a hard time of it, but did not know it. It was the sort of time that all of the Offal Court boys had; therefore he supposed it was the correct and comfortable thing. When he came home empty-handed at night, he knew his father would curse him and thrash him first, and that when he was done the awful grandmother would do it all over again and improve on it, and that away in the night his starving mother would slip to him stealthily with any mis-erable scrap or crust she had been able to save for him by going hungry herself, notwithstanding she was often caught in that sort of treason and soundly beaten for it by her hus-band.

No, Tom's life went along well enough, especially in summer. He only begged just enough to save himself, for the laws against mendicancy were stringent and the penal-ties heavy; so he put in a good deal of his time listening to good Father Andrew's charming old tales and legends about giants and fairies, dwarfs and genii, and enchanted castles, and gorgeous kings and princes. His head grew to be full of these wonderful things, and many a night as he lay in the dark on his scant and offensive straw, tired, hungry, and smarting from a thrashing, he unleashed his imagination and soon forgot his aches and pains in delicious picturings to himself of the charmed life of a petted prince in a regal palace. One desire came in time to haunt him day and night:

it was to see a real prince, with his own eyes. He spoke of it once to some of his Offal Court comrades, but they jeered him and scoffed him so unmercifully that he was glad to keep his dream to himself after that.

He often read the priest's old books and got him to explain and enlarge upon them. His dreamings and readings worked certain changes in him by and by. His dream people were so fine that he grew to lament his shabby clothing and his dirt and to wish to be clean and better clad. He went on playing in the mud just the same, and enjoying it too; but instead of splashing around in the Thames solely for the fun of it, he began to find an added value in it because of the washings and cleansings it afforded.

Tom could always find something going on around the Maypole in Cheapside and at the fairs; and now and then he and the rest of London had a chance to see a military parade when some famous unfortunate was carried prisoner to the Tower by land or boat. One summer's day he saw poor Anne Askew and three men burned at the stake in Smithfield and heard an ex-bishop preach a sermon to them which did not interest him. Yes, Tom's life was varied and pleasant enough on the whole.

By and by Tom's reading and dreaming about princely life wrought such a strong effect upon him that he began to *act* the prince, unconsciously. His speech and manners became curiously ceremonious and courtly, to the vast admiration and amusement of his intimates. But Tom's influence among these young people began to grow now day by day, and in time he came to be looked up to by them, with a sort of wondering awe, as a superior being. He seemed to know so much! And he could do and say such marvelous things! And withal, he was so deep and wise! Tom's remarks and Tom's performances were reported by the boys to their elders; and these also presently began to discuss Tom Canty and to regard him as a most gifted and extraordinary creature. Full-grown people brought their perplexities to Tom for solution and were often astonished at the wit and wisdom of his decisions. In fact he was become a hero to all who knew him except his own family—these only saw nothing in him.

Privately, after a while, Tom organized a royal court! He was the prince; his special comrades were guards, chamberlains, equerries, lords- and ladies-in-waiting, and the royal family. Daily the mock prince was received with elaborate ceremonials borrowed by Tom from his romantic readings; daily the great affairs of the mimic kingdom were discussed in the royal council; and daily his mimic highness issued decrees to his imaginary armies, navies, and viceroyalties.

After which, he would go forth in his rags and beg a few farthings, eat his poor crust, take his customary cuffs and abuse, and then stretch himself upon his handful of foul straw and resume his empty grandeurs in his dreams.

And still his desire to look just once upon a real prince in the flesh grew upon him, day by day, and week by week, until at last it absorbed all other desires and became the one passion of his life.

One January day, on his usual begging tour, he tramped despondently up and down the region round about Mincing Lane and Little East Cheap, hour after hour, barefooted and cold, looking in at cookshop windows and longing for the dreadful pork pies and other deadly inventions displayed there; for to him these were dainties fit for the angels; that is, judging by the smell they were, for it had never been his good luck to own and eat one. There was a cold drizzle of rain; the atmosphere was murky; it was a melancholy day. At night Tom reached home so wet and tired and hungry that it was not possible for his father and grandmother to observe his forlorn condition and not be moved—after their fashion; wherefore they gave him a brisk cuffing at once and sent him to bed. For a long time his pain and hunger and the swearing and fighting going on in the building kept him awake; but at last his thoughts drifted away to far, romantic lands, and he fell asleep in the company of jeweled and gilded princelings who lived in vast palaces and had servants salaaming before them or fiying to execute their orders. And then as usual, he dreamed that *he* was a princeling himself.

All night long the glories of his royal estate shone upon him: he moved among great lords and ladies in a blaze of light, breathing perfumes, drinking in delicious music, and answering the reverent obeisances of the glittering throng as it parted to make way for him, with here a smile and there a nod of his princely head.

And when he awoke in the morning and looked upon

the wretchedness about him, his dream had had its usual effect: it had intensified the sordidness of his surroundings a thousandfold. Then came bitterness, and heartbreak, and tears.

3

Tom's Meeting with the Prince

Tom got up hungry, and sauntered hungry away, but with his thoughts busy with the shadowy splendors of his night's dreams. He wandered here and there in the city, hardly noticing where he was going or what was happening around him. People jostled him, and some gave him rough speech; but it was all lost on the musing boy. By and by he found himself at Temple Bar, the farthest from home he had ever traveled in that direction. He stopped and considered a moment, then fell into his imaginings again, and passed on outside the walls of London. The Strand had ceased to be a country road then and regarded itself as a street, but by a strained construction; for though there was a tolerably compact row of houses on one side of it, there were only some scattering great buildings on the other, these being palaces of rich nobles, with ample and beautiful grounds stretching to the river—grounds that are now closely packed with grim acres of brick and stone.

Tom discovered Charing Village presently and rested himself at the beautiful cross built there by a bereaved king of earlier days; then idled down a quiet, lovely road past the great cardinal's stately palace, toward a far more mighty and majestic palace beyond—Westminster. Tom stared in glad wonder at the vast pile of masonry, the wide-spreading wings, the frowning bastions and turrets, the huge stone gateway, with its gilded bars and its magnificent array of colossal granite lions, and the other signs and symbols of English royalty. Was the desire of his soul to be satisfied at last? Here indeed was a king's palace. Might he not hope to see a prince now, a prince of flesh and blood, if heaven were willing?

At each side of the gilded gate stood a living statue, that is to say, an erect and stately and motionless man-at-arms clad from head to heel in shining steel armor. At a respect-

ful distance were many country folk and people from the
city waiting for any chance glimpse of royalty that might
offer. Splendid carriages with splendid people in them and
splendid servants outside were arriving and departing by
several other noble gateways that pierced the royal enclo-
sure.

Poor little Tom, in his rags, approached and was moving
slow and timidly past the sentinels, with a beating heart and
a rising hope, when all at once he caught sight through the
golden bars of a spectacle that almost made him shout for
joy. Within was a comely boy, tanned and brown with sturdy
outdoor sports and exercises, whose clothing was all of
lovely silks and satins, shining with jewels—at his hip a
little jeweled sword and dagger, dainty buskins on his feet,
with red heels, and on his head a jaunty crimson cap with
drooping plumes fastened with a great sparkling gem. Several gorgeous gentlemen stood near—his servants, without
a doubt. Oh! He was a prince—a prince, a living prince, a
real prince—without the shadow of a question; and the
prayer of the pauper-boy's heart was answered at last.

Tom's breath came quick and short with excitement, and
his eyes grew big with wonder and delight. Everything gave
way in his mind instantly to one desire: that was to get close
to the prince and have a good, devouring look at him. Before he knew what he was about, he had his face against the
gate bars. The next instant one of the soldiers snatched him
rudely away and sent him spinning among the gaping crowd
of country gawks and London idlers.

The soldier said, "Mind thy manners, thou young beggar!"

The crowd jeered and laughed, but the young prince
sprang to the gate with his face flushed and his eyes flashing
with indignation and cried out, "How darst thou use a poor
lad like that! How darst thou use the king my father's meanest subject so! Open the gates and let him in!"

You should have seen that fickle crowd snatch off their
hats then. You should have heard them cheer and shout,
"Long live the Prince of Wales!"

The soldiers presented arms with their halberds, opened
the gates, and presented again as the little Prince of Poverty
passed in, in his fluttering rags, to join hands with the Prince
of Limitless Plenty.

Edward Tudor said, "Thou lookest tired and hungry: thou'st been treated ill. Come with me."

Half a dozen attendants sprang forward to—I don't know what; interfere, no doubt. But they were waved aside with a right royal gesture, and they stopped stock-still where they were, like so many statues. Edward took Tom to a rich apartment in the palace, which he called his cabinet. By his command a repast was brought such as Tom had never encountered before except in books. The prince, with princely delicacy and breeding, sent away the servants so that his humble guest might not be embarrassed by their critical presence; then he sat nearby and asked questions while Tom ate.

"What is thy name, lad?"

"Tom Canty, an' it please thee, sir."

" 'Tis an odd one. Where dost live?"

"In the city, please thee, sir. Offal Court, out of Pudding Lane."

"Offal Court! Truly 'tis another odd one. Hast parents?"

"Parents have I, sir, and a grandam likewise that is but indifferently precious to me—God forgive me if it be offense to say it—also twin sisters, Nan and Bet."

"Then is thy grandam not over kind to thee, I take it."

"Neither to any other is she, so please your Worship. She hath a wicked heart and worketh evil all her days."

"Doth she mistreat thee?"

"There be times that she stayeth her hand, being asleep or overcome with drink; but when she hath her judgment clear again, she maketh it up to me with goodly beatings."

A fierce look came into the little prince's eyes, and he cried out, "What! Beatings?"

"Oh, indeed, yes, please you, sir."

"*Beatings!* And thou so frail and little. Hark ye; before the night come she shall hie her to the Tower. The king my father—"

"In sooth, you forget, sir, her low degree. The Tower is for the great alone."

"True, indeed. I had not thought of that. I will consider of her punishment. Is thy father kind to thee?"

"Not more than Gammer Canty, sir."

"Fathers be alike, mayhap. Mine hath not a doll's temper. He smiteth with a heavy hand, yet spareth me; he spareth me not always with his tongue, though, sooth to say. How doth thy mother use thee?"

"She is good, sir, and giveth me neither sorrow nor pain of any sort. And Nan and Bet are like to her in this."

"How old be these?"

"Fifteen, an' it please you, sir."

"The lady Elizabeth, my sister, is fourteen, and the lady Jane Grey, my cousin, is of mine own age, and comely and gracious withal; but my sister the lady Mary, with her gloomy mien and— Look you; do thy sisters forbid their servants to smile, lest the sin destroy their souls?"

"They? Oh, dost think, sir, that *they* have servants?"

The little prince contemplated the little pauper gravely a moment, then said, "And prithee, why not? Who helpeth them undress at night? Who attireth them when they rise?"

"None, sir. Wouldst have them take off their garment and sleep without—like beasts?"

"Their garment! Have they but one?"

"Ah, good your Worship, what would they do with more? Truly they have not two bodies each."

"It is a quaint and marvelous thought! Thy pardon, I had not meant to laugh. But thy good Nan and thy Bet shall have raiment and lackeys enow, and that soon too; my cofferer shall look to it. No, thank me not; 'tis nothing. Thou speakest well; thou hast an easy grace in it. Art learned?"

"I know not if I am or not, sir. The good priest that is called Father Andrew taught me, of his kindness, from his books."

"Knowst thou the Latin?"

"But scantly, sir, I doubt."

"Learn it, lad; 'tis hard only at first. The Greek is harder; but neither these nor any tongues else, I think, are hard to the lady Elizabeth and my cousin. Thou shouldst hear those damsels at it! But tell me of thy Offal Court. Hast thou a pleasant life there?"

"In truth, yes, so please you, sir, save when one is hungry. There be Punch-and-Judy shows, and monkeys—oh, such antic creatures, and so bravely dressed!—and there be plays wherein they that play do shout and fight till all are slain, and 'tis so fine to see, and costeth but a farthing, albeit 'tis main hard to get the farthing, please your Worship."

"Tell me more."

"We lads of Offal Court do strive against each other with the cudgel, like to the fashion of the 'prentices, sometimes."

The prince's eyes flashed. Said he, "Marry, that would not I mislike. Tell me more."

"We strive in races, sir, to see who of us shall be fleetest."

"That I would like also. Speak on."

"In summer, sir, we wade and swim in the canals and in the river, and each doth duck his neighbor, and spatter him with water, and dive and shout and tumble and——"

" 'Twould be worth my father's kingdom but to enjoy it once! Prithee go on."

"We dance and sing about the Maypole in Cheapside; we play in the sand, each covering his neighbor up; and times we make mud pastry—oh, the lovely mud, it hath not its like for delightfulness in all the world!—we do fairly wallow in the mud, sir, saving your worship's presence."

"Oh, prithee say no more; 'tis glorious! If that I could but clothe me in raiment like to thine, and strip my feet, and revel in the mud once, just once, with none to rebuke me or forbid, meseemeth I could forgo the crown!"

"And if that I could clothe me once, sweet sir, as thou art clad, just once——"

"Oho, wouldst like it? Then so shall it be. Doff thy rags and don these splendors, lad! It is a brief happiness, but will be not less keen for that. We will have it while we may, and change again before any come to molest."

A few minutes later the little Prince of Wales was garlanded with Tom's fluttering odds and ends, and the little Prince of Pauperdom was tricked out in the gaudy plumage of royalty. The two went and stood side by side before a great mirror, and lo, a miracle: there did not seem to have been any change made! They stared at each other, then at the glass, then at each other again. At last the puzzled princeling said, "What dost thou make of this?"

"Ah, good your worship, require me not to answer. It is not meet that one of my degree should utter the thing."

"Then will *I* utter it. Thou hast the same hair, the same eyes, the same voice and manner, the same form and stature, the same face and countenance that I bear. Fared we forth naked, there is none could say which was you, and which the Prince of Wales. And now that I am clothed as thou wert clothed, it seemeth I should be able the more nearly to feel as thou didst when the brute soldier— Hark ye, is not this a bruise upon your hand?''

''Yes; but it is a slight thing, and your Worship knoweth that the poor man-at-arms——''

''Peace! It was a shameful thing and a cruel!'' cried the little prince, stamping his bare foot. ''If the king— Stir not a step till I come again! It is a command!''

In a moment he had snatched up and put away an article of national importance that lay upon a table, and was out at the door and flying through the palace grounds in his bannered rags, with a hot face and glowing eyes. As soon as he reached the great gate, he seized the bars and tried to shake them, shouting, ''Open! Unbar the gates!''

The soldier that had maltreated Tom obeyed promptly; and as the prince burst through the portal, half smothered with royal wrath, the soldier fetched him a sounding box on the ear that sent him whirling to the roadway and said, ''Take that, thou beggar's spawn, for what thou got'st me from his Highness!''

The crowd roared with laughter. The prince picked himself out of the mud and made fiercely at the sentry, shouting, ''I am the Prince of Wales, my person is sacred; and thou shalt hang for laying thy hand upon me!''

The soldier brought his halberd to a present arms and said mockingly, ''I salute your gracious Highness.'' Then angrily, ''Be off, thou crazy rubbish!''

Here the jeering crowd closed around the poor little prince and hustled him far down the road, hooting him and shouting, ''Way for his royal Highness! Way for the Prince of Wales!''

4

The Prince's Troubles Begin

After hours of persistent pursuit and persecution, the little prince was at last deserted by the rabble and left to himself. As long as he had been able to rage against the mob, and threaten it royally, and royally utter commands that were good stuff to laugh at, he was very entertaining; but when weariness finally forced him to be silent, he was no longer of use to his tormentors and they sought amusement elsewhere. He looked about him now but could not recognize the locality. He was within the city of London—that was all he knew. He moved on aimlessly, and in a little while the houses thinned and the passersby were infrequent. He bathed his bleeding feet in the brook which flowed then where Farrington Street now is, rested a few moments, then passed on, and presently came upon a great space with only a few scattered houses in it and a prodigious church. He recognized this church. Scaffoldings were about everywhere, and swarms of workmen, for it was undergoing elaborate repairs. The prince took heart at once; he felt that his troubles were at an end now. He said to himself, "It is the ancient Grey Friars' Church, which the king my father hath taken from the monks and given for a home forever for poor and forsaken children, and new-named it Christ's Church. Right gladly will they serve the son of him who hath done so generously by them, and the more that that son is himself as poor and as forlorn as any that be sheltered here this day, or ever shall be."

He was soon in the midst of a crowd of boys who were running, jumping, playing at ball and leapfrog, and otherwise disporting themselves, and right noisily too. They were all dressed alike, and in the fashion which in that day prevailed among servingmen and 'prentices*—that is to say,

*See Note 1 at end of volume.

each had on the crown of his head a flat black cap about the
size of a saucer, which was not useful as a covering, it being
of such scanty dimensions; neither was it ornamental; from
beneath it the hair fell, unparted, to the middle of the forehead, and was cropped straight around; a clerical band at
the neck; a blue gown that fitted closely and hung as low as
the knees or lower; full sleeves; a broad red belt; bright-
yellow stockings, gartered above the knees; low shoes with
large metal buckles. It was a sufficiently ugly costume.

The boys stopped their play and flocked about the prince,
who said with native dignity, "Good lads, say to your master that Edward, Prince of Wales, desireth speech with
him."

A great shout went up at this, and one rude fellow said,
"Marry, art thou his Grace's messenger, beggar?"

The prince's face flushed with anger, and his ready hand
flew to his hip, but there was nothing there. There was a
storm of laughter, and one boy said, "Didst mark that? He
fancied he had a sword—belike he is the prince himself."

This sally brought more laughter. Poor Edward drew himself up proudly and said, "I am the prince, and it ill beseem-
eth you that feed upon the king my father's bounty to use
me so."

This was vastly enjoyed, as the laughter testified. The
youth who had first spoken shouted to his comrades, "Ho,
swine, slaves, pensioners of his Grace's princely father,
where be your manners? Down on your marrow-bones, all
of ye, and do reverence to his kingly port and royal rags!"

With boisterous mirth they dropped upon their knees in
a body and did mock homage to their prey. The prince
spurned the nearest boy with his foot and said fiercely,
"Take thou that till the morrow come and I build thee a
gibbet!"

Ah, but this was not a joke; this was going beyond fun.
The laughter ceased on the instant, and fury took its place.
A dozen shouted, "Hale him forth! To the horsepond, to
the horsepond! Where be the dogs? Ho, there, Lion! Ho,
Fangs!"

Then followed such a thing as England had never seen
before—the sacred person of the heir to the throne rudely
buffeted by plebeian hands and set upon and torn by dogs.

As night drew to a close that day, the prince found himself far down in the close-built portion of the city. His body

was bruised, his hands were bleeding, and his rags were all besmirched with mud. He wandered on and on, and grew more and more bewildered, and so tired and faint he could hardly drag one foot after the other. He had ceased to ask questions of anyone, since they brought him only insult instead of information. He kept muttering to himself, "Offal Court—that is the name; if I can but find it before my strength is wholly spent and I drop, then am I saved, for his people will take me to the palace and prove that I am none of theirs, but the true prince, and I shall have mine own again." And now and then his mind reverted to his treatment by those rude Christ's Hospital boys, and he said, "When I am king, they shall not have bread and shelter only, but also teachings out of books, for a full belly is little worth where the mind is starved, and the heart. I will keep this diligently in my remembrance, that this day's lesson be not lost upon me, and my people suffer thereby; for learning softeneth the heart and breedeth gentleness and charity."*

The lights began to twinkle, it came on to rain, the wind rose, and a raw and gusty night set in. The houseless prince, the homeless heir to the throne of England, still moved on, drifting deeper into the maze of squalid alleys where the swarming hives of poverty and misery were massed together.

Suddenly a great drunken ruffian collared him and said, "Out to this time of night again, and hast not brought a farthing home, I warrant me! If it be so, an' I do not break all the bones in thy lean body, then am I not John Canty, but some other."

The prince twisted himself loose, unconsciously brushed his profaned shoulder, and eagerly said, "Oh, art *his* father, truly? Sweet heaven grant it be so; then wilt thou fetch him away and restore me!"

"*His* father? I know not what thou meanst; I but know I am *thy* father, as thou shalt soon have cause to——"

"Oh, jest not, palter not, delay not! I am worn, I am wounded, I can bear no more. Take me to the king my father, and he will make thee rich beyond thy wildest dreams. Believe me, man, believe me! I speak no lie, but only the truth! Put forth thy hand and save me! I am indeed the Prince of Wales!"

*See Note 2 at end of volume.

The man stared down, stupefied, upon the lad, then shook his head and muttered, "Gone stark mad as any Tom o' Bedlam!"—then collared him once more and said with a coarse laugh and an oath, "But mad or no mad, I and thy Gammer Canty will soon find where the soft places in thy bones lie, or I'm no true man!"

With this he dragged the frantic and struggling prince away and disappeared up a front court followed by a delighted and noisy swarm of human vermin.

5

Tom as a Patrician

Tom Canty, left alone in the prince's cabinet, made good use of his opportunity. He turned himself this way and that before the great mirror, admiring his finery; then walked away, imitating the prince's high-bred carriage, and still observing results in the glass. Next he drew the beautiful sword and bowed, kissing the blade and laying it across his breast as he had seen a noble knight do, by way of salute to the lieutenant of the Tower, five or six weeks before, when delivering the great lords of Norfolk and Surrey into his hands for captivity. Tom played with the jeweled dagger that hung upon his thigh; he examined the costly and exquisite ornaments of the room; he tried each of the sumptuous chairs and thought how proud he would be if the Offal Court herd could only peep in and see him in his grandeur. He wondered if they would believe the marvelous tale he should tell when he got home or if they would shake their heads and say his overtaxed imagination had at last upset his reason.

At the end of half an hour it suddenly occurred to him that the prince was gone a long time; then right away he began to feel lonely; very soon he fell to listening and longing, and ceased to toy with the pretty things about him; he grew uneasy, then restless, then distressed. Suppose someone should come and catch him in the prince's clothes, and the prince not there to explain. Might they not hang him at once and inquire into his case afterward? He had heard that the great were prompt about small matters. His fears rose higher and higher, and trembling, he softly opened the door to the antechamber, resolved to fly and seek the prince, and through him, protection and release. Six gorgeous gentlemen servants and two young pages of high degree, clothed like butterflies, sprung to their feet and bowed low before him. He stepped quickly back and shut the door. He said,

"Oh, they mock at me! They will go and tell. Oh! Why came I here to cast away my life?"

He walked up and down the floor, filled with nameless fears, listening, starting at every trifling sound. Presently the door swung open and a silken page said, "The lady Jane Grey."

The door closed, and a sweet young girl, richly clad, bounded toward him. But she stopped suddenly and said in a distressed voice, "Oh, what aileth thee, my lord?"

Tom's breath was nearly failing him, but he made shift to stammer out, "Ah, be merciful, thou! In sooth I am no lord, but only poor Tom Canty of Offal Court in the city. Prithee let me see the prince, and he will of his grace restore to me my rags and let me hence unhurt. Oh, be thou merciful and save me!"

By this time the boy was on his knees and supplicating with his eyes and uplifted hands as well as with his tongue. The young girl seemed horror-stricken. She cried out, "Oh, my lord, on thy knees? And to *me!*"

Then she fled away in fright; and Tom, smitten with despair, sank down, murmuring, "There is no help, there is no hope. Now will they come and take me."

Whilst he lay there benumbed with terror, dreadful tidings were speeding through the palace. The whisper, for it was whispered always, flew from menial to menial, from lord to lady, down all the long corridors, from story to story, from saloon to saloon, "The prince hath gone mad, the prince hath gone mad!" Soon every saloon, every marble hall, had its group of glittering lords and ladies and other groups of dazzling lesser folk, talking earnestly together in whispers, and every face had in it dismay. Presently a splendid official came marching by these groups, making solemn proclamation, "In the name of the king! Let none list to this false and foolish matter, upon pain of death, nor discuss the same, nor carry it abroad. In the name of the king!"

The whispering ceased as suddenly as if the whisperers had been stricken dumb.

Soon there was a general buzz along the corridors of, "The prince! See, the prince comes!"

Poor Tom came slowly walking past the low-bowing groups, trying to bow in return, and meekly gazing upon his strange surroundings with bewildered and pathetic eyes. Great nobles walked upon each side of him, making him lean upon them, and so steady his steps. Behind him followed the court physicians and some servants.

Presently Tom found himself in a noble apartment of the palace and heard the door close behind him. Around him stood those who had come with him. Before him, at a little distance, reclined a very large and very fat man with a wide, pulpy face and a stern expression. His large head was very gray; and his whiskers, which he wore only around his face, like a frame, were gray also. His clothing was of rich stuff, but old and slightly frayed in places. One of his swollen legs had a pillow under it and was wrapped in bandages. There was silence now, and there was no head there but was bent in reverence, except this man's. This stern-countenanced invalid was the dread Henry VIII. He said—and his face grew gentle as he began to speak—"How now, my lord Edward, my prince? Hast been minded to cozen me, the good king thy father, who loveth thee and kindly useth thee, with a sorry jest?"

Poor Tom was listening, as well as his dazed faculties would let him, to the beginning of this speech; but when the words "me, the good king" fell upon his ear, his face blanched and he dropped as instantly upon his knees as if a shot had brought him there. Lifting up his hands, he exclaimed, "Thou the *king?* Then am I undone indeed!"

This speech seemed to stun the king. His eyes wandered from face to face aimlessly, then rested, bewildered, upon the boy before him. Then he said in a tone of deep disappointment, "Alack, I had believed the rumor disproportioned to the truth, but I fear me 'tis not so." He breathed a heavy sigh and said in a gentle voice, "Come to thy father, child; thou art not well."

Tom was assisted to his feet, and approached the Majesty of England, humble and trembling. The king took the frightened face between his hands and gazed earnestly and lovingly into it awhile, as if seeking some grateful sign of returning reason there, then pressed the curly head against his breast and patted it tenderly. Presently he said, "Dost not know thy father, child? Break not mine old heart; say thou knowst me. Thou *dost* know me, dost thou not?"

"Yea, thou art my dread lord the king, whom God preserve!"

"True, true—that is well—be comforted, tremble not so;

there is none here would hurt thee; there is none here but loves thee. Thou art better now; thy ill dream passeth; is't not so? And thou knowest thyself now also; is't not so? Thou wilt not miscall thyself again, as they say thou didst a little while agone?"

"I pray thee of thy Grace believe me, I did but speak the truth, most dread lord, for I am the meanest among thy subjects, being a pauper born, and 'tis by a sore mischance and accident I am here, albeit I was therein nothing blameful. I am but young to die, and thou canst save me with one little word. Oh, speak it, sir!"

"Die? Talk not so, sweet prince; peace, peace, to thy troubled heart; thou shalt not die!"

Tom dropped upon his knees with a glad cry, "God requite thy mercy, O my king, and save thee long to bless thy land!" Then springing up, he turned a joyful face toward the two lords-in-waiting and exclaimed, "Thou heardst it! I am not to die; the king hath said it!" There was no movement, save that all bowed with grave respect; but no one spoke. He hesitated, a little confused, then turned timidly toward the king, saying, "I may go now?"

"Go? Surely, if thou desirest. But why not tarry yet a little? Whither wouldst go?"

Tom dropped his eyes and answered humbly, "Peradventure I mistook; but I did think me free, and so was I moved to seek again the kennel where I was born and bred to misery, yet which harboreth my mother and my sisters, and so is home to me; whereas these pomps and splendors whereunto I am not used— Oh, please you, sir, to let me go!"

The king was silent and thoughtful awhile, and his face betrayed a growing distress and uneasiness. Presently he said, with something of hope in his voice, "Perchance he is but mad upon this one strain and hath his wits unmarred as toucheth other matter. God send it may be so! We will make trial."

Then he asked Tom a question in Latin, and Tom answered him lamely in the same tongue. The king was delighted, and showed it. The lords and doctors manifested their gratification also. The king said, " 'Twas not according to his schooling and ability, but sheweth that his mind is but diseased, not stricken fatally. How say you, sir?"

The physician addressed bowed low and replied, "It jumpeth with mine own conviction, sire, that thou hast divined aright."

The king looked pleased with this encouragement, coming as it did from so excellent authority, and continued with good heart, "Now mark ye all; we will try him further."

He put a question to Tom in French. Tom stood silent a moment, embarrassed by having so many eyes centered upon him, then said diffidently, "I have no knowledge of this tongue, so please your majesty."

The king fell back upon his couch. The attendants flew to his assistance; but he put them aside and said, "Trouble me not—it is nothing but a scurvy faintness. Raise me! There, 'tis sufficient. Come hither, child; there, rest thy poor troubled head upon thy father's heart and be at peace. Thou'lt soon be well; 'tis but a passing fantasy. Fear thou not; thou'lt soon be well." Then he turned toward the company; his gentle manner changed, and baleful lightnings began to play from his eyes. He said, "List ye all! This my son is mad, but it is not permanent. Overstudy hath done this, and somewhat too much of confinement. Away with his books and teachers! See ye to it. Pleasure him with sports, beguile him in wholesome ways, so that his health come again." He raised himself higher still and went on with energy, "He is mad, but he is my son and England's heir, and mad or sane, still shall he reign! And hear ye further, and proclaim it: whoso speaketh of this his distemper worketh against the peace and order of these realms and shall to the gallows! Give me to drink—I burn: this sorrow sappeth my strength. There, take away the cup. Support me. There, that is well. Mad, is he? Were he a thousand times mad, yet is he Prince of Wales, and I the king will confirm it. This very morrow shall he be installed in his princely dignity in due and ancient form. Take instant order for it, my lord Hertford."

One of the nobles knelt at the royal couch and said, "The king's majesty knoweth that the Hereditary Great Marshal of England lieth attainted in the Tower. It were not meet that one attainted——"

"Peace! Insult not mine ears with his hated name. Is this man to live forever? Am I to be balked of my will? Is the prince to tarry uninstalled because, forsooth, the realm lacketh an earl marshal free of treasonable taint to invest him with his honors? No, by the splendor of God! Warn my Parliament to bring me Norfolk's doom before the sun rise again, else shall they answer for it grievously!''*

Lord Hertford said, "The king's will is law," and rising, returned to his former place.

Gradually the wrath faded out of the old king's face, and he said, "Kiss me, my prince. There. What fearest thou? Am I not thy loving father?''

"Thou art good to me that am unworthy, O mighty and gracious lord; that in truth I know. But—but—it grieveth me to think of him that is to die, and——''

"Ah, 'tis like thee, 'tis like thee! I know thy heart is still the same, even though thy mind hath suffered hurt, for thou wert ever of a gentle spirit. But this duke standeth between thee and thine honors; I will have another in his stead that shall bring no taint to his great office. Comfort thee, my prince; trouble not thy poor head with this matter.''

"But is it not I that speed him hence, my liege? How long might he not live, but for me?''

"Take no thought of him, my prince; he is not worthy. Kiss me once again and go to thy trifles and amusements, for my malady distresseth me. I am aweary and would rest. Go with thine uncle Hertford and thy people, and come again when my body is refreshed.''

Tom, heavyhearted, was conducted from the presence, for this last sentence was a deathblow to the hope he had cherished that now he would be set free. Once more he heard the buzz of low voices exclaiming, "The prince, the prince comes!''

His spirits sank lower and lower as he moved between the glittering files of bowing courtiers, for he recognized that he was indeed a captive now and might remain forever shut up in this gilded cage, a forlorn and friendless prince, except God in his mercy take pity on him and set him free.

And turn where he would, he seemed to see floating in

*See Note 3 at end of volume.

the air the severed head and the remembered face of the great Duke of Norfolk, the eyes fixed on him reproachfully.

His old dreams had been so pleasant, but this reality was so dreary!

6

Tom Receives Instructions

Tom was conducted to the principal apartment of a noble suite and made to sit down, a thing which he was loath to do since there were elderly men and men of high degree about him. He begged them to be seated also, but they only bowed their thanks or murmured them and remained standing. He would have insisted, but his "uncle" the Earl of Hertford whispered in his ear, "Prithee, insist not, my lord; it is not meet that they sit in thy presence."

The lord St. John was announced, and after making obeisance to Tom, he said, "I come upon the king's errand, concerning a matter which requireth privacy. Will it please your royal Highness to dismiss all that attend you here, save my lord the Earl of Hertford?"

Observing that Tom did not seem to know how to proceed, Hertford whispered him to make a sign with his hand and not trouble himself to speak unless he chose. When the waiting gentlemen had retired, Lord St. John said, "His Majesty commandeth that for due and weighty reasons of state, the prince's grace shall hide his infirmity in all ways that be within his power till it be passed and he be as he was before. To wit, that he shall deny to none that he is the true prince and heir to England's greatness; that he shall uphold his princely dignity and shall receive, without word or sign of protest, that reverence and observance which unto it do appertain of right and ancient usage; that he shall cease to speak to any of that lowly birth and life his malady hath conjured out of the unwholesome imaginings of o'er-wrought fancy; that he shall strive with diligence to bring unto his memory again those faces which he was wont to know—and where he faileth he shall hold his peace, neither betraying by semblance of surprise or other sign that he hath forgot; that upon occasions of state, whensoever any matter shall perplex him as to the thing he should do or the utterance he should make, he shall show nought of unrest to the curious that look on, but take advice in that matter of the lord Hertford or my humble self, which are commanded of the king to be upon this service and close at call till this commandment be dissolved. Thus saith the king's majesty, who sendeth greeting to your royal Highness and prayeth that God will of his mercy quickly heal you and have you now and ever in his holy keeping."

The lord St. John made reverence and stood aside. Tom replied resignedly, "The king hath said it. None may palter with the king's command or fit it to his ease, where it doth chafe, with deft evasions. The king shall be obeyed."

Lord Hertford said, "Touching the king's majesty's ordainment concerning books and such like serious matters, it may peradventure please your Highness to ease your time with lightsome entertainment, lest you go wearied to the banquet and suffer harm thereby."

Tom's face showed inquiring surprise, and a blush followed when he saw Lord St. John's eyes bent sorrowfully upon him. His lordship said, "Thy memory still wrongeth thee, and thou hast shown surprise; but suffer it not to trouble thee, for 'tis a matter that will not bide, but depart with thy mending malady. My lord of Hertford speaketh of the city's banquet which the king's majesty did promise, some two months flown, your Highness should attend. Thou recallest it now?"

"It grieves me to confess it had indeed escaped me," said Tom in a hesitating voice, and blushed again.

At this moment the lady Elizabeth and the lady Jane Grey were announced. The two lords exchanged significant glances, and Hertford stepped quickly toward the door. As the young girls passed him, he said in a low voice, "I pray ye, ladies, seem not to observe his humors nor show surprise when his memory doth lapse, it will grieve you to note how it doth stick at every trifle."

Meantime Lord St. John was saying in Tom's ear, "Please you, sir, keep diligently in mind his Majesty's desire. Remember all thou canst, *seem* to remember all else. Let them not perceive that thou art much changed from thy wont, for thou knowest how tenderly thy old play-fellows bear thee in their hearts and how 'twould grieve them. Art willing, sir, that I remain? And thine uncle?"

Tom signified assent with a gesture and a murmured word,

for he was already learning, and in his simple heart was resolved to acquit himself as best he might, according to the king's command.

In spite of every precaution, the conversation among the young people became a little embarrassing at times. More than once, in truth, Tom was near to breaking down and confessing himself unequal to his tremendous part; but the tact of the princess Elizabeth saved him, or a word from one or the other of the vigilant lords, thrown in apparently by chance, had the same happy effect. Once the little lady Jane turned to Tom and dismayed him with this question, "Hast paid thy duty to the queen's majesty today, my lord?"

Tom hesitated, looked distressed, and was about to stammer out something at hazard when Lord St. John took the word and answered for him with the easy grace of a courtier accustomed to encounter delicate difficulties and to be ready for them, "He hath indeed, madam, and she did greatly hearten him, as touching his Majesty's condition; is it not so, your Highness?"

Tom mumbled something that stood for assent, but felt that he was getting upon dangerous ground. Somewhat later it was mentioned that Tom was to study no more at present, whereupon her little ladyship exclaimed, " 'Tis a pity, 'tis such a pity! Thou wert proceeding bravely. But bide thy time in patience; it will not be for long. Thou'lt yet be graced with learning like thy father, and make thy tongue master of as many languages as his, good my prince."

"My father!" cried Tom, off his guard for the moment. "I trow he cannot speak his own so that any but the swine that wallow in the sties may tell his meaning; and as for learning of any sort soever—"

He looked up and encountered a solemn warning in my lord St. John's eyes.

He stopped, blushed, then continued low and sadly, "Ah, my malady persecuteth me again, and my mind wandereth. I meant the king's grace no irreverence."

"We know it, sir," said the princess Elizabeth, taking her "brother's" hand between her two palms, respectfully but caressingly; "trouble not thyself as to that. The fault is none of thine, but thy distemper's."

"Thou'rt a gentle comforter, sweet lady," said Tom gratefully, "and my heart moveth me to thank thee for't, an' I may be so bold."

Once the giddy little lady Jane fired a simple Greek phrase at Tom. The princess Elizabeth's quick eye saw by the serene blankness of the target's front that the shaft was overshot, so she tranquilly delivered a return volley of sounding Greek on Tom's behalf and then straightway changed the talk to other matters.

Time wore on pleasantly, and likewise smoothly, on the whole. Snags and sandbars grew less and less frequent, and Tom grew more and more at his ease, seeing that all were so lovingly bent upon helping him and overlooking his mistakes. When it came out that the little ladies were to accompany him to the Lord Mayor's banquet in the evening, his heart gave a bound of relief and delight, for he felt that he should not be friendless now among that multitude of strangers, whereas an hour earlier the idea of their going with him would have been an insupportable terror to him.

Tom's guardian angels, the two lords, had had less comfort in the interview than the other parties to it. They felt much as if they were piloting a great ship through a dangerous channel; they were on the alert constantly, and found their office no child's play. Wherefore, at last, when the ladies' visit was drawing to a close and the lord Guilford Dudley was announced, they not only felt that their charge had been sufficiently taxed for the present, but also that they themselves were not in the best condition to take their ship back and make their anxious voyage all over again. So they respectfully advised Tom to excuse himself, which he was very glad to do, although a slight shade of disappointment might have been observed upon my lady Jane's face when she heard the splendid stripling denied admittance.

There was a pause now, a sort of waiting silence which Tom could not understand. He glanced at Lord Hertford, who gave him a sign, but he failed to understand that also. The ready Elizabeth came to the rescue with her usual easy grace. She made reverence and said, "Have we leave of the prince's grace my brother to go?"

Tom said, "Indeed your ladyships can have whatsoever of me they will for the asking; yet would I rather give them any other thing that in my poor power lieth than leave to take the light and blessing of their presence hence. Give ye good dén, and God be with ye!" Then he smiled inwardly at the thought; " 'Tis not for nought I have dwelt but among princes in my reading and taught my tongue some slight trick of their broidered and gracious speech withal!''

When the illustrious maidens were gone, Tom turned wearily to his keepers and said, ''May it please your lordships to grant me leave to go into some corner and rest me?''

Lord Hertford said, ''So please your Highness, it is for you to command, it is for us to obey. That thou shouldst rest is indeed a needful thing, since thou must journey to the city presently.''

He touched a bell, and a page appeared, who was ordered to desire the presence of Sir William Herbert. This gentleman came straightway and conducted Tom to an inner apartment. Tom's first movement there was to reach for a cup of water; but a silk-and-velvet servitor seized it, dropped upon one knee, and offered it to him on a golden salver.

Next the tired captive sat down and was going to take off his buskins, timidly asking leave with his eye, but another silk-and-velvet discomforter went down upon his knees and took the office from him. He made two or three further efforts to help himself, but being promptly forestalled each time, he finally gave up with a sigh of resignation and a murmured, ''Beshrew me but I marvel they do not require to breathe for me also!'' Slippered and wrapped in a sumptuous robe, he laid himself down at last to rest, but not to sleep, for his head was too full of thoughts and the room too full of people. He could not dismiss the former, so they stayed; he did not know enough to dismiss the latter, so they stayed also, to his vast regret—and theirs.

Tom's departure had left his two noble guardians alone. They mused awhile, with much headshaking and walking the floor; then Lord St. John said, ''Plainly, what dost thou think?''

''Plainly, then, this. The king is near his end, my nephew is mad, mad will mount the throne, and mad remain. God protect England, since she will need it!''

''Verily it promiseth so, indeed. But—have you no misgivings as to—as to—''

The speaker hesitated and finally stopped. He evidently felt that he was upon delicate ground. Lord Hertford stopped before him, looked into his face with a clear, frank eye, and said, "Speak on; there is none to hear but me. Misgivings as to what?"

"I am full loath to word the thing that is in my mind, and thou so near to him in blood, my lord. But craving pardon if I do offend, seemeth it not strange that madness could so change his port and manner! Not but that his port and speech are princely still, but that they *differ* in one unweighty trifle or another from what his custom was aforetime. Seemeth it not strange that madness should filch from his memory his father's very lineaments; the customs and observances that are his due from such as be about him; and, leaving him his Latin, strip him of his Greek and French? My Lord, be not offended, but ease my mind of its disquiet and receive my grateful thanks. It haunteth me, his saying he was not the prince, and so——"

"Peace, my lord, thou utterest treason! Hast forgot the king's command? Remember I am party to thy crime if I but listen."

St. John paled and hastened to say, "I was in fault, I do confess it. Betray me not, grant me this grace out of thy courtesy, and I will neither think nor speak of this thing more. Deal not hardly with me, sir, else am I ruined."

"I am content, my lord. So thou offend not again, here or in the ears of others, it shall be as though thou hadst not spoken. But thou needst not have misgivings. He is my sister's son; are not his voice, his face, his form, familiar to me from his cradle? Madness can do all the odd conflicting things thou seest in him, and more. Dost not recall how that the old baron Marley, being mad, forgot the favor of his own countenance that he had known for sixty years, and held it was another's; nay, even claimed he was the son of Mary Magdalene and that his head was made of Spanish glass; and sooth to say, he suffered none to touch it, lest by mischance some heedless hand might shiver it. Give thy misgivings easement, good my lord. This is the very prince, I know him well—and soon will be thy king; it may advantage thee to bear this in mind and more dwell upon it than the other."

After some further talk, in which the lord St. John covered up his mistake as well as he could by repeated protests that his faith was thoroughly grounded now and could not be assailed by doubts again, the lord Hertford relieved his fellow keeper and sat down to keep watch and ward alone.

He was soon deep in meditation. And evidently the longer he thought, the more he was bothered. By and by he began to pace the floor and mutter.

"Tush, he *must* be the prince! Will any he in all the land maintain there can be two, not of one blood and birth, so marvelously twinned? And even were it so, 'twere yet a stranger miracle that chance should cast the one into the other's place. Nay, 'tis folly, folly, folly!"

Presently he said, "Now were he impostor and called himself prince, look you *that* would be natural; that would be reasonable. But lived ever an impostor yet who, being called prince by the king, prince by the court, prince by all, *denied* his dignity and pleaded against his exaltation? *No!* By the soul of St. Swithin, no! This is the true prince, gone mad!''

Tom's First Royal Dinner

Somewhat after one in the afternoon, Tom resignedly underwent the ordeal of being dressed for dinner. He found himself as finely clothed as before, but everything different, everything changed, from his ruff to his stockings. He was presently conducted with much state to a spacious and ornate apartment, where a table was already set for one. Its furniture was all of massy gold, and beautified with designs which well-nigh made it priceless, since they were the work of Benvenuto. The room was half filled with noble servitors. A chaplain said grace, and Tom was about to fall to, for hunger had long been constitutional with him, but was interrupted by my lord the Early of Berkeley, who fastened a napkin about his neck, for the great post of Diaperers to the Princes of Wales was hereditary in this nobleman's family. Tom's cupbearer was present and forestalled all his attempts to help himself to wine. The Taster to his Highness the Prince of Wales was there also, prepared to taste any suspicious dish upon requirement and run the risk of being poisoned. He was only an ornamental appendage at this time and was seldom called upon to exercise his function; but there had been times, not many generations past, when the office of taster had its perils and was not a grandeur to be desired. Why they did not use a dog or a plumber seems strange, but all the ways of royalty are strange. My lord D'Arcy, First Groom of the Chamber, was there to do goodness knows what; but there he was—let that suffice. The Lord Chief Butler was there and stood behind Tom's chair, overseeing the solemnities under command of the Lord Great Steward and the Lord Head Cook, who stood near. Tom had three hundred and eighty-four servants beside these, but they were not all in that room, of course, nor the quarter of them; neither was Tom aware yet that they existed.

All those that were present had been well drilled within the hour to remember that the prince was temporarily out of his head and to be careful to show no surprise at his vagaries. These "vagaries" were soon on exhibition before them, but they only moved their compassion and their sorrow, not their mirth. It was a heavy affliction to them to see the beloved prince so stricken.

Poor Tom ate with his fingers mainly, but no one smiled at it or even seemed to observe it. He inspected his napkin curiously and with deep interest, for it was of a very dainty and beautiful fabric; then said with simplicity, "Prithee take it away, lest in mine unheedfulness it be soiled."

The Hereditary Diaperer took it away with reverent manner and without word or protest of any sort.

Tom examined the turnips and the lettuce with interest, and asked what they were and if they were to be eaten, for it was only recently that men had begun to raise these things in England in place of importing them as luxuries from Holland.* His question was answered with grave respect, and no surprise manifested. When he had finished his dessert, he filled his pockets with nuts; but nobody appeared to be aware of it or disturbed by it. But the next moment he was himself disturbed by it and showed discomposure, for this was the only service he had been permitted to do with his own hands during the meal, and he did not doubt that he had done a most improper and unprincely thing. At that moment the muscles of his nose began to twitch, and the end of that organ to lift and wrinkle. This continued, and Tom began to evince a growing distress. He looked appealingly, first at one and then another of the lords about him, and tears came into his eyes. They sprang forward with dismay in their faces and begged to know his trouble. Tom said with genuine anguish, "I crave your indulgence; my nose itcheth cruelly. What is the custom and usage in this emergence? Prithee speed, for 'tis but a little time that I can bear it."

None smiled, but all were sore perplexed and looked one to the other in deep tribulation for counsel. But behold, here was a dead wall, and nothing in English history to tell how to get over it. The Master of Ceremonies was not present; there was no one who felt safe to venture upon this un-

*See Note 4 at end of volume.

charted sea or risk the attempt to solve this solemn problem.
Alas! There was no Hereditary Scratcher. Meantime the
tears had overflowed their banks and begun to trickle down
Tom's cheeks. His twitching nose was pleading more ur-
gently than ever for relief. At last nature broke down the
barriers of etiquette: Tom lifted up an inward prayer for
pardon if he was doing wrong and brought relief to the bur-
dened hearts of his court by scratching his nose himself.

His meal being ended, a lord came and held before him
a broad, shallow, golden dish with fragrant rose water in it
to cleanse his mouth and fingers with; and my lord the Hereditary Diaperer stood by with a napkin for his use. Tom
gazed at the dish a puzzled moment or two, then raised it
to his lips and gravely took a draft. Then he returned it to
the waiting lord and said, "Nay, it likes me not, my lord;
it hath a pretty flavor, but it wanteth strength."

This new eccentricity of the prince's ruined mind made
all the hearts about him ache, but the sad sight moved none
to merriment.

Tom's next unconscious blunder was to get up and leave
the table just when the chaplain had taken his stand behind
his chair, and with uplifted hands and closed, uplifted eyes
was in the act of beginning the blessing. Still nobody
seemed to perceive that the prince had done a thing unusual.

By his own request, our small friend was now conducted
to his private cabinet and left there alone to his own devices.
Hanging upon hooks in the oaken wainscotting were the
several pieces of a suit of shining steel armor, covered all
over with beautiful designs exquisitely inlaid in gold. This
martial panoply belonged to the true prince, a recent present from Madam Parr, the queen. Tom put on the greaves,
the gauntlets, the plumed helmet, and such other pieces as
he could don without assistance, and for a while was minded
to call for help and complete the matter, but bethought him
of the nuts he had brought away from dinner and the joy it
would be to eat them with no crowd to eye him and no
Grand Hereditaries to pester him with undesired services;
so he restored the pretty things to their several places and
soon was cracking nuts and feeling almost naturally happy
for the first time since God for his sins had made him a
prince. When the nuts were all gone, he stumbled upon
some inviting books in a closet, among them one about the

etiquette of the English court. This was a prize. He lay down upon a sumptuous divan and proceeded to instruct himself with honest zeal. Let us leave him there for the present.

8

*The Question
of the Seal*

About five o'clock Henry VIII awoke out of an unrefreshing nap and muttered to himself, "Troublous dreams, troublous dreams! Mine end is now at hand; so say these warnings, and my failing pulses do confirm it." Presently a wicked light flamed up in his eye, and he muttered, "Yet will not I die till *he* go before."

His attendants perceiving that he was awake, one of them asked his pleasure concerning the Lord Chancellor, who was waiting without.

"Admit him, admit him!" exclaimed the king eagerly.

The Lord Chancellor entered and knelt by the king's couch, saying, "I have given order, and according to the king's command, the peers of the realm, in their robes, do now stand at the bar of the House, where, having confirmed the Duke of Norfolk's doom, they humbly wait his Majesty's further pleasure in the matter."

The king's face lit up with a fierce joy. Said he, "Lift me up! In mine own person will I go before my Parliament, and with mine own hand will I seal the warrant that rids me of—"

His voice failed, an ashen pallor swept the flush from his cheeks, and the attendants eased him back upon his pillows and hurriedly assisted him with restoratives. Presently he said sorrowfully, "Alack, how have I longed for this sweet hour! And lo, too late it cometh, and I am robbed of this so coveted chance. But speed ye, speed ye! Let others do this happy office sith 'tis denied to me. I put my Great Seal in commission; choose thou the lords that shall compose it, and get ye to your work. Speed ye, man! Before the sun shall rise and set again, bring me his head, that I may see it."

"According to the king's command, so shall it be. Will't

please your Majesty to order that the Seal be now restored
to me, so that I may forth upon the business?''

"The Seal? Who keepeth the Seal but thou?''

''Please your Majesty, you did take it from me two days
since, saying it should no more do its office till your own
royal hand should use it upon the Duke of Norfolk's warrant.''

"Why, so in sooth I did; I do remember it. What did I
with it? I am very feeble. So oft these days doth my memory
play the traitor with me. 'Tis strange, strange—''

The king dropped into inarticulate mumblings, shaking
his gray head weakly from time to time and gropingly trying
to recollect what he had done with the Seal.

At last my lord Hertford ventured to kneel and offer information, ''Sire, if that I may be so bold, here be several
that do remember with me how that you gave the Great Seal
into the hands of his Highness the Prince of Wales to keep
against the day that——''

"True, most true!'' interrupted the king. "Fetch it! Go;
time flieth!''

Lord Hertford flew to Tom, but returned to the king before very long troubled and empty-handed. He delivered
himself to this effect: "It grieveth me, my lord the king, to
bear so heavy and unwelcome tidings; but it is the will of
God that the prince's affliction abideth still, and he cannot
recall to mind that he received the Seal. So came I quickly
to report, thinking it were waste of precious time and little
worth withal that any should attempt to search the long array of chambers and saloons that belong unto his royal
High——''

A groan from the king interrupted my lord at this point.
After a little while his Majesty said, with a deep sadness in
his tone, "Trouble him no more, poor child. The hand of
God lieth heavy upon him, and my heart goeth out in loving
compassion for him, and sorrow that I may not bear his
burden on mine own old trouble-weighted shoulders, and
so bring him peace.''

He closed his eyes, fell to mumbling, and presently was
silent. After a time he opened his eyes again and gazed
vacantly around until his glance rested upon the kneeling
Lord Chancellor. Instantly his face flushed with wrath:
"What, thou here yet! By the glory of God, an' thou gettest

not about that traitor's business, thy miter shall have holiday the morrow for lack of a head to grace withal!''

The trembling Chancellor answered, ''Good your Majesty, I cry you mercy! I but waited for the Seal.''

''Man, hast lost thy wits? The small Seal which aforetime I was wont to take with me abroad lieth in my treasury. And since the Great Seal hath flown away, shall not it suffice? Hast lost thy wits? Begone! And hark ye; come no more till thou do bring his head.''

The poor Chancellor was not long in removing himself from this dangerous vicinity, nor did the commission waste time in giving the royal assent to the work of the slavish Parliament and appointing the morrow for the beheading of the premier peer of England, the luckless Duke of Norfolk.*

9

The River Pageant

At nine in the evening the whole vast river-front of the palace was blazing with light. The river itself, as far as the eye could reach citywards, was so thickly covered with watermen's boats and with pleasure barges, all fringed with colored lanterns and gently agitated by the waves, that it resembled a glowing and limitless garden of flowers stirred to soft motion by summer winds. The grand terrace of stone steps leading down to the water, spacious enough to mass the army of a German principality upon, was a picture to see, with its ranks of royal halberdiers in polished armor and its troops of brilliantly costumed servitors flitting up and down, and to and fro, in the hurry of preparation.

Presently a command was given, and immediately all living creatures vanished from the steps. Now the air was heavy with the hush of suspense and expectancy. As far as one's vision could carry, he might see the myriads of people in the boats rise up, and shade their eyes from the glare of lanterns and torches, and gaze toward the palace.

A file of forty or fifty state barges drew up to the steps. They were richly gilt, and their lofty prows and sterns were elaborately carved. Some of them were decorated with banners and streamers, some with cloth of gold and arras embroidered with coats of arms, others with silken flags that had numberless little silver bells fastened to them which shook out tiny showers of joyous music whenever the breezes fluttered them; others of yet higher pretensions, since they belonged to nobles in the prince's immediate service, had their sides picturesquely fenced with shields gorgeously emblazoned with armorial bearings. Each state barge was towed by a tender. Besides the rowers, these tenders carried each a number of men-at-arms in glossy helmet and breastplate, and a company of musicians.

The advance guard of the expected procession now appeared in the great gateway, a troop of halberdiers. They were dressed in striped hose of black and tawny, velvet caps graced at the sides with silver roses, and doublets of murrey-and-blue cloth embroidered on the front and back with the three feathers, the prince's blazon, woven in gold. Their halberd staves were covered with crimson velvet, fastened with gilt nails, and ornamented with gold tassels. Filing off on the right and left, they formed two long lines, extending from the gateway of the palace to the water's edge. A thick, rayed cloth, or carpet, was then unfolded and laid down between them by attendants in the gold-and-crimson liveries of the prince. This done, a flourish of trumpets resounded from within. A lively prelude arose from the musicians on the water, and two ushers with white wands marched with a slow and stately pace from the portal. They were followed by an officer bearing the civic mace, after whom came another carrying the city's sword; then several sergeants of the city guard, in their full accouterments and with badges on their sleeves; then the garter king-at-arms, in his tabard; then several knights of the bath, each with a white lace on his sleeve; then their esquires; then the judges, in their robes of scarlet and coifs; then the lord High Chancellor of England, in a robe of scarlet, open before and purified with miniver; then a deputation of aldermen, in their scarlet cloaks; and then the heads of the different civic companies, in their robes of state. Now came twelve French gentlemen, in splendid habiliments, consisting of pourpoints of white damask barred with gold, short mantles of crimson velvet lined with violet taffeta, and carnation-colored *hauts-de-chausses*, and took their way down the steps. They were of the suite of the French ambassador, and were followed by twelve cavaliers of the suite of the Spanish ambassador, clothed in black velvet unrelieved by any ornament. Following these came several great English nobles with their attendants.

There was a flourish of trumpets within; and the prince's uncle, the future great Duke of Somerset, emerged from the gateway arrayed in a doublet of black cloth of gold and a cloak of crimson satin flowered with gold and ribanded with nets of silver. He turned, doffed his plumed cap, bent his body in a low reverence, and began to step backward, bowing at each step. A prolonged trumpet blast followed, and a proclamation, "Way for the high and mighty, the lord

Edward, Prince of Wales!'' High aloft on the palace walls a long line of red tongues of flame leaped forth with a thundercrash; the massed world on the river burst into a mighty roar of welcome; and Tom Canty, the cause and hero of it all, stepped into view and slightly bowed his princely head.

He was magnificently habited in a doublet of white satin, with a frontpiece of purple cloth of tissue, powdered with diamonds, and edged with ermine. Over this he wore a mantle of white cloth of gold pounced with the triple-feather crest, lined with blue satin, set with pearls and precious stones, and fastened with a clasp of brilliants. About his neck hung the Order of the Garter and several princely foreign orders, and wherever light fell upon him jewels responded with a blinding flash. O Tom Canty, born in a hovel, bred in the gutters of London, familiar with rags and dirt and misery, what a spectacle is this!

10

The Prince in the Toils

We left John Canty dragging the rightful prince into Offal Court, with a noisy and delighted mob at his heels. There was but one person in it who offered a pleading word for the captive, and he was not heeded; he was hardly even heard, so great was the turmoil. The prince continued to struggle for freedom and to rage against the treatment he was suffering, until John Canty lost what little patience was left in him and raised his oaken cudgel in a sudden fury over the prince's head. The single pleader for the lad sprang to stop the man's arm, and the blow descended upon his own wrist. Canty roared out, "Thou'lt meddle, wilt thou? Then have thy reward."

His cudgel crashed down upon the meddler's head; there was a groan, a dim form sank to the ground among the feet of the crowd, and the next moment it lay there in the dark alone. The mob pressed on, their enjoyment nothing disturbed by this episode.

Presently the prince found himself in John Canty's abode, with the door closed against the outsiders. By the vague light of a tallow candle which was thrust into a bottle he made out the main features of the loathsome den and also the occupants of it. Two frowzy girls and a middle-aged woman cowered against the wall in one corner with the aspect of animals habituated to harsh usage and expecting and dreading it now. From another corner stole a withered hag with streaming gray hair and malignant eyes. John Canty said to this one, "Tarry! There's fine mummeries here. Mar them not till thou'st enjoyed them; then let thy hand be heavy as thou wilt. Stand forth, lad. Now say thy foolery again, an' thou'st not forgot it. Name thy name. Who art thou?"

The insulted blood mounted to the little prince's cheek once more, and he lifted a steady and indignant gaze to the man's face and said, " 'Tis but ill breeding in such as thou to command me to speak. I tell thee now, as I told thee before, I am Edward, Prince of Wales, and none other.''

The stunning surprise of this reply nailed the hag's feet to the floor where she stood, and almost took her breath. She stared at the prince in stupid amazement, which so amused her ruffianly son that he burst into a roar of laughter. But the effect upon Tom Canty's mother and sisters was different. Their dread of bodily injury gave way at once to distress of a different sort. They ran forward with woe and dismay in their faces, exclaiming, "O poor Tom, poor lad!''

The mother fell on her knees before the prince, put her hands upon his shoulders, and gazed yearningly into his face through her rising tears. Then she said, "O my poor boy! Thy foolish reading hath wrought its woeful work at last and ta'en thy wit away. Ah! Why didst thou cleave to it when I so warned thee 'gainst it? Thou'st broke thy mother's heart.''

The prince looked into her face and said gently, "Thy son is well and hath not lost his wits, good dame. Comfort thee; let me to the palace where he is, and straightway will the king my father restore him to thee.''

"The king thy father! O my child! Unsay these words that be freighted with death for thee and ruin for all that be near to thee. Shake off this gruesome dream. Call back thy poor wandering memory. Look upon me. Am not I thy mother that bore thee and loveth thee?''

The prince shook his head and reluctantly said, "God knoweth I am loath to grieve thy heart, but truly have I never looked upon thy face before.''

The woman sank back to a sitting posture on the floor, and covering her eyes with her hands, gave way to heart-broken sobs and wailings.

"Let the show go on!'' shouted Canty. "What, Nan! What, Bet! Mannerless wenches! Will ye stand in the prince's presence? Upon your knees, ye pauper scum, and do him reverence!''

He followed this with another horselaugh. The girls began to plead timidly for their brother, and Nan said, "An' thou wilt but let him to bed, Father, rest and sleep will heal his madness; prithee, do.''

"Do, Father,'' said Bet; "he is more worn than is his

wont. Tomorrow will he be himself again, and will beg with diligence, and come not empty home again.''

This remark sobered the father's joviality and brought his mind to business. He turned angrily upon the prince and said, ''The morrow must we pay two pennies to him that owns this hole; two pennies, mark ye—all this money for a half year's rent, else out of this we go. Show what thou'st gathered with thy lazy begging.''

The prince said, ''Offend me not with thy sordid matters. I tell thee again I am the king's son.''

A sounding blow upon the prince's shoulder from Canty's broad palm sent him staggering into goodwife Canty's arms, who clasped him to her breast and sheltered him from a pelting rain of cuffs and slaps by interposing her own person. The frightened girls retreated to their corner, but the grandmother stepped eagerly forward to assist her son. The prince sprang away from Mrs. Canty, exclaiming, ''Thou shalt not suffer for me, madam. Let these swine do their will upon me alone.''

This speech infuriated the swine to such a degree that they set about their work without waste of time. Between them they belabored the boy right soundly, and then gave the girls and their mother a beating for showing sympathy for the victim.

''Now,'' said Canty, ''to bed, all of ye. The entertainment has tired me.''

The light was put out, and the family retired. As soon as the snorings of the head of the house and his mother showed that they were asleep, the young girls crept to where the prince lay and covered him tenderly from the cold with straw and rags; and their mother crept to him also, and stroked his hair, and cried over him, whispering broken words of comfort and compassion in his ear the while. She had saved a morsel for him to eat also, but the boy's pains had swept away all appetite, at least for black and tasteless crusts. He was touched by her brave and costly defense of him and by her commiseration, and he thanked her in very noble and princely words, and begged her to go to her sleep and try to forget her sorrows. And he added that the king his father would not let her loyal kindness and devotion go unrewarded. This return to his ''madness'' broke her heart anew, and she strained him to her breast again and again and then went back, drowned in tears, to her bed.

As she lay thinking and mourning, the suggestion began to creep into her mind that there was an undefinable something about this boy that was lacking in Tom Canty, mad or sane. She could not describe it, she could not tell just what it was, and yet her sharp mother instinct seemed to detect it and perceive it. What if the boy were really not her son after all? Oh, absurd! She almost smiled at the idea, spite of her griefs and troubles. No matter, she found that it was an idea that would not "down," but persisted in haunting her. It pursued her, it harassed her, it clung to her, and refused to be put away or ignored. At last she perceived that there was not going to be any peace for her until she should devise a test that should prove, clearly and without question, whether this lad was her son or not, and so banish these wearing and worrying doubts. Ah yes, this was plainly the right way out of the difficulty; therefore she set her wits to work at once to contrive that test. But it was an easier thing to propose than to accomplish. She turned over in her mind one promising test after another, but was obliged to relinquish them all: none of them were absolutely sure, absolutely perfect; and an imperfect one could not satisfy her. Evidently she was racking her head in vain; it seemed manifest that she must give the matter up. While this depressing thought was passing through her mind, her ear caught the regular breathing of the boy, and she knew he had fallen asleep. And while she listened, the measured breathing was broken by a soft, startled cry, such as one utters in a troubled dream. This chance occurrence furnished her instantly with a plan worth all her labored tests combined. She at once set herself feverishly but noiselessly to work to relight her candle, muttering to herself, "Had I but seen him *then*, I should have known! Since that day, when he was little, that the powder burst in his face, he hath never been startled of a sudden out of his dreams or out of his thinkings, but he hath cast his hand before his eyes, even as he did that day; and not as others would do it, with the palm inward, but always with the palm turned outward. I have seen it a hundred times, and it hath never varied nor ever failed. Yes, I shall soon know now!"

By this time she had crept to the slumbering boy's side with the candle, shaded, in her hand. She bent heedfully and warily over him, scarcely breathing in her suppressed excitement, and suddenly flashed the light in his face and struck the floor by his ear with her knuckles. The sleeper's eyes sprung wide open, and he cast a startled stare about him, but he made no special movement with his hands.

The poor woman was smitten almost helpless with surprise and grief, but she contrived to hide her emotions and to soothe the boy to sleep again; then she crept apart and communed miserably with herself upon the disastrous result of her experiment. She tried to believe that her Tom's madness had banished this habitual gesture of his, but she could not do it. "No," she said, "his *hands* are not mad; they could not unlearn so old a habit in so brief a time. Oh, this is a heavy day for me!"

Still, hope was as stubborn now as doubt had been before; she could not bring herself to accept the verdict of the test; she must try the thing again: the failure must have been only an accident; so she startled the boy out of his sleep a second and a third time, at intervals, with the same result which had marked the first test; then she dragged herself to bed and fell sorrowfully asleep, saying, "But I cannot give him up. Oh, no, I cannot, I cannot; he *must* be my boy!"

The poor mother's interruptions having ceased and the prince's pains having gradually lost their power to disturb him, utter weariness at last sealed his eyes in a profound and restful sleep. Hour after hour slipped away, and still he slept like the dead. Thus four or five hours passed. Then his stupor began to lighten. Presently while half asleep and half awake, he murmured, "Sir William!"

After a moment, "Ho, Sir William Herbert! Hie thee hither, and list to the strangest dream that ever. Sir William! Dost hear? Man, I did think me changed to a pauper, and— Ho there! Guards! Sir William! What! Is there no groom of the chamber in waiting? Alack, it shall go hard with——"

"What aileth thee?" asked a whisper near him. "Who art thou calling?"

"Sir William Herbert. Who art thou?"

"I? Who should I be but thy sister Nan? Oh, Tom, I had forgot! Thou'rt mad yet; poor lad thou'rt mad yet; would I had never woke to know it again! But prithee master thy tongue, lest we be all beaten till we die!"

The startled prince sprang partly up, but a sharp reminder from his stiffened bruises brought him to himself, and he sunk back among his foul straw with a moan and the ejaculation, "Alas, it was no dream then!"

In a moment all the heavy sorrow and misery which sleep
had banished were upon him again, and he realized that he
was no longer a petted prince in a palace with the adoring
eyes of a nation upon him, but a pauper, an outcast, clothed
in rags, prisoner in a den fit only for beasts, and consorting
with beggars and thieves.

In the midst of his grief he began to be conscious of
hilarious noises and shoutings, apparently but a block or
two away. The next moment there were several sharp raps
at the door; John Canty ceased from snoring and said, "Who
knocketh? What wilt thou?"

A voice answered, "Knowst thou who it was thou laid
thy cudgel on?"

"No. Neither know I, nor care."

"Belike thou'lt change thy note eftsoons. An' thou would
save thy neck, nothing but flight may stead thee. The man
is this moment delivering up the ghost. 'Tis the priest Father
Andrew!"

"God-a-mercy!" exclaimed Canty. He roused his family
and hoarsely commanded, "Up with ye all and fly, or bide
where ye are and perish!"

Scarcely five minutes later the Canty household were in
the street and flying for their lives. John Canty held the
prince by the wrist and hurried him along the dark way,
giving him this caution in a low voice, "Mind thy tongue,
thou mad fool, and speak not our name. I will choose me
a new name speedily to throw the law's dogs off the scent.
Mind thy tongue, I tell thee!" He growled these words to
the rest of the family: "If it so chance that we be separated,
let each make for London Bridge; whoso findeth himself as
far as the last linen-draper's shop on the bridge, let him
tarry there till the others be come; then will we flee into
Southwark together."

At this moment the party burst suddenly out of darkness
into light, and not only into light, but into the midst of a
multitude of singing, dancing, and shouting people massed
together on the river frontage. There was a line of bonfires
stretching as far as one could see, up and down the Thames;
London Bridge was illuminated; Southwark Bridge likewise; the entire river was aglow with the flash and sheen of
colored lights; and constant explosions of fireworks filled
the skies with an intricate commingling of shooting splendors and a thick rain of dazzling sparks that almost turned

night into day; everywhere were crowds of revelers; all London seemed to be at large.

John Canty delivered himself of a furious curse and commanded a retreat, but it was too late. He and his tribe were swallowed up in that swarming hive of humanity and hopelessly separated from each other in an instant. We are not considering that the prince was one of his tribe; Canty still kept his grip upon him. The prince's heart was beating high with hopes of escape now. A burly waterman, considerably exalted with liquor, found himself rudely shoved by Canty in his efforts to plow through the crowd; he laid his great hand on Canty's shoulder and said, "Nay, whither so fast, friend? Dost canker thy soul with sordid business when all that be leal men and true make holiday?"

"Mine affairs are mine own; they concern thee not," answered Canty roughly; "take away thy hand and let me pass."

"Sith that is thy humor, thou'lt *not* pass till thou'st drunk to the Prince of Wales, I tell thee that," said the waterman, barring the way resolutely.

"Give me the cup, then, and make speed, make speed!"

Other revelers were interested by this time. They cried out, "The loving cup, the loving cup! Make the sour knave drink the loving cup, else will we feed him to the fishes."

So a huge loving cup was brought; the waterman, grasping it by one of its handles, and with his other hand bearing up the end of an imaginary napkin, presented it in due and ancient form to Canty, who had to grasp the opposite handle with one of his hands and take off the lid with the other, according to ancient custom.* This left the prince hand-free for a second of course. He wasted no time, but dived among the forest of legs about him and disappeared. In another moment he could not have been harder to find under that tossing sea of life if its billows had been the Atlantic's and he a lost sixpence.

He very soon realized this fact and straightway busied himself about his own affairs without further thought of John Canty. He quickly realized another thing too. To wit, that a spurious Prince of Wales was being feasted by the city in his stead. He easily concluded that the pauper lad, Tom

*See Note 6 at end of volume.

Canty, had deliberately taken advantage of his stupendous opportunity and become a usurper.

Therefore there was but one course to pursue—find his way to the Guildhall, make himself known, and denounce the impostor. He also made up his mind that Tom should be allowed a reasonable time for spiritual preparation and then be hanged, drawn, and quartered according to the law and usage of the day in cases of high treason.

11

At Guildhall

The royal barge, attended by its gorgeous fleet, took its stately way down the Thames through the wilderness of illuminated boats. The air was laden with music; the river banks were beruffled with joy flames; the distant city lay in a soft luminous glow from its countless invisible bonfires; above it rose many a slender spire into the sky, encrusted with sparkling lights, wherefore in their remoteness they seemed like jeweled lances thrust aloft; as the fleet swept along, it was greeted from the banks with a continuous hoarse roar of cheers and the ceaseless flash and boom of artillery.

To Tom Canty, half buried in his silken cushions, these sounds and this spectacle were a wonder unspeakably sublime and astonishing. To his little friends at his side, the princess Elizabeth and the lady Jane Grey, they were nothing.

Arrived at the Dowgate, the fleet was towed up the limpid Walbrook (whose channel has now been for two centuries buried out of sight under acres of buildings) to Bucklersbury, past houses and under bridges populous with merrymakers and brilliantly lighted, and at last came to a halt in a basin where now is Barge Yard, in the center of the ancient city of London. Tom disembarked, and he and his gallant procession crossed Cheapside and made a short march through the Old Jewry and Basinghall street to the Guildhall.

Tom and his little ladies were received with due ceremony by the Lord Mayor and the Fathers of the City, in their gold chains and scarlet robes of state, and conducted to a rich canopy of estate at the head of the great hall, preceded by heralds making proclamation, and by the mace and the city sword. The lords and ladies who were to attend upon Tom and his two small friends took their places behind their chairs.

At a lower table the court grandees and other guests of noble degree were seated with the magnates of the city; the commoners took places at a multitude of tables on the main floor of the hall. From their lofty vantage ground the giants Gog and Magog, the ancient guardians of the city, contemplated the spectacle below them with eyes grown familiar to it in forgotten generations. There was a bugle blast and a proclamation, and a fat butler appeared in a high perch in the leftward wall, followed by his servitors bearing with impressive solemnity a royal Baron of Beef, smoking hot and ready for the knife.

After grace, Tom (being instructed) rose—and the whole house with him—and drank from a portly golden loving cup with the princess Elizabeth; from her it passed to the lady Jane and then traversed the general assemblage. So the banquet began.

By midnight the revelry was at its height. Now came one of those picturesque spectacles so admired in that old day. A description of it is still extant in the quaint wording of a chronicler who witnessed it:

"Space being made, presently entered a baron and an earl appareled after the Turkish fashion in long robes of bawdkin powdered with gold, hats on their heads of crimson velvet, with great rolls of gold, girded with two swords called scimitars hanging by great bawdricks of gold. Next came yet another baron and another earl, in two long gowns of yellow satin, traversed with white satin, and in every bend of white was a bend of crimson satin, after the fashion of Russia, with furred hats of gray on their heads, either of them having an hatchet in their hands and boots with pikes" (points a foot long), "turned up. And after them came a knight, then the Lord High Admiral, and with him five nobles, in doublets of crimson velvet, voyded low on the back and before to the cannell-bone, laced on the breasts with chains of silver; and over that, short cloaks of crimson satin, and on their heads hats after the dancers' fashion, with pheasants' feathers in them. These were appareled after the fashion of Prussia. The torchbearers, which were about an hundred, were appareled in crimson satin and green, like Moors, their faces black. Next came in a *mommarye*. Then the minstrels, which were disguised, danced; and the lords and ladies did wildly dance also, that it was a pleasure to behold.''

And while Tom, in his high seat, was gazing upon this "wild" dancing, lost in admiration of the dazzling commingling of kaleidoscopic colors which the whirling turmoil of gaudy figures below him presented, the ragged but real little Prince of Wales was proclaiming his rights and his wrongs, denouncing the impostor, and clamoring for admission at the gates of Guildhall! The crowd enjoyed this episode prodigiously and pressed forward and craned their necks to see the small rioter. Presently they began to taunt him and mock at him, purposely to goad him to a higher and still more entertaining fury. Tears of mortification sprung to his eyes, but he stood his ground and defied the mob right royally. Other taunts followed, added mockings stung him, and he exclaimed, "I tell ye again, you pack of unmannerly curs, I am the Prince of Wales! And all forlorn and friendless as I be, with none to give me word of grace or help me in my need, yet will not I be driven from my ground, but will maintain it!''

"Though thou be prince or no prince, 'tis all one; thou be'st a gallant lad, and not friendless neither! Here stand I by thy side to prove it; and mind I tell thee thou mightst have a worser friend than Miles Hendon and yet not tire thy legs with seeking. Rest thy small jaw, my child; I talk the language of these base kennel-rats like to a very native.''

The speaker was a sort of Don Caesar de Bazan in dress, aspect, and bearing. He was tall, trim-built, muscular. His doublet and trunks were of rich material, but faded and threadbare, and their gold-lace adornments were sadly tarnished; his ruff was rumpled and damaged; the plume in his slouched hat was broken and had a bedraggled and disreputable look; at his side he wore a long rapier in a rusty iron sheath; his swaggering carriage marked him at once as a ruffler of the camp. The speech of this fantastic figure was received with an explosion of jeers and laughter. Some cried, " 'Tis another prince in disguise!'' " 'Ware thy tongue, friend; belike he is dangerous!'' "Marry, he looketh it; mark his eye!'' "Pluck the lad from him; to the horsepond wi' the cub!''

Instantly a hand was laid upon the prince, under the impulse of this happy thought; as instantly the stranger's long sword was out and the meddler went to the earth under a

sounding thump with the flat of it. The next moment a score
of voices shouted, "Kill the dog! Kill him! Kill him!" And
the mob closed in on the warrior, who backed himself
against a wall and began to lay about him with his long
weapon like a madman. His victims sprawled this way and
that, but the mobtide poured over their prostrate forms and
dashed itself against the champion with undiminished fury.
His moments seemed numbered, his destruction certain, when
suddenly a trumpet blast sounded, a voice shouted, "Way
for the king's messenger!" and a troop of horsemen came
charging down upon the mob, who fled out of harm's reach
as fast as their legs could carry them. The bold stranger
caught up the prince in his arms and was soon far away
from danger and the multitude.

Return we within the Guildhall. Suddenly, high above the
jubilant roar and thunder of the revel, broke the clear peal
of a bugle note. There was instant silence, a deep hush;
then a single voice rose—that of the messenger from the
palace—and began to pipe forth a proclamation, the whole
multitude standing, listening.

The closing words, solemnly pronounced, were, "The
king is dead!"

The great assemblage bent their heads upon their breasts
with one accord, remained so in profound silence a few
moments; then all sunk upon their knees in a body, stretched
out their hands toward Tom; and a mighty shout burst forth
that seemed to shake the building, "Long live the king!"

Poor Tom's dazed eyes wandered abroad over this stupe-
fying spectacle and finally rested dreamily upon the kneeling princesses beside him a moment, then upon the Earl of
Hertford. A sudden purpose dawned in his face. He said in
a low tone at Lord Hertford's ear, "Answer me truly, on
thy faith and honor! Uttered I here a command, the which
none but a king might hold privilege and prerogative to utter, would such commandment be obeyed, and none rise up
to say me nay?"

"None, my liege, in all these realms. In thy person bides
the majesty of England. Thou art the king; thy word is law."

Tom responded in a strong, earnest voice, and with great
animation, "Then shall the king's law be law of mercy from
this day, and never more be law of blood! Up from thy
knees and away! To the Tower and say the king decrees the
Duke of Norfolk shall not die!"

The words were caught up and carried eagerly from lip to lip far and wide over the hall, and as Hertford hurried from the presence, another prodigious shout burst forth, "The reign of blood is ended! Long live Edward, King of England!"

The Prince
and His Deliverer

As soon as Miles Hendon and the little prince were clear of the mob, they struck down through back lanes and alleys toward the river. Their way was unobstructed until they approached London Bridge; then they plowed into the multitude again, Hendon keeping a fast grip upon the prince's— no, the king's—wrist. The tremendous news was already abroad, and the boy learned it from a thousand voices at once—"The king is dead!" The tidings struck a chill to the heart of the poor little waif and sent a shudder through his frame. He realized the greatness of his loss and was filled with a bitter grief, for the grim tyrant who had been such a terror to others had always been gentle with him. The tears sprung to his eyes and blurred all objects. For an instant he felt himself the most forlorn, outcast, and forsaken of God's creatures; then another cry shook the night with its far-reaching thunder, "Long live King Edward the Sixth!" And this made his eyes kindle and thrilled him with pride to his finger's ends. "Ah," he thought, "how grand and strange it seems—I AM KING!"

Our friends threaded their way slowly through the throngs upon the bridge. This structure, which had stood for six hundred years and had been a noisy and populous thoroughfare all that time, was a curious affair, for a closely packed rank of stores and shops, with family quarters overhead, stretched along both sides of it, from one bank of the river to the other. The bridge was a sort of town to itself; it had its inn, its beer houses, it bakeries, its haberdasheries, its food markets, its manufacturing industries, and even its church. It looked upon the two neighbors which it linked together—London and Southwark—as being well enough as suburbs, but not otherwise particularly important. It was a close corporation, so to speak; it was a narrow town, of a single street a fifth of a mile long; its population was but a village population, and everybody in it knew all his fellow townsmen intimately and had known their fathers and mothers before them—and all their little family affairs into the bargain. It had its aristocracy, of course—its fine old families of butchers, and bakers, and what-not, who had occupied the same old premises for five or six hundred years and knew the great history of the bridge from beginning to end, and all its strange legends, and who always talked bridgy talk, and thought bridgy thoughts, and lied in a long, level, direct, substantial bridgy way. It was just the sort of population to be narrow and ignorant and self-conceited. Children were born on the bridge, were reared there, grew to old age and finally died without ever having set a foot upon any part of the world but London Bridge alone. Such people would naturally imagine that the mighty and interminable procession which moved through its street night and day, with its confused roar of shouts and cries, its neighings and bellowings and bleatings and its muffled thunder-tramp, was the one great thing in this world, and themselves somehow the proprietors of it. And so they were, in effect; at least they could exhibit it from their windows, and did—for a consideration—whenever a returning king or hero gave it a fleeting splendor, for there was no place like it for affording a long, straight, uninterrupted view of marching columns.

Men born and reared upon the bridge found life unendurably dull and inane elsewhere. History tells of one of these who left the bridge at the age of seventy-one and retired to the country. But he could only fret and toss in his bed; he could not go to sleep, the deep stillness was so painful, so awful, so oppressive. When he was worn out with it at last, he fled back to his old home, a lean and haggard specter, and fell peacefully to rest and pleasant dreams under the lulling music of the lashing waters and the boom and crash and thunder of London Bridge.

In the times of which we are writing, the bridge furnished "object lessons" in English history for its children, namely, the livid and decaying heads of renowned men impaled upon iron spikes atop of its gateways. But we digress.

Hendon's lodgings were in the little inn on the bridge. As he neared the door with his small friend, a rough voice said, "So, thou'rt come at last! Thou'lt not escape again, I warrant thee; and if pounding thy bones to a pudding can teach thee somewhat, thou'lt not keep us waiting another time, mayhap." And John Canty put out his hand to seize the boy.

Miles Hendon stepped in the way and said, "Not too fast, friend. Thou art needlessly rough, methinks. What is the lad to thee?"

"If it be any business of thine to make and meddle in others' affairs, he is my son."

" 'Tis a lie!" cried the little king hotly.

"Boldly said, and I believe thee, whether thy small head-piece be sound or cracked, my boy. But whether this scurvy ruffian be thy father or no, 'tis all one; he shall not have thee to beat thee and abuse, according to his threat, so thou prefer to bide with me."

"I do, I do—I know him not, I loathe him, and will die before I will go with him."

"Then 'tis settled, and there is nought more to say."

"We will see as to that!" exclaimed John Canty, striding past Hendon to get at the boy. "By force shall he——"

"If thou do but touch him, thou animated offal, I will spit thee like a goose!" said Hendon, barring the way and laying his hand upon his sword hilt. Canty drew back. "Now mark ye," continued Hendon, "I took this lad under my protection when a mob of such as thou would have mishandled him, mayhap killed him; dost imagine I will desert him now to a worser fate? For whether thou art his father or no—and sooth to say, I think it is a lie—a decent swift death were better for such a lad than life in such brute hands as thine. So go thy ways, and set quick about it, for I like not much bandying of words, being not overpatient in my nature."

John Canty moved off, muttering threats and curses, and was swallowed from sight in the crowd. Hendon ascended three flights of stairs to his room, with his charge, after ordering a meal to be sent thither. It was a poor apartment, with a shabby bed and some odds and ends of old furniture in it, and was vaguely lighted by a couple of sickly candles. The little king dragged himself to the bed and lay down upon it, almost exhausted with hunger and fatigue. He had been on his feet a good part of a day and a night, for it was now two or three o'clock in the morning, and had eaten nothing meantime. He murmured drowsily, "Prithee call me when the table is spread," and sunk into a deep sleep immediately.

A smile twinkled in Hendon's eye, and he said to himself,

"By the mass, the little beggar takes to one's quarters and usurps one's bed with as natural and easy a grace as if he owned them—with never a by-your-leave or so-please-it-you, or anything of the sort. In his diseased ravings he called himself the Prince of Wales, and bravely doth he keep up the character. Poor little friendless rat, doubtless his mind has been disordered with ill usage. Well, I will be his friend; I have saved him, and it draweth me strongly to him; already I love the bold-tongued little rascal. How soldierlike he faced the smutty rabble and flung back his high defiance! And what a comely, sweet, and gentle face he hath, now that sleep hath conjured away its troubles and its griefs. I will teach him, I will cure his malady; yea, I will be his elder brother, and care for him and watch over him; and whoso would shame him or do him hurt may order his shroud, for though I be burnt for it he shall need it!"

He bent over the boy and contemplated him with kind and pitying interest, tapping the young cheek tenderly and smoothing back the tangled curls with his great brown hand. A slight shiver passed over the boy's form. Hendon muttered, "See, now, how like a man it was to let him lie here uncovered and fill his body with deadly rheums. Now what shall I do? 'Twill wake him to take him up and put him within the bed, and he sorely needeth sleep."

He looked about for extra covering, but finding none, doffed his doublet and wrapped the lad in it, saying, "I am used to nipping air and scant apparel; 'tis little I shall mind the cold''; then walked up and down the room to keep his blood in motion, soliloquizing as before. "His injured mind persuades him he is Prince of Wales; 'twill be odd to have a Prince of Wales still with us, now that he that *was* the prince is prince no more, but king—for this poor mind is set upon the one fantasy and will not reason out that now it should cast by the prince and call itself the king. If my father liveth still, after these seven years that I have heard nought from home in my foreign dungeon, he will welcome the poor lad and give him generous shelter for my sake; so will my good elder brother, Arthur; my other brother, Hugh—but I will crack his crown, an' *he* interfere, the fox-hearted, ill-conditioned animal! Yes, thither will we fare—and straightway too."

A servant entered with a smoking meal, disposed it upon a small deal table, placed the chairs,' and took his departure, leaving such cheap lodgers as these to wait upon themselves. The door slammed after him, and the noise woke the boy, who sprung to a sitting posture and shot a glad glance about him; then a grieved look came into his face and he murmured to himself with a deep sigh, "Alack, it was but a dream, woe is me." Next he noticed Miles Hendon's doublet—glanced from that to Hendon, comprehended the sacrifice that had been made for him, and said gently, "Thou art good to me; yes, thou art very good to me. Take it and put it on; I shall not need it more."

Then he got up and walked to the washstand in the corner, and stood there, waiting. Hendon said in a cheery voice, "We'll have a right hearty sup and bite now, for everything is savory and smoking hot, and that and thy nap together will make thee a little man again, never fear!"

The boy made no answer, but bent a steady look that was filled with grave surprise and also somewhat touched with impatience upon the tall knight of the sword. Hendon was puzzled and said, "What's amiss?"

"Good sir, I would wash me."

"Oh, is that all! Ask no permission of Miles Hendon for aught thou cravest. Make thyself perfectly free here, and welcome, with all that are his belongings."

Still the boy stood, and moved not; more, he tapped the floor once or twice with his small impatient foot. Hendon was wholly perplexed. Said he, "Bless us, what is it?"

"Prithee pour the water, and make not so many words!"

Hendon, suppressing a horselaugh and saying to himself, "By all the saints, but this is admirable!" stepped briskly forward and did the small insolent's bidding; then stood by in a sort of stupefaction until the command, "Come, the towel!" woke him sharply up. He took up a towel from under the boy's nose and handed it to him without comment. He now proceeded to comfort his own face with a wash, and while he was at it his adopted child seated himself at the table and prepared to fall to. Hendon dispatched his ablutions with alacrity, then drew back the other chair and was about to place himself at table when the boy said indignantly, "Forbear! Wouldst sit in the presence of the king?"

This blow staggered Hendon to his foundations. He muttered to himself, "Lo, the poor thing's madness is up with the time! It hath changed with the great change that is come to the realm, and now in fancy is he *king!* Good lack, I must humor the conceit too—there is no other way—faith, he would order me to the Tower, else!''

And pleased with this jest, he removed the chair from the table, took his stand behind the king, and proceeded to wait upon him in the courtliest way he was capable of.

While the king ate, the rigor of his royal dignity relaxed a little, and with his growing contentment came a desire to talk. He said, ''I think thou callest thyself Miles Hendon, if I heard thee aright?''

''Yes, sire,'' Miles replied; then observed to himself, ''If I *must* humor the poor lad's madness, I must sire him, I must majesty him, I must not go by halves, I must stick at nothing that belongeth to the part I play, else shall I play it ill and work evil to this charitable and kindly cause.''

The king warmed his heart with a second glass of wine and said, ''I would know thee—tell me thy story. Thou hast a gallant way with thee, and a noble—art nobly born?''

''We are of the tail of the nobility, good your Majesty. My father is a baronet—one of the smaller lords, by knight service*—Sir Richard Hendon, of Hendon Hall, by Monk's Holm, in Kent.''

''The name has escaped my memory. Go on—tell me thy story.''

'' 'Tis not much, your Majesty, yet perchance it may beguile a short half hour for want of a better. My father, Sir Richard, is very rich and of a most generous nature. My mother died whilst I was yet a boy. I have two brothers: Arthur, my elder, with a soul like to his father's; and Hugh, younger than I, a mean spirit, covetous, treacherous, vicious, underhanded—a reptile. Such was he from the cradle; such was he ten years past, when I last saw him—a ripe rascal at nineteen, I being twenty then and Arthur twenty-two. There is none other of us but the lady Edith, my cousin—she was sixteen then—beautiful, gentle, good, the daughter of an earl, the last of her race, heiress of a great fortune and a lapsed title. My father was her guardian. I loved her and she loved me, but she was betrothed to Arthur from the cradle, and Sir Richard would not suffer the con-

---

*He refers to the order of baronets, or baronettes—the *barones minores,* as distinct from the parliamentary barons—not, it need hardly be said, the baronets of later creation.

tract to be broken. Arthur loved another maid and bade us be of good cheer and hold fast to the hope that delay and luck together would some day give success to our several causes. Hugh loved the lady Edith's fortune, though in truth he said it was herself he loved; but then 'twas his way, alway, to say the one thing and mean the other. But he lost his arts upon the girl; he could deceive my father, but none else. My father loved him best of us all and trusted and believed him, for he was the youngest child and others hated him—these qualities being in all ages sufficient to win a parent's dearest love; and he had a smooth persuasive tongue, with an admirable gift of lying—and these be qualities which do mightily assist a blind affection to cozen itself. I was wild—in troth I might go yet farther and say *very* wild, though 'twas a wildness of an innocent sort, since it hurt none but me, brought shame to none, nor loss, nor had in it any taint of crime or baseness or what might not beseem mine honorable degree.

"Yet did my brother Hugh turn these faults to good account, he seeing that our brother Arthur's health was but indifferent, and hoping the worst might work him profit were I swept out of the path— But 'twere a long tale, good my liege, and little worth the telling. Briefly, then, this brother did deftly magnify my faults and make them crimes, ending his base work with finding a silken ladder in mine apartments—conveyed thither by his own means—and did convince my father by this and suborned evidence of servants and other lying knaves that I was minded to carry off my Edith and marry her in rank defiance of his will.

"Three years of banishment from home and England might make a soldier and a man of me, my father said, and teach me some degree of wisdom. I fought out my long probation in the continental wars, tasting sumptuously of hard knocks, privation, and adventure; but in my last battle I was taken captive, and during the seven years that have waxed and waned since then, a foreign dungeon hath harbored me. Through wit and courage I won to the free air at last and fled hither straight, and am but just arrived, right poor in purse and raiment, and poorer still in knowledge of what these dull seven years have wrought at Hendon Hall, its people and belongings. So please you, sir, my meager tale is told."

"Thou hast been shamefully abused!" said the little king

with a flashing eye. "But I will right thee—by the cross will I! The king hath said it."

Then, fired by the story of Miles's wrongs, he loosed his tongue and poured the history of his own recent misfortunes into the ears of his astonished listener.

When he had finished, Miles said to himself, "Lo, what an imagination he hath! Verily this is no common mind, else, crazed or sane, it could not weave so straight and gaudy a tale as this out of the airy nothings wherewith it hath wrought this curious romaunt. Poor ruined little head, it shall not lack friend or shelter whilst I bide with the living. He shall never leave my side; he shall be my pet, my little comrade. And he shall be cured! Aye, made whole and sound; then will he make himself a name; and proud shall I be to say, 'Yes, he is mine—I took him, a homeless little ragamuffin, but I saw what was in him, and I said his name would be heard some day—behold him, observe him—was I right?' "

The king spoke in a thoughtful, measured voice, "Thou didst save me injury and shame, perchance my life, and so my crown. Such service demandeth rich reward. Name thy desire, and so it be within the compass of my royal power, it is thine."

This fantastic suggestion startled Hendon out of his reverie. He was about to thank the king and put the matter aside with saying he had only done his duty and desired no reward, but a wiser thought came into his head, and he asked leave to be silent a few moments and consider the gracious offer—an idea which the king gravely approved, remarking that it was best to be not too hasty with a thing of such great import.

Miles reflected during some moments, then said to himself, "Yes, that is the thing to do; by any other means it were impossible to get at it, and certes, this hour's experience has taught me 'twould be most wearing and inconvenient to continue as it is. Yes, I will propose it; 'twas a happy accident that I did not throw the chance away." Then he dropped upon one knee and said, "My poor service went not beyond the limit of a subject's simple duty and therefore hath no merit, but since your Majesty is pleased to hold it worthy some reward, I take heart of grace to make petition to this effect. Near four hundred years ago, as your Grace knoweth, there being ill blood betwixt John, king of England, and the king of France, it was decreed that two champions should fight together in the lists and so settle the dispute by what is called the arbitrament of God. These two kings, and the Spanish king, being assembled to witness and judge the conflict, the French champion appeared; but so redoubtable was he that our English knights refused to measure weapons with him. So the matter, which was a weighty one, was like to go against the English monarch by default. Now in the Tower lay the lord De Courcy, the mightiest arm in England, stripped of his honors and possessions, and wasting with long captivity. Appeal was made to him; he gave assent and came forth arrayed for battle; but no sooner did the Frenchman glimpse his huge frame and hear his famous name but he fled away, and the French king's cause was lost. King John restored De Courcy's titles and possessions and said, 'Name thy wish and thou shalt have it, though it cost me half my kingdom'; whereat De Courcy, kneeling, as I do now, made answer, 'This, then, I ask, my liege; that I and my successors may have and hold the privilege of remaining covered in the presence of the kings of England, henceforth while the throne shall last.' The boon was granted, as your Majesty knoweth; and there hath been no time these four hundred years that that line has failed of an heir; and so, even unto this day, the head of that ancient house still weareth his hat or helm before the king's majesty, without let or hindrance, and this none other may do.* Invoking this precedent in aid of my prayer, I beseech the king to grant to me but this one grace and privilege—to my more than sufficient reward—and none other, to wit: that I and my heirs forever may *sit* in the presence of the Majesty of England!''

''Rise, Sir Miles Hendon, knight,'' said the king gravely, giving the accolade with Hendon's sword; ''rise, and seat thyself. Thy petition is granted. Whilst England remains, and the crown continues, the privilege shall not lapse.''

His Majesty walked apart, musing, and Hendon dropped into a chair at table, observing to himself, '' 'Twas a brave thought and hath wrought me a mighty deliverance; my legs are grievously wearied. An' I had not thought of that, I must have had to stand for weeks, till my poor lad's wits are

---

*The lords of Kingsale, descendants of De Courcy, still enjoy this curious privilege.

cured.'' After a little, he went on, ''And so I am become a knight of the Kingdom of Dreams and Shadows! A most odd and strange position truly for one so matter-of-fact as I. I will not laugh—no, God forbid, for this thing which is so substanceless to me is *real* to him. And to me also, in one way, it is not a falsity, for it reflects with truth the sweet and generous spirit that is in him.'' After a pause: ''Ah, what if he should call me by my fine title before folk! There'd be a merry contrast betwixt my glory and my raiment! But no matter; let him call me what he will, so it please him, I shall be content.''

The Disappearance
of the Prince

A heavy drowsiness presently fell upon the two comrades. The king said, "Remove these rags," meaning his clothing.

Hendon disappareled the boy without dissent or remark, tucked him up in bed, then glanced about the room, saying to himself ruefully, "He hath taken my bed again, as before; marry, what shall *I* do?"

The little king observed his perplexity and dissipated it with a word. He said sleepily, "Thou wilt sleep athwart the door and guard it." In a moment more he was out of his troubles, in a deep slumber.

"Dear heart, he should have been born a king!" muttered Hendon admiringly. "He playeth the part to a marvel."

Then he stretched himself across the door, on the floor, saying contentedly, "I have lodged worse for seven years; 'twould be but ill gratitude to Him above to find fault with this."

He dropped asleep as the dawn appeared. Toward noon he rose, uncovered his unconscious ward—a section at a time—and took his measure with a string. The king awoke just as he had completed his work, complained of the cold, and asked what he was doing.

" 'Tis done now, my liege," said Hendon; "I have a bit of business outside, but will presently return; sleep thou again—thou needest it. There—let me cover thy head also—thou'lt be warm the sooner."

The king was back in dreamland before this speech was ended. Miles slipped softly out and slipped as softly in again in the course of thirty or forty minutes, with a complete secondhand suit of boy's clothing, of cheap material and showing signs of wear, but tidy and suited to the season of the year. He seated himself and began to overhaul his purchase, mumbling to himself, "A longer purse would have got a better sort, but when one has not the long purse one must be content with what a short one may do:

> " 'There was a woman in our town
> In our town did dwell—'

"He stirred, methinks. I must sing in a less thunderous key; 'tis not good to mar his sleep, with this journey before him and he so wearied out, poor chap. This garment—'tis well enough—a stitch here and another there will set it aright. This other is better, albeit a stitch or two will not come amiss in it likewise. *These* be very good and sound, and will keep his small feet warm and dry—an odd new thing to him, belike, since he has doubtless been used to foot it bare, winters and summers the same. Would thread were bread, seeing one getteth a year's sufficiency for a farthing, and such a brave big needle without cost, for mere love. Now shall I have the demon's own time to thread it!"

And so he had. He did as men have always done, and probably always will do, to the end of time—held the needle still and tried to thrust the thread through the eye, which is the opposite of a woman's way. Time and time again the thread missed the mark, going sometimes on one side of the needle, sometimes on the other, sometimes doubling up against the shaft; but he was patient, having been through these experiences before when he was soldiering. He succeeded at last and took up the garment that had lain waiting meantime across his lap and began his work.

"The inn is paid—the breakfast that is to come, included—and there is wherewithal left to buy a couple of donkeys and meet our little costs for the two or three days betwixt this and the plenty that awaits us at Hendon Hall:

> " 'She loved her hus—'

"Body o' me! I have driven the needle under my nail! It matters little—'tis not a novelty—yet 'tis not a convenience neither. We shall be merry there, little one, never doubt it! Thy troubles will vanish, there, and likewise thy sad distemper:

> " 'She loved her husband dearilee,
> But another man—'

"These be noble large stitches!"—holding the garment up and viewing it admiringly. "They have a grandeur and a majesty that do cause these small stingy ones of the tailor-man to look mightily paltry and plebeian:

> " 'She loved her husband dearilee,
> But another man he loved she—'

"Marry, 'tis done—a goodly piece of work, too, and wrought with expedition. Now will I wake him, apparel him, pour for him, feed him, and then will we hie us to the mart by the Tabard Inn in Southwark and—be pleased to rise, my liege!—he answereth not—what ho, my liege!—of a truth must I profane his sacred person with a touch, sith his slumber is deaf to speech. What!"

He threw back the covers; the boy was gone!

He stared about him in speechless astonishment for a moment, noticed for the first time that his ward's ragged raiment was also missing; then he began to rage and storm and shout for the innkeeper. At that moment a servant entered with the breakfast.

"Explain, thou limb of Satan, or thy time is come!" roared the man of war, and made so savage a spring toward the waiter that this latter could not find his tongue for the instant, for fright and surprise. "Where is the boy?"

In disjointed and trembling syllables the man gave the information desired.

"You were hardly gone from the place, your worship, when a youth came running and said it was your worship's will that the boy come to you straight, at the bridge end on the Southwark side. I brought him hither, and when he woke the lad and gave his message, the lad did grumble some little for being disturbed 'so early,' as he called it, but straightway trussed on his rags and went with the youth, only saying it had been better manners that your worship came yourself, not sent a stranger; and so——"

"And so thou'rt a fool: a fool, and easily cozened; hang all thy breed! Yet mayhap no hurt is done. Possibly no harm is meant the boy. I will go fetch him. Make the table ready. Stay! The coverings of the bed were disposed as if one lay beneath them; happened that by accident?''

"I know not, good your worship. I saw the youth meddle with them—he that came for the boy.''

"Thousand deaths!'Twas done to deceive me—'tis plain 'twas done to gain time. Hark ye! Was that youth alone?''

"All alone, your worship.''

"Art sure?''

"Sure, your worship.''

"Collect thy scattered wits—bethink thee—take time, man.''

After a moment's thought the servant said, "When he came, none came with him; but now I remember me that as the two stepped into the throng of the bridge, a ruffian-looking man plunged out from some near place; and just as he was joining them——''

"What *then?* Out with it!'' thundered the impatient Hendon, interrupting.

"Just then the crowd lapped them up and closed them in, and I saw no more, being called by my master, who was in a rage because a joint that the scrivener had ordered was forgot, though I take all the saints to witness that to blame *me* for that miscarriage were like holding the unborn babe to judgment for sins com——''

"Out of my sight, idiot! Thy prating drives me mad! Hold! Whither art flying? Canst not bide still an instant? Went they toward Southwark?''

"Even so, your worship; for, as I said before, as to the detestable joint, the babe unborn is no whit more blameless than——''

"Art here *yet!* And prating still? Vanish, lest I throttle thee!'' The servitor vanished. Hendon followed after him, passed him, and plunged down the stairs two steps at a stride, muttering, " 'Tis that scurvy villain that claimed he was his son. I have lost thee, my poor little mad master—it is a bitter thought—and I had come to love thee so! No! By book and bell, *not* lost! Not lost, for I will ransack the land till I find thee again. Poor child, yonder is his breakfast and mine, but I have no hunger now; so let the rats have it. Speed, speed! That is the word!'' As he wormed his swift way through the noisy multitudes upon the bridge, he several times said to himself, clinging to the thought, as if it were a particularly pleasing one, "He grumbled, but he *went*—he went, yes, because he thought Miles Hendon asked it, sweet lad—he would ne'er have done it for another, I know it well."

14

"Le Roi Est Mort—Vive le Roi"

Toward daylight of the same morning, Tom Canty stirred out of a heavy sleep and opened his eyes in the dark. He lay silent a few moments, trying to analyze his confused thoughts and impressions and get some sort of meaning out of them; then suddenly he burst out in a rapturous but guarded voice, "I see it all, I see it all! Now God be thanked, I am indeed awake at last! Come, joy! Vanish, sorrow! Ho, Nan! Bet! Kick off your straw and hie ye hither to my side, till I do pour into your unbelieving ears the wildest madcap dream that ever the spirits of night did conjure up to astonish the soul of man withal! Ho, Nan, I say! Bet!"

A dim form appeared at his side, and a voice said, "Wilt deign to deliver thy commands?"

"Commands? Oh, woe is me, I know thy voice! Speak, thou—who am I?"

"Thou? In sooth, yesternight wert thou the prince of Wales; today art thou my most gracious liege, Edward, king of England."

Tom buried his head among his pillows, murmuring plaintively, "Alack, it was no dream! Go to thy rest, sweet sir; leave me to my sorrows."

Tom slept again, and after a time he had this pleasant dream. He thought it was summer and he was playing all alone in the fair meadow called Goodman's Fields, when a dwarf only a foot high, with long red whiskers and a humped back, appeared to him suddenly and said, "Dig, by that stump." He did so and found twelve bright new pennies—wonderful riches! Yet this was not the best of it, for the dwarf said, "I know thee. Thou art a good lad and a deserving; thy distresses shall end, for the day of thy reward is come. Dig here every seventh day, and thou shalt find always the same treasure, twelve bright new pennies. Tell none—keep the secret.'' Then the dwarf vanished, and Tom flew to Offal Court with his prize, saying to himself, ''Every night will I give my father a penny; he will think I begged it, it will glad his heart, and I shall no more be beaten. One penny every week the good priest that teacheth me shall have; Mother, Nan, and Bet the other four. We be done with hunger and rags now, done with fears and frets and savage usage.''

In his dream he reached his sordid home all out of breath, but with eyes dancing with grateful enthusiasm, cast four of his pennies into his mother's lap, and cried out, ''They are for thee! All of them, every one! For thee and Nan and Bet—and honestly come by, not begged nor stolen!''

The happy and astonished mother strained him to her breast and exclaimed, ''It waxeth late; may it please your Majesty to rise?''

Ah, that was not the answer he was expecting. The dream had snapped asunder—he was awake.

He opened his eyes; the richly clad First Lord of the Bedchamber was kneeling by his couch. The gladness of the lying dream faded away; the poor boy recognized that he was still a captive and a king. The room was filled with courtiers clothed in purple mantles—the mourning color—and with noble servants of the monarch. Tom sat up in bed and gazed out from the heavy silken curtains upon this fine company.

The weighty business of dressing began, and one courtier after another knelt and paid his court and offered to the little king his condolences upon his heavy loss whilst the dressing proceeded. In the beginning, a shirt was taken up by the Chief Equerry-in-Waiting, who passed it to the First Lord of the Buckhounds, who passed it to the Second Gentleman of the Bedchamber, who passed it to the Head Ranger of Windsor Forest, who passed it to the Third Groom of the Stole, who passed it to the Chancellor Royal of the Duchy of Lancaster, who passed it to the Master of the Wardrobe, who passed it to Norroy King-at-Arms, who passed it to the Constable of the Tower, who passed it to the Chief Steward of the Household, who passed it to the Hereditary Grand Diaperer, who passed it to the Lord High Admiral of England, who passed it to the Archbishop of Canterbury, who passed it to the First Lord of the Bedchamber, who took what was left of it and put it on Tom. Poor little wondering chap, it reminded him of passing buckets at a fire.

Each garment in its turn had to go through this slow and solemn process; consequently Tom grew very weary of the ceremony, so weary that he felt an almost gushing gratefulness when he at last saw his long silken hose begin the journey down the line and knew that the end of the matter was drawing near. But he exulted too soon. The First Lord of the Bedchamber received the hose and was about to encase Tom's legs in them when a sudden flush invaded his face and he hurriedly hustled the things back into the hands of the Archbishop of Canterbury with an astounded look and a whispered, "See, my lord!"—pointing to a something connected with the hose. The Archbishop paled, then flushed, and passed the hose to the Lord High Admiral, whispering, "See, my lord!" The admiral passed the hose to the Hereditary Grand Diaperer and had hardly breath enough in his body to ejaculate, "See, my lord!" The hose drifted backward along the line, to the Chief Steward of the Household, the Constable of the Tower, Norroy King-at-Arms, the Master of the Wardrobe, the Chancellor Royal of the Duchy of Lancaster, the Third Groom of the Stole, the Head Ranger of Windsor Forest, the Second Gentleman of the Bedchamber, the First Lord of the Buckhounds, accompanied always with that amazed and frightened "See! see!"—till they finally reached the hands of the Chief Equerry-in-Waiting, who gazed a moment, then hoarsely whispered, "Body of my life, a tag gone from a trusspoint! To the Tower with the Head Keeper of the King's Hose!"—after which he leaned upon the shoulder of the First Lord of the Buckhounds to regather his vanished strength whilst fresh hose, without any damaged strings to them, were brought.

But all things must have an end, and so in time Tom Canty was in a condition to get out of the bed. The proper official poured water, the proper official engineered the washing, the proper official stood by with a towel, and by and by Tom got safely through the purifying stage and was ready for the services of the Hairdresser Royal. When he at length emerged from this master's hands, he was a gracious figure and as pretty as a girl in his mantle and trunks of purple satin and purple-plumed cap. He now moved in state toward his breakfast room through the midst of the courtly assemblage; and as he passed, these fell back, leaving his way free, and dropped upon their knees.

After breakfast he was conducted, with regal ceremony, attended by his great officers and his guard of fifty Gentlemen Pensioners bearing gilt battle axes, to the throne room, where he proceeded to transact business of state. His "uncle," Lord Hertford, took his stand by the throne to assist the royal mind with wise counsel.

The body of illustrious men named by the late king as his executors appeared to ask Tom's approval of certain acts of theirs—rather a form, and yet not wholly a form, since there was no Protector as yet. The Archbishop of Canterbury made report of the decree of the Council of Executors concerning the obsequies of his late most illustrious Majesty and finished by reading the signatures of the executors, to wit: the Archbishop of Canterbury, the Lord Chancellor of England, William Lord St. John, John Lord Russell, Edward Earl of Hertford, John Viscount Lisle, Cuthbert Bishop of Durham—

Tom was not listening; an earlier clause of the document was puzzling him. At this point he turned and whispered to Lord Hertford, "What day did he say the burial hath been appointed for?"

"The sixteenth of the coming month, my liege."

" 'Tis a strange folly. Will he keep?"

Poor chap, he was still new to the customs of royalty; he was used to seeing the forlorn dead of Offal Court hustled out of the way with a very different sort of expedition. However, the lord Hertford set his mind at rest with a word or two.

A secretary of state presented an order of the council appointing the morrow at eleven for the reception of the foreign ambassadors, and desired the king's assent.

Tom turned an inquiring look toward Hertford, who whispered, "Your Majesty will signify consent. They come to testify their royal masters' sense of the heavy calamity which hath visited your Grace and the realm of England."

Tom did as he was bidden. Another secretary began to read a preamble concerning the expenses of the late king's household, which had amounted to £28,000 during the preceding six months—a sum so vast that it made Tom Canty gasp; he gasped again when the fact appeared that £20,000 of this money were still owing and unpaid, and once more when it appeared that the king's coffers were about empty and his twelve hundred servants much embarrassed for lack of the wages due them. Tom spoke out with lively apprehension, "We be going to the dogs, 'tis plain. 'Tis meet and necessary that we take a smaller house and set the servants at large, sith they be of no value but to make delay, and trouble one with offices that harass the spirit and shame the soul, they misbecoming any but a doll, that hath nor brains nor hands to help itself withal. I remember me of a small house that standeth over against the fish market, by Billingsgate——"

A sharp pressure upon Tom's arm stopped his foolish tongue and sent a blush to his face; but no countenance there betrayed any sign that this strange speech had been remarked or given concern.

A secretary made report that forasmuch as the late king had provided in his will for conferring the ducal degree upon the Earl of Hertford and raising his brother, Sir Thomas Seymour, to the peerage, and likewise Hertford's son to an earldom, together with similar aggrandizements to other great servants of the Crown, the council had resolved to hold a sitting on the sixteenth of February for the delivering and confirming of these honors; and that meantime, the late king not having granted in writing estates suitable to the support of these dignities, the council, knowing his private wishes in that regard, had thought proper to grant to Seymour "£500 lands," and to Hertford's son "800 pound lands and 300 pound of the next bishop's lands which should fall vacant,"* his present Majesty being willing.

Tom was about to blurt out something about the propriety of paying the late king's debts first before squandering all this money, but a timely touch upon his arm from the thoughtful Hertford saved him this indiscretion, wherefore he gave the royal assent, without spoken comment but with much inward discomfort. While he sat reflecting a moment over the ease with which he was doing strange and glittering miracles, a happy thought shot into his mind: why not make his mother Duchess of Offal Court and give her an estate? But a sorrowful thought swept it instantly away: he was only a king in name, these grave veterans and great nobles were his masters; to them his mother was only the creature of a

*Hume.

diseased mind; they would simply listen to his project with unbelieving ears, then send for the doctor.

The dull work went tediously on. Petitions were read, and proclamations, patents, and all manner of wordy, repetitious, and wearisome papers relating to the public business; and at last Tom sighed pathetically and murmured to himself, "In what have I offended, that the good God should take me away from the fields and the free air and the sunshine to shut me up here and make me a king and afflict me so?" Then his poor muddled head nodded awhile and presently drooped to his shoulder, and the business of the empire came to a standstill for want of that august factor the ratifying power. Silence ensued around the slumbering child, and the sages of the realm ceased from their deliberations.

During the forenoon Tom had an enjoyable hour, by permission of his keepers, Hertford and St. John, with the lady Elizabeth and the little lady Jane Grey, though the spirits of the princesses were rather subdued by the mighty stroke that had fallen upon the royal house; and at the end of the visit his "elder sister"—afterwards the "Bloody Mary" of history—chilled him with a solemn interview which had but one merit in his eyes, its brevity. He had a few moments to himself, and then a slim lad of about twelve years of age was admitted to his presence, whose clothing, except his snowy ruff and the laces about his wrists, was of black—doublet, hose and all. He bore no badge of mourning but a knot of purple ribbon on his shoulder. He advanced hesitatingly with head bowed and bare and dropped upon one knee in front of Tom. Tom sat still and contemplated him soberly a moment. Then he said, "Rise, lad. Who art thou? What wouldst have?"

The boy rose and stood at graceful ease, but with an aspect of concern in his face. He said "Of a surety thou must remember me, my lord. I am thy whipping boy."

"My *whipping* boy?"

"The same, your Grace. I am Humphrey—Humphrey Marlow."

Tom perceived that here was someone whom his keepers ought to have posted him about. The situation was delicate. What should he do? Pretend he knew this lad, and then betray by his every utterance that he had never heard of him before? No, that would not do. An idea came to his relief:

accidents like this might be likely to happen with some frequency now that business urgencies would often call Hertford and St. John from his side, they being members of the council of executors; therefore perhaps it would be well to strike out a plan himself to meet the requirements of such emergencies. Yes, that would be a wise course; he would practice on this boy, and see what sort of success he might achieve. So he stroked his brow perplexedly a moment or two and presently said, "Now I seem to remember thee somewhat, but my wit is clogged and dim with suffering—"

"Alack, my poor master!" ejaculated the whipping boy with feeling, adding to himself, "In truth 'tis as they said—his mind is gone; alas, poor soul! But misfortune catch me, how am I forgetting! They said one must not seem to observe that aught is wrong with him."

"'Tis strange how my memory doth wanton with me these days," said Tom. "But mind it not—I mend apace—a little clue doth often serve to bring me back again the things and names which had escaped me. [And not they only, forsooth, but e'en such as I ne'er heard before—as this lad shall see.] Give thy business speech."

"'Tis matter of small weight, my liege, yet will I touch upon it an' it please your Grace. Two days gone by, when your Majesty faulted thrice in your Greek in the morning lessons—dost remember it?"

"Y-e-s—methinks I do. [It is not much of a lie—an' I had meddled with the Greek at all, I had not faulted simply thrice, but forty times.] Yes, I do recall it now; go on."

"The master, being wroth with what he termed such slovenly and doltish work, did promise that he would soundly whip me for it, and——"

"Whip *thee!*" said Tom, astonished out of his presence of mind. "Why should he whip *thee* for faults of mine?"

"Ah, your Grace forgetteth again. He always scourgeth me when thou dost fail in thy lessons."

"True, true—I had forgot. Thou teachest me in private; then if I fail, he argueth that thy office was lamely done, and——"

"Oh, my liege, what words are these? I, the humblest of thy servants, presume to teach *thee?*"

"Then where is thy blame? What riddle is this? Am I in truth gone mad, or is it thou? Explain—speak out."

"But good your Majesty, there's nought that needeth simplifying. None may visit the sacred person of the Prince of Wales with blows, wherefore when he faulteth, 'tis I that take them; and meet it is and right, for that it is mine office and my livelihood.''*

Tom stared at the tranquil boy, observing to himself, ''Lo, it is a wonderful thing—a most strange and curious trade; I marvel they have not hired a boy to take my combings and my dressings for me—would heaven they would!—an' they will do this thing, I will take my lashings in mine own person, giving God thanks for the change.'' Then he said aloud, ''And hast thou been beaten, poor friend, according to the promise?''

''No, good your Majesty, my punishment was appointed for this day, and peradventure it may be annulled as unbefitting the season of mourning that is come upon us; I know not, and so have made bold to come hither and remind your Grace about your gracious promise to intercede in my behalf——''

''With the master? To save thee thy whipping?''

''Ah, thou dost remember!''

''My memory mendeth, thou seest. Set thy mind at ease; thy back shall go unscathed; I will see to it.''

''Oh, thanks, my good lord!'' cried the boy, dropping upon his knee again. ''Mayhap I have ventured far enow; and yet——''

Seeing Master Humphrey hesitate, Tom encouraged him to go on, saying he was ''in the granting mood.''

''Then will I speak it out, for it lieth near my heart. Sith thou art no more Prince of Wales, but king, thou canst order matters as thou wilt, with none to say thee nay; wherefore it is not in reason that thou wilt longer vex thyself with dreary studies, but wilt burn thy books and turn thy mind to things less irksome. Then am I ruined, and mine orphan sisters with me!''

''Ruined? Prithee how?''

''My back is my bread, O my gracious liege! If it go idle, I starve. An' thou cease from study, mine office is gone, thou'lt need no whipping boy. Do not turn me away!''

Tom was touched with this pathetic distress. He said, with a right royal burst of generosity, ''Discomfort thyself no further, lad. Thine office shall be permanent in thee and thy

*See Note 8 at end of volume.

line forever.'' Then he struck the boy a light blow on the shoulder with the flat of his sword, exclaiming, ''Rise, Humphrey Marlow, Hereditary Grand Whipping Boy to the royal house of England! Banish sorrow; I will betake me to my books again and study so ill that they must in justice treble thy wage, so mightily shall the business of thine office be augmented.''

The grateful Humphrey responded fervidly, ''Thanks, O most noble master; this princely lavishness doth far surpass my most distempered dreams of fortune. Now shall I be happy all my days, and all the house of Marlow after me.''

Tom had wit enough to perceive that here was a lad who could be useful to him. He encouraged Humphrey to talk, and he was nothing loath. He was delighted to believe that he was helping in Tom's ''cure,'' for always, as soon as he had finished calling back to Tom's diseased mind the various particulars of his experiences and adventures in the royal schoolroom and elsewhere about the palace, he noticed that Tom was then able to ''recall'' the circumstances quite clearly. At the end of an hour Tom found himself well freighted with very valuable information concerning personages and matters pertaining to the court, so he resolved to draw instruction from this source daily, and to this end he would give order to admit Humphrey to the royal closet whenever he might come, provided the majesty of England was not engaged with other people. Humphrey had hardly been dismissed when my lord Hertford arrived with more trouble for Tom.

He said that the lords of the council, fearing that some overwrought report of the king's damaged health might have leaked out and got abroad, they deemed it wise and best that his Majesty should begin to dine in public after a day or two—his wholesome complexion and vigorous step, assisted by a carefully guarded repose of manner and ease and grace of demeanor, would more surely quiet the general pulse, in case any evil rumors *had* gone about, than any other scheme that could be devised.

Then the earl proceeded very delicately to instruct Tom as to the observances proper to the stately occasion, under the rather thin disguise of ''reminding'' him concerning things already known to him; but to his vast gratification it turned out that Tom needed very little help in this line: he had been making use of Humphrey in that direction, for

Humphrey had mentioned that within a few days he was to begin to dine in public, having gathered it from the swift-winged gossip of the court. Tom kept these facts to himself, however.

Seeing the royal memory so improved, the earl ventured to apply a few tests to it, in an apparently casual way, to find out how far its amendment had progressed. The results were happy, here and there, in spots—spots where Humphrey's tracks remained; and on the whole my lord was greatly pleased and encouraged. So encouraged was he, indeed, that he spoke up and said in a quite hopeful voice, "Now am I persuaded that if your Majesty will but tax your memory yet a little further, it will resolve the puzzle of the Great Seal—a loss which was of moment yesterday, although of none today, since its term of service ended with our late lord's life. May it please your Grace to make the trial?"

Tom was at sea—a Great Seal was a something which he was totally unacquainted with. After a moment's hesitation he looked up innocently and asked, "What was it like, my lord?"

The earl started, almost imperceptibly, muttering to himself, "Alack, his wits are flown again! It was ill wisdom to lead him on to strain them." Then he deftly turned the talk to other matters, with the purpose of sweeping the unlucky Seal out of Tom's thoughts—a purpose which easily succeeded.

Tom as King

The next day the foreign ambassadors came, with their gorgeous trains; and Tom, throned in awful state, received them. The splendors of the scene delighted his eye and fired his imagination at first, but the audience was long and dreary, and so were most of the addresses; wherefore, what began as a pleasure grew into weariness and homesickness by and by. Tom said the words which Hertford put into his mouth from time to time and tried hard to acquit himself satisfactorily, but he was too new to such things and too ill at ease to accomplish more than a tolerable success. He looked sufficiently like a king, but he was ill able to feel like one. He was cordially glad when the ceremony was ended.

The larger part of his day was "wasted"—as he termed it in his own mind—in labors pertaining to his royal office. Even the two hours devoted to certain princely pastimes and recreations were rather a burden to him than otherwise, they were so fettered by restrictions and ceremonious observances. However, he had a private hour with his whipping boy, which he counted clear gain, since he got both entertainment and needful information out of it.

The third day of Tom Canty's kingship came and went much as the others had done, but there was a lifting of his cloud in one way: he felt less uncomfortable than at first; he was getting a little used to his circumstances and surroundings; his chains still galled, but not all the time; he found that the presence and homage of the great afflicted and embarrassed him less and less sharply with every hour that drifted over his head.

But for one single dread, he could have seen the fourth day approach without serious distress—the dining in public; it was to begin that day. There were greater matters in the program, for on that day he would have to preside at a coun-

cil which would take his views and commands concerning
the policy to be pursued toward various foreign nations scattered far and near over the great globe; on that day too,
Hertford would be formally chosen to the grand office of
Lord Protector; other things of note were appointed for that
fourth day also, but to Tom they were all insignificant com-
pared with the ordeal of dining all by himself with a multitude of curious eyes fastened upon him and a multitude of
mouths whispering comments upon his performance—and
upon his mistakes, if he should be so unlucky as to make
any.

Still, nothing could stop that fourth day, and so it came.
It found poor Tom low-spirited and absentminded, and this
mood continued; he could not shake it off. The ordinary
duties of the morning dragged upon his hands and wearied
him. Once more he felt the sense of captivity heavy upon
him.

Late in the forenoon he was in a large audience chamber,
conversing with the Earl of Hertford and dully awaiting the
striking of the hour appointed for a visit of ceremony from
a considerable number of great officials and courtiers.

After a little while Tom, who had wandered to a window
and become interested in the life and movement of the great
highway beyond the palace gates—and not idly interested,
but longing with all his heart to take part in person in its
stir and freedom—saw the van of a hooting and shouting
mob of disorderly men, women, and children of the lowest
and poorest degree approaching from up the road.

"I would I knew what 'tis about!" he exclaimed with all
a boy's curiosity in such happenings.

"Thou art the king!" solemnly responded the earl with
a reverence. "Have I your Grace's leave to act?"

"Oh, blithely, yes! Oh, gladly, yes!" exclaimed Tom excitedly, adding to himself with a lively sense of satisfaction,
"In truth, being a king is not all dreariness; it hath its com-
pensations and conveniences."

The earl called a page and sent him to the captain of the
guard with the order, "Let the mob be halted, and inquiry
made concerning the occasion of its movement. By the
king's command!"

A few seconds later a long rank of the royal guards, cased
in flashing steel, filed out at the gates and formed across
the highway in front of the multitude. A messenger returned

to report that the crowd were following a man, a woman, and a young girl to execution for crimes committed against the peace and dignity of the realm.

Death—and a violent death—for these poor unfortunates! The thought wrung Tom's heartstrings. The spirit of compassion took control of him, to the exclusion of all other considerations: he never thought of the offended laws or of the grief or loss which these three criminals had inflicted upon their victims, he could think of nothing but the scaffold and the grisly fate hanging over the heads of the condemned. His concern made him even forget for the moment that he was but the false shadow of a king, not the substance; and before he knew it he had blurted out the command, "Bring them here!"

Then he blushed scarlet, and a sort of apology sprung to his lips; but observing that his order had wrought no sort of surprise in the earl or the waiting page, he suppressed the words he was about to utter. The page, in the most matter-of-fact way, made a profound obeisance and retired backwards out of the room to deliver the command. Tom experienced a glow of pride and a renewed sense of the compensating advantages of the kingly office. He said to himself, "Truly it is like what I was used to feel when I read the old priest's tales and did imagine mine own self a prince, giving law and command to all, saying, 'Do this, do that,' whilst none durst offer let or hindrance to my will."

Now the doors swung open; one high-sounding title after another was announced, the personages owning them followed, and the place was quickly half filled with noble folk and finery. But Tom was hardly conscious of the presence of these people, so wrought up was he and so intensely absorbed in that other and more interesting matter. He seated himself absently in his chair of state and turned his eyes upon the door with manifestations of impatient expectancy, seeing which, the company forebore to trouble him and fell to chatting a mixture of public business and court gossip one with another.

In a little while the measured tread of military men was heard approaching, and the culprits entered the presence in charge of an undersheriff and escorted by a detail of the king's guard. The civil officer knelt before Tom, then stood aside; the three doomed persons knelt also and remained so; the guard took position behind Tom's chair. Tom scanned the prisoners curiously. Something about the dress or appearance of the man had stirred a vague memory in him. "Methinks I have seen this man ere now, but the when or the where fail me—" Such was Tom's thought. Just then the man glanced quickly up, and quickly dropped his face again, not being able to endure the awful port of sovereignty; but the one full glimpse of the face which Tom got was sufficient. He said to himself, "Now is the matter clear; this is the stranger that plucked Giles Witt out of the Thames and saved his life that windy, bitter, first day of the new year—a brave good deed; pity he hath been doing baser ones and got himself in this sad case. I have not forgot the day, neither the hour; by reason that an hour after, upon the stroke of eleven, I did get a hiding by the hand of Gammer Canty which was of so goodly and admired severity that all that went before or followed after it were but fondlings and caresses by comparison."

Tom now ordered that the woman and the girl be removed from the presence for a little time, then addressed himself to the undersheriff, saying, "Good sir, what is this man's offense?"

The officer knelt and answered, "So please your Majesty, he hath taken the life of a subject by poison."

Tom's compassion for the prisoner and admiration of him as the daring rescuer of a drowning boy experienced a most damaging shock.

"The thing was proven upon him?" he asked.

"Most clearly, sire."

Tom sighed and said, "Take him away—he hath earned his death. 'Tis a pity, for he was a brave heart—na—na, I mean he hath the *look* of it!"

The prisoner clasped his hands together with sudden energy and wrung them despairingly, at the same time appealing imploringly to the "king" in broken and terrified phrases, "O my lord the king, an' thou canst pity the lost, have pity upon me! I am innocent—neither hath that wherewith I am charged been more than but lamely proved—yet I speak not of that; the judgment is gone forth against me and may not suffer alteration; yet in mine extremity I beg a boon, for my doom is more than I can bear. A grace, a grace, my lord the king! In thy royal compassion grant my prayer; give commandment that I be hanged!"

Tom was amazed. This was not the outcome he had looked for.

"Odds my life, a strange *boon!* Was it not the fate intended thee?"

"O good my liege, not so! It is ordered that I be *boiled alive!*"

The hideous surprise of these words almost made Tom spring from his chair. As soon as he could recover his wits he cried out, "Have thy wish, poor soul! An' thou had poisoned a hundred men thou shouldst not suffer so miserable a death."

The prisoner bowed his face to the ground and burst into passionate expressions of gratitude, ending with, "If ever thou shouldst know misfortune—which God forefend!—may thy goodness to me this day be remembered and requited!"

Tom turned to the Earl of Hertford and said, "My lord, is it believable that there was warrant for this man's ferocious doom?"

"It is the law, your Grace—for poisoners. In Germany coiners be boiled to death in *oil*—not cast in of a sudden, but by a rope let down into the oil by degrees, and slowly; first the feet, then the legs, then——"

"Oh, prithee no more, my lord; I cannot bear it!" cried Tom, covering his eyes with his hands to shut out the picture. "I beseech your good lordship that order be taken to change this law. Oh, let no more poor creatures be visited with its tortures."

The earl's face showed profound gratification, for he was a man of merciful and generous impulses—a thing not very common with his class in that fierce age. He said, "These your Grace's noble words have sealed its doom. History will remember it to the honor of your royal house."

The undersheriff was about to remove his prisoner; Tom gave him a sign to wait; then he said, "Good sir, I would look into this matter further. The man has said his deed was but lamely proved. Tell me what thou knowest."

"If the king's grace please, it did appear upon the trial that this man entered into a house in the hamlet of Islington where one lay sick—three witnesses say it was at ten of the clock in the morning and two say it was some minutes later—the sick man being alone at the time, and sleeping; and presently the man came forth again and went his way.

The sick man died within the hour, being torn with spasms and retchings.''

"Did any see the poison given? Was poison found?''

"Marry, no, my liege.''

"Then how doth one know there was poison given at all?''

"Please your Majesty, the doctors testified that none die with such symptoms but by poison.''

Weighty evidence, this—in that simple age. Tom recognized its formidable nature and said, "The doctor knoweth his trade; belike they were right. The matter hath an ill look for this poor man.''

"Yet was not this all, your Majesty; there is more and worse. Many testified that a witch, since gone from the village, none know whither, did foretell, and speak it privately in their ears, that the sick man *would die by poison,* and more, that a stranger would give it—a stranger with brown hair and clothed in a worn and common garb; and surely this prisoner doth answer woundily to the bill. Please your Majesty to give the circumstance that solemn weight which is its due, seeing it was *foretold.*''

This was an argument of tremendous force in that superstitious day. Tom felt that the thing was settled; if evidence was worth anything, this poor fellow's guilt was proved. Still he offered the prisoner a chance, saying, "If thou canst say aught in thy behalf, speak.''

"Nought that will avail, my king. I am innocent, yet cannot I make it appear. I have no friends, else might I show that I was not in Islington that day; so also might I show that at that hour they name I was above a league away, seeing I was at Wapping Old Stairs; yea more, my king, for I could show that whilst they say I was *taking* life, I was *saving* it. A drowning boy——''

"Peace! Sheriff, name the day the deed was done!''

"At ten in the morning, or some minutes later, the first day of the new year, most illustrious——''

"Let the prisoner go free; it is the king's will!''

Another blush followed this unregal outburst, and he covered his indecorum as well as he could by adding, "It enrageth me that a man should be hanged upon such idle, harebrained evidence!''

A low buzz of admiration swept through the assemblage. It was not admiration of the decree that had been delivered by Tom, for the propriety or expediency of pardoning a convicted poisoner was a thing which few there would have felt justified in either admitting or admiring—no, the admiration was for the intelligence and spirit which Tom had displayed. Some of the low-voiced remarks were to this effect: "This is no mad king; he hath his wits sound." "How sanely he put his questions; how like his former natural self was this abrupt, imperious disposal of the matter!" "God be thanked his infirmity is spent! This is no weakling, but a king. He hath borne himself like to his own father."

The air being filled with applause, Tom's ear necessarily caught a little of it. The effect which this had upon him was to put him greatly at his ease and also to charge his system with very gratifying sensations.

However, his juvenile curiosity soon rose superior to these pleasant thoughts and feelings; he was eager to know what sort of deadly mischief the woman and the little girl could have been about; so, by his command the two terrified and sobbing creatures were brought before him.

"What is it that these have done?" he inquired of the sheriff.

"Please your Majesty, a black crime is charged upon them, and clearly proven; wherefore the judges have decreed, according to the law, that they be hanged. They sold themselves to the devil; such is their crime."

Tom shuddered. He had been taught to abhor people who did this wicked thing. Still, he was not going to deny himself the pleasure of feeding his curiosity, for all that; so he asked, "Where was this done? And when?"

"On a midnight, in December, in a ruined church, your Majesty."

Tom shuddered again.

"Who was there present?"

"Only these two, your Grace—and *that other*."

"Have these confessed?"

"Nay, not so, sire; they do deny it."

"Then prithee, how was it known?"

"Certain witnesses did see them wending thither, good your Majesty; this bred the suspicion, and dire effects have since confirmed and justified it. In particular, it is in evidence that through the wicked power so obtained, they did invoke and bring about a storm that wasted all the region round about. Above forty witnesses have proved the storm;

and sooth one might have had a thousand, for all had reason to remember it, sith all had suffered by it.''

"Certes this is a serious matter." Tom turned this dark piece of scoundrelism over in his mind awhile, then asked, "Suffered the woman also by the storm?"

Several old heads among the assemblage nodded their recognition of the wisdom of this question. The sheriff, however, saw nothing consequential in the inquiry; he answered with simple directness, "Indeed did she, your Majesty, and most righteously, as all aver. Her habitation was swept away, and herself and child left shelterless."

"Methinks the power to do herself so ill a turn was dearly bought. She had been cheated had she paid but a farthing for it; that she paid her soul, and her child's, argueth that she is mad; if she is mad she knoweth not what she doth, therefore sinneth not."

The elderly heads nodded recognition of Tom's wisdom once more, and one individual murmured, "An' the king be mad himself, according to report, then is it a madness of a sort that would improve the sanity of some I wot of, if by the gentle providence of God they could but catch it."

"What age hath the child?" asked Tom.

"Nine years, please your Majesty."

"By the law of England may a child enter into covenant and sell itself, my lord?" asked Tom, turning to a learned judge.

"The law doth not permit a child to make or meddle in any weighty matter, good my liege, holding that its callow wit unfitteth it to cope with the riper wit and evil schemings of them that are its elders. The *devil* may buy a child if he so choose, and the child agree thereto, but not an Englishman; in this latter case the contract would be null and void."

"It seemeth a rude, unchristian thing, and ill-contrived, that English law denieth privileges to Englishmen, to waste them on the devil!" cried Tom with honest heat.

This novel view of the matter excited many smiles, and was stored away in many heads to be repeated about the court as evidence of Tom's originality as well as progress toward mental health.

The elder culprit had ceased from sobbing and was hanging upon Tom's words with an excited interest and a growing hope. Tom noticed this, and it strongly inclined his sympathies toward her in her perilous and unfriended situation. Presently he asked, "How wrought they to bring the storm?"

"*By pulling off their stockings,* sire."

This astonished Tom and also fired his curiosity to fever heat. He said eagerly, "It is wonderful! Hath it always this dread effect?"

"Always, my liege, at least if the woman desire it and utter the needful words, either in her mind or with her tongue."

Tom turned to the woman and said with impetuous zeal, "Exert thy power; I would see a storm!"

There was a sudden paling of cheeks in the superstitious assemblage, and a general though unexpressed desire to get out of the place, all of which was lost upon Tom, who was dead to everything but the proposed cataclysm. Seeing a puzzled and astonished look in the woman's face, he added excitedly, "Never fear; thou shalt be blameless. More, thou shalt go free; none shall touch thee. Exert thy power."

"Oh, my lord the king, I have it not; I have been falsely accused."

"Thy fears stay thee. Be of good heart; thou shalt suffer no harm. Make a storm; it mattereth not how small a one— I require nought great or harmful, but indeed prefer the opposite; do this and thy life is spared; thou shalt go out free, with thy child, bearing the king's pardon, and safe from hurt or malice from any in the realm."

The woman prostrated herself and protested with tears that she had no power to do the miracle, else she would gladly win her child's life alone and be content to lose her own, if by obedience to the king's command so precious a grace might be acquired.

Tom urged; the woman still adhered to her declarations. Finally he said, "I think the woman hath said true. An' *my* mother were in her place and gifted with the devil's functions, she had not stayed a moment to call her storms and lay the whole land in ruins if the saving of my forfeit life were the price she got! It is argument that other mothers are made in like mold. Thou art free, goodwife—thou and thy child—for I do think thee innocent. *Now* thou'st nought to fear, being pardoned, pull off thy stockings! An' thou canst make me a storm, thou shalt be rich!"

The redeemed creature was loud in her gratitude and proceeded to obey, whilst Tom looked on with eager expectancy, a little marred by apprehension, the courtiers at the same time manifesting decided discomfort and uneasiness. The woman stripped her own feet and her little girl's also, and plainly did her best to reward the king's generosity with an earthquake, but it was all a failure and a disappointment.

Tom sighed and said, "There, good soul, trouble thyself no further; thy power is departed out of thee. Go thy way in peace; and if it return to thee at any time, forget me not, but fetch me a storm."

16

The State Dinner

The dinner hour drew near, yet strangely enough the thought brought but slight discomfort to Tom, and hardly any terror. The morning's experiences had wonderfully built up his confidence; the poor little ash-cat was already more wonted to his strange garret after four days' habit than a mature person could have become in a full month. A child's facility in accommodating itself to circumstances was never more strikingly illustrated.

Let us privileged ones hurry to the great banqueting room and have a glance at matters there whilst Tom is being made ready for the imposing occasion. It is a spacious apartment, with gilded pillars and pilasters, and pictured walls and ceilings. At the door stand tall guards, as rigid as statues, dressed in rich and picturesque costumes, and bearing halberds. In a high gallery which runs all around the place is a band of musicians and a packed company of citizens of both sexes in brilliant attire. In the center of the room, upon a raised platform, is Tom's table. Now let the ancient chronicler speak:

"A gentleman enters the room bearing a rod, and along with him another bearing a tablecloth, which, after they have both kneeled three times with the utmost veneration, he spreads upon the table, and after kneeling again they both retire; then come two others, one with the rod again, the other with a salt cellar, a plate, and bread; when they have kneeled as the others had done and placed what was brought upon the table, they too retire with the same ceremonies performed by the first; at last come two nobles, richly clothed, one bearing a tasting knife, who, after prostrating themselves three times in the most graceful manner, approach and rub the table with bread and salt with as much awe as if the king had been present."*

*Leigh Hunt's *The Town*, p. 408, quotation from an earlier tourist.

So end the solemn preliminaries. Now, far down the echoing corridors we hear a bugle blast and the indistinct cry, "Place for the king! Way for the king's most excellent majesty!" These sounds are momently repeated—they grow nearer and nearer—and presently, almost in our faces, the martial note peals and the cry rings out, "Way for the king!" At this instant the shining pageant appears and files in at the door with a measured march. Let the chronicler speak again:

"First come gentlemen, barons, earls, knights of the Garter, all richly dressed and bareheaded; next comes the Chancellor, between two, one of which carries the royal scepter, the other the Sword of State in a red scabbard studded with golden fleurs-de-lis, the point upwards; next comes the king himself, whom, upon his appearing, twelve trumpets and many drums salute with a great burst of welcome, whilst all in the galleries rise in their places, crying, 'God save the king!' After him come nobles attached to his person, and on his right and left march his guard of honor, his fifty gentlemen pensioners, with gilt battle-axes."

This was all fine and pleasant. Tom's pulse beat high, and a glad light was in his eyes. He bore himself right gracefully, and all the more so because he was not thinking of how he was doing it, his mind being charmed and occupied with the blithe sights and sounds about him; and besides, nobody can be very ungraceful in nicely fitting beautiful clothes after he has grown a little used to them, especially if he is for the moment unconscious of them. Tom remembered his instructions and acknowledged his greeting with a slight inclination of his plumed head and a courteous, "I thank ye, my good people."

He seated himself at table without removing his cap, and did it without the least embarrassment, for to eat with one's cap on was the one solitary royal custom upon which the kings and the Cantys met upon common ground, neither party having any advantage over the other in the matter of old familiarity with it. The pageant broke up and grouped itself picturesquely, and remained bareheaded.

Now, to the sound of gay music, the yeomen of the guard entered, "the tallest and mightiest men in England, they being carefully selected in this regard." But we will let the chronicler tell about it:

"The yeomen of the guard entered, bareheaded, clothed

in scarlet, with golden roses upon their backs; and these went and came, bringing in each turn a course of dishes, served in plate. These dishes were received by a gentleman in the same order they were brought, and placed upon the table, while the taster gave to each guard a mouthful to eat of the particular dish he had brought, for fear of any poison.''

Tom made a good dinner, notwithstanding he was conscious that hundreds of eyes followed each morsel to his mouth and watched him eat it with an interest which could not have been more intense if it had been a deadly explosive and was expected to blow him up and scatter him all about the place. He was careful not to hurry, and equally careful not to do anything whatever for himself, but wait till the proper official knelt down and did it for him. He got through without a mistake—flawless and precious triumph.

When the meal was over at last and he marched away in the midst of his bright pageant, with the happy noises in his ears of blaring bugles, rolling drums, and thundering acclamations, he felt that if he had seen the worst of dining in public, it was an ordeal which he would be glad to endure several times a day if by that means he could but buy himself free from some of the more formidable requirements of his royal office.

Foo-foo the First

Miles Hendon hurried along toward the Southwark end of
the bridge, keeping a sharp lookout for the persons he sought
and hoping and expecting to overtake them presently. He
was disappointed in this, however. By asking questions, he
was enabled to track them part of the way through Southwark; then all traces ceased, and he was perplexed as to
how to proceed. Still, he continued his efforts as best he
could during the rest of the day. Nightfall found him leg-
weary, half famished, and his desire as far from accomplishment as ever; so he supped at the Tabard Inn and went
to bed, resolved to make an early start in the morning and
give the town an exhaustive search. As he lay thinking and
planning, he presently began to reason thus: The boy would
escape from the ruffian, his reputed father, if possible;
would he go back to London and seek his former haunts?
No, he would not do that; he would avoid recapture. What,
then, would he do? Never having had a friend in the world
or a protector until he met Miles Hendon, he would naturally try to find that friend again, provided the effort did not
require him to go toward London and danger. He would
strike for Hendon Hall, that is what he would do, for he
knew Hendon was homeward bound and there he might ex-
pect to find him. Yes, the case was plain to Hendon—he
must lose no more time in Southwark, but move at once
through Kent, toward Monk's Holm, searching the wood
and inquiring as he went. Let us return to the vanished little
king now.

The ruffian whom the waiter at the inn on the bridge saw
"about to join" the youth and the king did not exactly join
them, but fell in close behind them and followed their steps.
He said nothing. His left arm was in a sling, and he wore a
large green patch over his left eye; he limped slightly and
used an oaken staff as a support. The youth led the king a

rooked course through Southwark, and by and by struck
into the high road beyond. The king was irritated now and
said he would stop here—it was Hendon's place to come to
him, not his to go to Hendon. He would not endure such
insolence; he would stop where he was. The youth said,
"Thou'lt tarry here, and thy friend lying wounded in the
wood yonder? So be it then."

The king's manner changed at once. He cried out, "Wound-
d? And who hath dared to do it? But that is apart; lead on,
lead on! Faster, sirrah! Art shod with lead? Wounded, is
e? Now though the doer of it be a duke's son, he shall rue
t!"

It was some distance to the wood, but the space was
speedily traversed. The youth looked about him, discovered
a bough sticking in the ground, with a small bit of rag tied
to it, then led the way into the forest, watching for similar
boughs and finding them at intervals: they were evidently
guides to the point he was aiming at. By and by an open
place was reached, where were the charred remains of a
farmhouse, and near them a barn which was falling to ruin
and decay. There was no sign of life anywhere, and utter
silence prevailed. The youth entered the barn, the king following eagerly upon his heels. No one there! The king shot
a surprised and suspicious glance at the youth and asked,
"Where is he?"

A mocking laugh was his answer. The king was in a rage
in a moment; he seized a billet of wood and was in the act
of charging upon the youth when another mocking laugh
fell upon his ear. It was from the lame ruffian who had been
following at a distance. The king turned and said angrily,
"Who art thou? What is thy business here?"

"Leave thy foolery," said the man, "and quiet thyself.
My disguise is none so good that thou canst pretend thou
knowest not thy father through it."

"Thou art not my father. I know thee not. I am the king.
If thou hast hid my servant, find him for me, or thou shalt
sup sorrow for what thou hast done."

John Canty replied in a stern and measured voice, "It is
plain thou art mad, and I am loath to punish thee; but if
thou provoke me, I must. Thy prating doth no harm here,
where there are no ears that need to mind thy follies, yet is
it well to practice thy tongue to wary speech, that it may do
no hurt when our quarters change. I have done a murder

and may not tarry at home; neither shalt thou, seeing I nee
thy service. My name is changed, for wise reasons; it i
Hobbs—John Hobbs; thine is Jack; charge thy memory ac
cordingly. Now then, speak. Where is thy mother? Wher
are thy sisters? They came not to the place appointed
knowest thou whither they went?''

The king answered sullenly, "Trouble me not with thes
riddles. My mother is dead; my sisters are in the palace.'

The youth nearby burst into a derisive laugh, and the kin
would have assaulted him, but Canty—or Hobbs, as he now
called himself—prevented him, and said, "Peace, Hugc
vex him not; his mind is astray, and thy ways fret him. S
thee down, Jack, and quiet thyself; thou shalt have a morse
to eat, anon.''

Hobbs and Hugo fell to talking together in low voices
and the king removed himself as far as he could from the
disagreeable company. He withdrew into the twilight of th
farther end of the barn, where he found the earthen floc
bedded a foot deep with straw. He lay down here, drev
straw over himself in lieu of blankets, and was soon at
sorbed in thinking. He had many griefs, but the minor one
were swept almost into forgetfulness by the supreme one
the loss of his father. To the rest of the world the name c
Henry VIII brought a shiver and suggested an ogre whos
nostrils breathed destruction and whose hand dealt scourg
ings and death; but to this boy the name brought only ser
sations of pleasure, the figure it invoked wore a countenanc
that was all gentleness and affection. He called to mind
long succession of loving passages between his father an
himself and dwelt fondly upon them, his unstinted tears a
testing how deep and real was the grief that possessed h:
heart. As the afternoon wasted away, the lad, wearied wit
his troubles, sunk gradually into a tranquil and healin
slumber.

After a considerable time—he could not tell how long—
his senses struggled to a half consciousness, and as he la
with closed eyes vaguely wondering where he was and wha
had been happening, he noted a murmurous sound, the su
len beating of rain upon the roof. A snug sense of comfo
stole over him, which was rudely broken the next momer
by a chorus of piping cackles and coarse laughter. It startle
him disagreeably, and he unmuffled his head to see whenc
this interruption proceeded. A grim and unsightly pictur

met his eye. A bright fire was burning in the middle of the floor at the other end of the barn; and around it, and lit weirdly up by the red glare, lolled and sprawled the motliest company of tattered gutter scum and ruffians, of both sexes, he had ever read or dreamed of. There were huge, stalwart men, brown with exposure, long-haired, and clothed in fantastic rags; there were middle-sized youths of truculent countenance, and similarly clad; there were blind mendicants with patched or bandaged eyes, crippled ones with wooden legs and crutches; there was a villain-looking peddler with his pack, a knife-grinder, a tinker, and a barber-surgeon with the implements of their trades; some of the females were hardly grown girls, some were at prime, some were old and wrinkled hags, and all were loud, brazen, foul-mouthed; and all soiled and slatternly; there were three sore-faced babies; there were a couple of starveling curs, with strings about their necks, whose office was to lead the blind.

The night was come, the gang had just finished feasting, an orgy was beginning, the can of liquor was passing from mouth to mouth. A general cry broke forth, "A song! A song from the Bat and Dick Dot-and-Go-One!"

One of the blind men got up and made ready by casting aside the patches that sheltered his excellent eyes and the pathetic placard which recited the cause of his calamity. Dot-and-Go-One disencumbered himself of his timber leg and took his place, upon sound and healthy limbs, beside his fellow rascal; then they roared out a rollicking ditty, and were reenforced by the whole crew at the end of each stanza in a rousing chous. By the time the last stanza was reached, the half-drunken enthusiasm had risen to such a pitch that everybody joined in and sang it clear through from the beginning, producing a volume of villainous sound that made the rafters quake. These were the inspiring words:

> Bien Darkmans then, Bouse Mort and Ken,
> The bien Coves bings awast,
> On Chates to trine by Rome Coves dine
> For his long lib at last.
> Bing'd out bien Morts and toure, and toure,
> Bing out of the Rome vile bine,

And toure the Cove that cloy'd your duds,
Upon the Chates to trine.*

Conversation followed; not in the thieves' dialect of the song, for that was only used in talk when unfriendly ears might be listening. In the course of it, it appeared that "John Hobbs" was not altogether a new recruit, but had trained in the gang at some former time. His later history was called for, and when he said he had "accidentally" killed a man, considerable satisfaction was expressed; when he added that the man was a priest, he was roundly applauded and had to take a drink with everybody. Old acquaintances welcomed him joyously, and new ones were proud to shake him by the hand. He was asked why he had "tarried away so many months." He answered, "London is better than the country, and safer these late years, the laws be so bitter and so diligently enforced. An' I had not had that accident, I had stayed there. I had resolved to stay and never more venture countrywards, but the accident has ended that."

He inquired how many persons the gang numbered now. The "Ruffler," or chief, answered, "Five and twenty sturdy budges, bulks, files, clapperdogeons and maunders, counting the dells and doxies and other morts.** Most are here; the rest are wandering eastward along the winter lay. We follow at dawn."

"I do not see the Wen among the honest folk about me. Where may he be?"

"Poor lad, his diet is brimstone now, and over hot for a delicate taste. He was killed in a brawl, somewhere about midsummer."

"I sorrow to hear that; the Wen was a capable man, and brave."

"That was he, truly. Black Bess, his dell, is of us yet, but absent on the eastward tramp; a fine lass, of nice ways and orderly conduct, none ever seeing her drunk above four days in the seven."

"She was ever strict—I remember it well—a goodly wench and worthy all commendation. Her mother was more free and less particular, a troublesome and ugly tempered beldame, but furnished with a wit above the common."

*From *The English Rogue;* London, 1665.
**Canting terms for various kinds of thieves, beggars, and vagabonds and their female companions.

"We lost her through it. Her gift of palmistry and other sorts of fortune-telling begot for her at last a witch's name and fame. The law roasted her to death at a slow fire. It did touch me to a sort of tenderness to see the gallant way she met her lot—cursing and reviling all the crowd that gaped and gazed around her, whilst the flames licked upward toward her face and catched her thin locks and crackled about her old gray head. Cursing them, said I? Cursing them! Why, an' thou shouldst live a thousand years thou'dst never hear so masterful a cursing. Alack, her art died with her. There be base and weakling imitations left, but no true blasphemy."

The Ruffler sighed; the listeners sighed in sympathy; a general depression fell upon the company for a moment, for even hardened outcasts like these are not wholly dead to sentiment, but are able to feel a fleeting sense of loss and affliction at wide intervals and under peculiarly favoring circumstances—as in cases like to this, for instance, when genius and culture depart and leave no heir. However, a deep drink all round soon restored the spirits of the mourners.

"Have any others of our friends fared hardly?" asked Hobbs.

"Some—yes. Particularly newcomers, such as small husbandmen turned shiftless and hungry upon the world because their farms were taken from them to be changed to sheep ranges. They begged, and were whipped at the cart's tail, naked from the girdle up, till the blood ran, then set in the stocks to be pelted; they begged again, were whipped again, and deprived of an ear; they begged a third time—poor devils, what else could they do?—and were branded on the cheek with a red-hot iron, then sold for slaves; they ran away, were hunted down, and hanged. 'Tis a brief tale, and quickly told. Others of us have fared less hardly. Stand forth, Yokel, Burns, and Hodge—show your adornments!"

These stood up and stripped away some of their rags, exposing their backs, crisscrossed with ropy old welts left by the lash; one turned up his hair and showed the place where a left ear had once been; another showed a brand upon his shoulder—the letter V—and a mutilated ear; the third said, "I am Yokel, once a farmer and prosperous, with loving wife and kids, now am I somewhat different in estate and calling, and the wife and kids are gone; mayhap they are in heaven, mayhap in—in the other place; but the kindly

God be thanked, they bide no more in *England!* My good old blameless mother strove to earn bread by nursing the sick; one of these died, the doctors knew not how, so my mother was burnt for a witch, whilst my babes looked on and wailed. English law! Up, all, with your cups! Now altogether and with a cheer! Drink to the merciful English law that delivered *her* from the English hell! Thank you, mates, one and all. I begged, from house to house—I and the wife—bearing with us the hungry kids; but it was crime to be hungry in England, so they stripped us and lashed us through three towns. Drink ye all again to the merciful English law! For its lash drank deep of my Mary's blood and its blessed deliverance came quick. She lies there, in the potter's field, safe from all harms. And the kids—well, whilst the law lashed me from town to town, they starved. Drink, lads—only a drop—a drop to the poor kids, that never did any creature harm. I begged again—begged for a crust, and got the stocks and lost an ear—see, here bides the stump; I begged again, and here is the stump of the other to keep me minded of it. And still I begged again, and was sold for a slave—here on my cheek under this stain, if I washed it off, ye might see the red S the branding iron left there! A *slave!* Do ye understand that word! An English *slave!* That is he that stands before ye. I have run from my master, and when I am found—the heavy curse of heaven fall on the law of the land that hath commanded it!—I shall hang!''*

A ringing voice came through the murky air, ''Thou shalt *not!* And this day the end of that law is come!''

All turned and saw the fantastic figure of the little king approaching hurriedly; as it emerged into the light and was clearly revealed, a general explosion of inquiries broke out: ''Who is it? *What* is it? Who art thou, manikin?''

The boy stood unconfused in the midst of all those surprised and questioning eyes and answered with princely dignity, ''I am Edward, king of England.''

A wild burst of laughter followed, partly of derision and partly of delight in the excellence of the joke. The king was stung. He said sharply, ''Ye mannerless vagrants, is this your recognition of the royal boon I have promised?''

He said more, with angry voice and excited gesture, but

*See Note 10 at end of volume.

it was lost in a whirlwind of laughter and mocking exclamations. "John Hobbs" made several attempts to make himself heard above the din, and at last succeeded, saying, "Mates, he is my son, a dreamer, a fool, and stark mad; mind him not—he thinketh he *is* the king."

"I *am* the king," said Edward, turning toward him, "as thou shalt know to thy cost, in good time. Thou hast confessed a murder—thou shalt swing for it."

"*Thou'lt* betray me? *Thou?* An' I get my hands upon thee—"

"Tut-tut!" said the burly Ruffler, interposing in time to save the king, and emphasizing this service by knocking Hobbs down with his fist. "Hast respect for neither king *nor* Rufflers? An' thou insult my presence so again, I'll hang thee up myself." Then he said to his Majesty, "Thou must make no threats against thy mates, lad; and thou must guard thy tongue from saying evil of them elsewhere. *Be* king, if it please thy mad humor, but be not harmful in it. Sink the title thou hast uttered—'tis treason; we be bad men in some few trifling ways, but none among us is so base as to be traitor to his king; we be loving and loyal hearts in that regard. Note if I speak truth. Now, all together: 'Long Live Edward, king of England!' "

"Long live Edward, king of England!"

The response came with such a thundergust from the motley crew that the crazy building vibrated to the sound. The little king's face lighted with pleasure for an instant, and he slightly inclined his head and said with grave simplicity, "I thank you, my good people."

This unexpected result threw the company into convulsions of merriment. When something like quiet was presently come again, the Ruffler said firmly but with an accent of good nature, "Drop it, boy; 'tis not wise nor well. Humor thy fancy if thou must, but choose some other title."

A tinker shrieked out a suggestion, "Foo-foo the First, king of the Mooncalves!"

The title "took" at once, every throat responded, and a roaring shout went up of "Long live Foo-foo the First, king of the Mooncalves!" followed by hootings, catcalls, and peals of laughter.

"Hale him forth and crown him!"

"Robe him!"

"Scepter him!"

"Throne him!"

These and twenty other cries broke out at once; and almost before the poor little victim could draw a breath he was crowned with a tin basin, robed in a tattered blanket, throned upon a barrel, and sceptered with the tinker's soldering iron. Then all flung themselves upon their knees about him and sent up a chorus of ironical wailings and mocking supplications, whilst they swabbed their eyes with their soiled and ragged sleeves and aprons: "Be gracious to us, O sweet king!" "Trample not upon thy beseeching worms, O noble Majesty!" "Pity thy slaves, and comfort them with a royal kick!" "Cheer us and warm us with thy gracious rays, O flaming sun of sovereignty!" "Sanctify the ground with the touch of thy foot, that we may eat the dirt and be ennobled!" "Deign to spit upon us, O sire, that our children's children may tell of thy princely condescension, and be proud and happy forever!"

But the humorous tinker made the "hit" of the evening and carried off the honors. Kneeling, he pretended to kiss the king's foot, and was indignantly spurned; whereupon he went about begging for a rag to paste over the place upon his face which had been touched by the foot, saying it must be preserved from contact with the vulgar air and that he should make his fortune by going to the highway and exposing it to view at the rate of a hundred shillings a sight. He made himself so killingly funny that he was the envy and admiration of the whole mangy rabble.

Tears of shame and indignation stood in the little monarch's eyes; and the thought in his heart was, "Had I offered them a deep wrong they could not be more cruel; yet have I proffered nought but to do them a kindness, and it is thus they use me for it!"

The Prince with the Tramps

The troop of vagabonds turned out at early dawn and set forward on their march. There was a lowering sky overhead, sloppy ground underfoot, and a winter chill in the air. All gaiety was gone from the company; some were sullen and silent, some were irritable and petulant, none were gentle-humored, all were thirsty.

The Ruffler put "Jack" in Hugo's charge, with some brief instructions, and commanded John Canty to keep away from him and let him alone; he also warned Hugo not to be too rough with the lad.

After a while the weather grew milder and the clouds lifted somewhat. The troop ceased to shiver, and their spirits began to improve. They grew more and more cheerful and finally began to chaff each other and insult passengers along the highway. This showed that they were awaking to an appreciation of life and its joys once more. The dread in which their sort was held was apparent in the fact that everybody gave them the road and took their ribald insolences meekly, without venturing to talk back. They snatched linen from the hedges occasionally, in full view of the owners, who made no protest but only seemed grateful that they did not take the hedges too.

By and by they invaded a small farmhouse and made themselves at home while the trembling farmer and his people swept the larder clean to furnish a breakfast for them. They chucked the housewife and her daughters under the chin whilst receiving the food from their hands, and made coarse jests about them, accompanied with insulting epithets and bursts of horselaughter. They threw bones and vegetables at the farmer and his sons, kept them dodging all the time, and applauded uproariously when a good hit was made. They ended by buttering the head of one of the daughters who resented some of their familiarities. When they took their leave they threatened to come back and burn the house over the heads of the family if any report of the doings got to the ears of the authorities.

About noon, after a long and heavy tramp, the gang came to a halt behind a hedge on the outskirts of a considerable village. An hour was allowed for rest, then the crew scattered themselves abroad to enter the village at different points to ply their various trades.

"Jack" was sent with Hugo. They wandered hither and thither for some time, Hugo watching for opportunities to do a stroke of business but finding none; so he finally said, "I see nought to steal; it is a paltry place. Wherefore we will beg."

"*We*, forsooth! Follow thy trade—it befits thee. But *I* will not beg."

"Thou'lt not beg!" exclaimed Hugo, eyeing the king with surprise. "Prithee, since when hast thou reformed?"

"What dost thou mean?"

"Mean? Hast thou not begged the streets of London all thy life?"

"I? Thou idiot!"

"Spare thy compliments—thy stock will last longer. Thy father says thou hast begged all thy days. Mayhap he lied. Peradventure you will even make so bold as to *say* he lied," scoffed Hugo.

"Him *you* call my father? Yes, he lied."

"Come, play not thy merry game of madman so far, mate; use it for thy amusement, not thy hurt. An' I tell him this, he will scorch thee finely for it."

"Save thyself the trouble. I will tell him."

"I like thy spirit, I do in truth; but I do not admire thy judgment. Bone-rackings and bastings be plenty enow in this life without going out of one's way to invite them. But a truce to these matters; *I* believe your father. I doubt not he can lie; I doubt not he *doth* lie upon occasion, for the best of us do that; but there is no occasion here. A wise man does not waste so good a commodity as lying for nought. But come; sith it is thy humor to give over begging, wherewithal shall we busy ourselves? With robbing kitchens?"

The king said impatiently, "Have done with this folly; you weary me!"

Hugo replied with temper, "Now harkee, mate; you will not beg, you will not rob; so be it. But I will tell you what

you *will* do. You will play decoy whilst *I* beg. Refuse, an'
you think you may venture!''

The king was about to reply contemptuously when Hugo
said, interrupting, ''Peace! Here comes one with a kindly
face. Now will I fall down in a fit. When the stranger runs
to me, set you up a wail and fall upon your knees, seeming
to weep; then cry out as all the devils of misery were in
your belly and say, 'Oh, sir, it is my poor afflicted brother,
and we be friendless; o' God's name cast through your merciful eyes one pitiful look upon a sick, forsaken, and most
miserable wretch; bestow one little penny out of thy riches
upon one smitten of God and ready to perish!' And mind
you, keep you *on* wailing, and abate not till we bilk him of
his penny, else shall you rue it.''

Then immediately Hugo began to moan, and groan, and
roll his eyes, and reel and totter about; and when the stranger
was close at hand, down he sprawled before him, with a
shriek, and began to writhe and wallow in the dirt, in seeming agony.

''Oh dear, oh dear!'' cried the benevolent stranger. ''Oh,
poor soul, poor soul, how he doth suffer! There, let me help
thee up.''

''Oh, noble sir, forbear, and God love you for a princely
gentleman—but it giveth me cruel pain to touch me when I
am taken so. My brother there will tell your worship how I
am racked with anguish when these fits be upon me. A
penny, dear sir, a penny to buy a little food; then leave me
to my sorrows.''

''A penny! Thou shalt have three, thou hapless creature''—and he fumbled in his pocket with nervous haste and
got them out. ''There, poor lad, take them, and most welcome. Now come hither, my boy, and help me carry thy
stricken brother to yon house, where——''

''I am not his brother,'' said the king, interrupting.

''What! Not his brother?''

''Oh, hear him!'' groaned Hugo, then privately ground
his teeth. ''He denies his own brother—and he with one foot
in the grave!''

''Boy, thou art indeed hard of heart if this is thy brother.
For shame! And he scarce able to move hand or foot. If he
is not thy brother, who is he then?''

''A beggar and a thief! He has got your money and has
picked your pocket likewise. An' thou wouldst do a healing

miracle, lay thy staff over his shoulders, and trust Providence for the rest.''

But Hugo did not tarry for the miracle. In a moment he was up and off like the wind, the gentleman following after and raising the hue and cry lustily as he went. The king, breathing deep gratitude to heaven for his own release, fled in the opposite direction and did not slacken his pace until he was out of harm's reach. He took the first road that offered and soon put the village behind him. He hurried along as briskly as he could during several hours, keeping a nervous watch over his shoulder for pursuit; but his fears left him at last, and a grateful sense of security took their place. He recognized now that he was hungry, and also very tired. So he halted at a farmhouse, but when he was about to speak he was cut short and driven rudely away. His clothes were against him.

He wandered on, wounded and indignant, and was resolved to put himself in the way of like treatment no more. But hunger is pride's master; so as the evening drew near he made an attempt at another farmhouse, but here he fared worse than before, for he was called hard names and was promised arrest as a vagrant except he moved on promptly

The night came on, chilly and overcast; and still the footsore monarch labored slowly on. He was obliged to keep moving, for every time he sat down to rest he was soon penetrated to the bone with the cold. All his sensations and experiences as he moved through the solemn gloom and the empty vastness of the night were new and strange to him. At intervals he heard voices approach, pass by, and fade into silence; and as he saw nothing more of the bodies they belonged to than a sort of formless drifting blur, there was something spectral and uncanny about it all that made him shudder. Occasionally he caught the twinkle of a light—always far away apparently, almost in another world; if he heard the tinkle of a sheep's bell, it was vague, distant indistinct; the muffled lowing of the herds floated to him on the night wind in vanishing cadences, a mournful sound now and then came the complaining howl of a dog over viewless expanses of field and forest; all sounds were remote; they made the little king feel that all life and activity were far removed from him and that he stood solitary, companionless, in the center of a measureless solitude.

He stumbled along through the gruesome fascinations o

this new experience, startled occasionally by the soft rustling of the dry leaves overhead, so like human whispers they seemed to sound; and by and by he came suddenly upon the freckled light of a tin lantern near at hand. He stepped back into the shadows and waited. The lantern stood by the open door of a barn. The king waited some time; there was no sound, and nobody stirring. He got so cold, standing still, and the hospitable barn looked so enticing that at last he resolved to risk everything and enter. He started swiftly and stealthily, and just as he was crossing the threshold he heard voices behind him. He darted behind a cask within the barn and stooped down. Two farm laborers came in, bringing the lantern with them, and fell to work, talking meanwhile. Whilst they moved about with the light, the king made good use of his eyes and took the bearings of what seemed to be a good-sized stall at the further end of the place, purposing to grope his way to it when he should be left to himself. He also noted the position of a pile of horse blankets, midway of the route, with the intent to levy upon them for the service of the Crown of England for one night.

By and by the men finished and went away, fastening the door behind them and taking the lantern with them. The shivering king made for the blankets with as good speed as the darkness would allow, gathered them up, and then groped his way safely to the stall. Of two of the blankets he made a bed, then covered himself with the remaining two. He was a glad monarch now, though the blankets were old and thin and not quite warm enough, and besides, gave out a pungent horsey odor that was almost suffocatingly powerful.

Although the king was hungry and chilly, he was also so tired and so drowsy that these latter influences soon began to get the advantage of the former, and he presently dozed off into a state of semiconsciousness. Then, just as he was on the point of losing himself wholly, he distinctly felt something touching him! He was broad awake in a moment, and gasping for breath. The cold horror of that mysterious touch in the dark almost made his heart stand still. He lay motionless and listened, scarcely breathing. But nothing stirred, and there was no sound. He continued to listen and wait during what seemed a long time, but still nothing stirred, and there was no sound. So he began to drop into a drowse once more at last; and all at once he felt that mysterious touch again! It was a grisly thing, this light touch from this noiseless and invisible presence; it made the boy sick with ghostly fears. What should he do? That was the question, but he did not know how to answer it. Should he leave these reasonably comfortable quarters and fly from this inscrutable horror? But fly whither? He could not get out of the barn, and the idea of scurrying blindly hither and thither in the dark within the captivity of the four walls, with this phantom gliding after him and visiting him with that soft, hideous touch upon cheek or shoulder at every turn, was intolerable. But to stay where he was and endure this living death all night? Was that better? No. What, then, was there left to do? Ah, there was but one course; he knew it well—he must put out his hand and find that thing!

It was easy to think this, but it was hard to brace himself up to try it. Three times he stretched his hand a little way out into the dark, gingerly, and snatched it suddenly back, with a gasp—not because it had encountered anything, but because he had felt so sure it was just *going* to. But the fourth time, he groped a little further, and his hand lightly swept against something soft and warm. This petrified him, nearly, with fright: his mind was in such a state that he could imagine the thing to be nothing else than a corpse newly dead and still warm. He thought he would rather die than touch it again. But he thought this false thought because he did not know the immortal strength of human curiosity. In no long time his hand was tremblingly groping again—against his judgment, and without his consent, but groping persistently on just the same. It encountered a bunch of long hair; he shuddered, but followed up the hair and found what seemed to be a warm rope; followed up the rope and found an innocent calf! For the rope was not a rope at all, but a calf's tail.

The king was cordially ashamed of himself for having gotten all that fright and misery out of so paltry a matter as a slumbering calf; but he need not have felt so about it, for it was not the calf that frightened him but a dreadful nonexistent something which the calf stood for; and any other boy in those old superstitious times would have acted and suffered just as he had done.

The king was not only delighted to find that the creature was only a calf, but delighted to have the calf's company, for he had been feeling so lonesome and friendless that the company and comradeship of even this humble animal was welcome. And he had been so buffeted, so rudely entreated by his own kind, that it was a real comfort to him to feel that he was at last in the society of a fellow creature that had at least a soft heart and a gentle spirit, whatever loftier attributes might be lacking. So he resolved to waive rank and make friends with the calf.

While stroking its sleek warm back—for it lay near him and within easy reach—it occurred to him that this calf might be utilized in more ways than one. Whereupon he rearranged his bed, spreading it down close to the calf; then he cuddled himself up to the calf's back, drew the covers up over himself and his friend, and in a minute or two was as warm and comfortable as he had ever been in the downy couches of the regal palace of Westminster.

Pleasant thoughts came at once; life took on a cheerfuller seeming. He was free of the bonds of servitude and crime, free of the companionship of base and brutal outlaws; he was warm, he was sheltered; in a word, he was happy. The night wind was rising; it swept by in fitful gusts that made the old barn quake and rattle; then its forces died down at intervals and went moaning and wailing around corners and projections; but it was all music to the king, now that he was snug and comfortable: let it blow and rage, let it batter and bang, let it moan and wail, he minded it not, he only enjoyed it. He merely snuggled the closer to his friend, in a luxury of warm contentment, and drifted blissfully out of consciousness into a deep and dreamless sleep that was full of serenity and peace. The distant dogs howled, the melancholy kine complained, and the winds went on raging, whilst furious sheets of rain drove along the roof; but the Majesty of England slept on, undisturbed, and the calf did the same, it being a simple creature and not easily troubled by storms or embarrassed by sleeping with a king.

19

The Prince with the Peasants

When the king awoke in the early morning, he found that a wet but thoughtful rat had crept into the place during the night and made a cozy bed for itself in his bosom. Being disturbed now, it scampered away. The boy smiled and said, "Poor fellow, why so fearful? I am forlorn as thou. 'Twould be a shame in me to hurt the helpless, who am myself so helpless. Moreover, I owe you thanks for a good omen; for when a king has fallen so low that the very rats do make a bed of him, it surely meaneth that his fortunes be upon the turn, since it is plain he can no lower go."

He got up and stepped out of the stall, and just then he heard the sound of children's voices. The barn door opened and a couple of little girls came in. As soon as they saw him their talking and laughing ceased, and they stopped and stood still, gazing at him with strong curiosity; they presently began to whisper together, then they approached nearer, and stopped again to gaze and whisper. By and by they gathered courage and began to discuss him aloud. One said, "He hath a comely face."

The other added, "And pretty hair."

"But is ill-clothed enow."

"And how starved he looketh."

They came still nearer, sidling shyly around and about him, examining him minutely from all points as if he were some strange new kind of animal, but warily and watchfully the while, as if they half feared he might be a sort of animal that would bite upon occasion. Finally they halted before him, holding each other's hands for protection, and took a good satisfying stare with their innocent eyes; then one of them plucked up all her courage and inquired with honest directness, "Who art thou, boy?"

"I am the king," was the grave answer.

The children gave a little start, and their eyes spread

themselves wide open and remained so during a speechless half minute. Then curiosity broke the silence, "The *king?* What king?"

"The king of England."

The children looked at each other, then at him, then at each other again—wonderingly, perplexedly; then one said, "Didst hear him, Margery? He saith he is the king. Can that be true?"

"How can it be else but true, Prissy? Would he say a lie? For look you, Prissy, an' it were not true, it *would* be a lie. It surely would be. Now think on't. For all things that be not true be lies; thou canst make nought else out of it."

It was a good tight argument, without a leak in it anywhere; and it left Prissy's half doubts not a leg to stand on. She considered a moment, then put the king upon his honor with the simple remark, "If thou art truly the king, then I believe thee."

"I am truly the king."

This settled the matter. His Majesty's royalty was accepted without further question or discussion, and the two little girls began at once to inquire into how he came to be where he was, and how he came to be so unroyally clad, and whither he was bound, and all about his affairs. It was a mighty relief to him to pour out his troubles where they would not be scoffed at or doubted, so he told his tale with feeling, forgetting even his hunger for the time; and it was received with the deepest and tenderest sympathy by the gentle little maids. But when he got down to his latest experiences and they learned how long he had been without food, they cut him short and hurried him away to the farmhouse to find a breakfast for him.

The king was cheerful and happy now and said to himself, "When I am come to mine own again, I will always honor little children, remembering how that these trusted me and believed in me in my time of trouble, whilst they that were older and thought themselves wiser mocked at me and held me for a liar."

The children's mother received the king kindly and was full of pity, for his forlorn condition and apparently crazed intellect touched her womanly heart. She was a widow and rather poor; consequently she had seen trouble enough to enable her to feel for the unfortunate. She imagined that the demented boy had wandered away from his friends or keepers, so she tried to find out whence to return him; but all her references to neighboring towns and villages, and all her inquiries in the same line, went for nothing: the boy's face, and his answers too, showed that the things she was talking of were not familiar to him. He spoke earnestly and simply about court matters and broke down more than once when speaking of the late king "his father"; but whenever the conversation changed to baser topics, he lost interest and became silent.

The woman was mightily puzzled, but she did not give up. As she proceeded with her cooking, she set herself to contriving devices to surprise the boy into betraying his real secret. She talked about cattle—he showed no concern; then about sheep—the same result, so her guess that he had been a shepherd boy was an error; she talked about mills; and about weavers, tinkers, smiths, trades, and tradesmen of all sorts; and about Bedlam, and jails, and charitable retreats; but no matter, she was baffled at all points. Not altogether, either, for she argued that she had narrowed the thing down to domestic service. Yes, she was sure she was on the right track now; he must have been a house servant. So she led up to that. But the result was discouraging. The subject of sweeping appeared to weary him; firebuilding failed to stir him; scrubbing and scouring awoke no enthusiasm. Then the goodwife touched, with a perishing hope, and rather as a matter of form, upon the subject of cooking. To her surprise and her vast delight, the king's face lighted at once! Ah, she had hunted him down at last, she thought; and she was right proud too of the devious shrewdness and tact which had accomplished it.

Her tired tongue got a chance to rest now, for the king's, inspired by gnawing hunger and the fragrant smells that came from the sputtering pots and pans, turned itself loose and delivered itself up to such an eloquent dissertation upon certain toothsome dishes that within three minutes the woman said to herself, "Of a truth I was right—he hath holpen in a kitchen!" Then he broadened his bill of fare, and discussed it with such appreciation and animation that the goodwife said to herself, "Good lack! How can he know so many dishes, and so fine ones withal? For these belong only upon the tables of the rich and great. Ah, now I see! Ragged outcast as he is, he must have served in the palace before his reason went astray; yes, he must have helped in the very kitchen of the king himself! I will test him.''

Full of eagerness to prove her sagacity, she told the king to mind the cooking a moment, hinting that he might manufacture and add a dish or two if he chose; then she went out of the room and gave her children a sign to follow after. The king muttered, ''Another English king had a commission like to this in a bygone time; it is nothing against my dignity to undertake an office which the great Alfred stooped to assume. But I will try to better serve my trust than he, for he let the cakes burn.''

The intent was good, but the performance was not answerable to it; for this king, like the other one, soon fell into deep thinkings concerning his vast affairs, and the same calamity resulted—the cookery got burned. The woman returned in time to save the breakfast from entire destruction, and she promptly brought the king out of his dreams with a brisk and cordial tongue-lashing. Then, seeing how troubled he was over his violated trust, she softened at once and was all goodness and gentleness toward him.

The boy made a hearty and satisfying meal, and was greatly refreshed and gladdened by it. It was a meal which was distinguished by this curious feature, that rank was waived on both sides; yet neither recipient of the favor was aware that it had been extended. The goodwife had intended to feed this young tramp with broken victuals in a corner like any other tramp or like a dog, but she was so remorseful for the scolding she had given him that she did what she could to atone for it by allowing him to sit at the family table and eat with his betters, on ostensible terms of equality with them; and the king, on his side, was so remorseful for having broken his trust after the family had been so kind to him that he forced himself to atone for it by humbling himself to the family level, instead of requiring the woman and her children to stand and wait upon him while he occupied their table in the solitary state due his birth and dignity. It does us all good to unbend sometimes. This good woman was made happy all the day long by the applauses which she got out of herself for her magnanimous condescension to a tramp, and the king was just as self-complacent over his gracious humility toward a humble peasant woman.

When breakfast was over, the housewife told the king to wash up the dishes. This command was a staggerer for a moment, and the king came near rebelling; but then he said to himself, "Alfred the Great watched the cakes; doubtless he would have washed the dishes too; therefore will I essay it."

He made a sufficiently poor job of it; and to his surprise too, for the cleaning of wooden spoons and trenchers had seemed an easy thing to do. It was a tedious and troublesome piece of work, but he finished it at last. He was becoming impatient to get away on his journey now; however, he was not to lose this thrifty dame's society so easily. She furnished him some little odds and ends of employment, which he got through with after a fair fashion and with some credit. Then she set him and the little girl to paring some winter apples, but he was so awkward at this service that she retired him from it and gave him a butcher knife to grind. Afterward she kept him carding wool until he began to think he had laid the good king Alfred about far enough in the shade for the present in the matter of showy menial heroisms that would read picturesquely in storybooks and histories, and so he was half minded to resign. And when, just after the noonday dinner, the goodwife gave him a basket of kittens to drown, he did resign. At least he was just going to resign—for he felt that he must draw the line somewhere, and it seemed to him that to draw it at kitten drowning was about the right thing—when there was an interruption. The interruption was John Canty, with a peddler's pack on his back, and Hugo!

The king discovered these rascals approaching the front gate before they had had a chance to see him; so he said nothing about drawing the line, but took up his basket of kittens and stepped quietly out the back way, without a word. He left the creatures in an outhouse and hurried on into a narrow lane at the rear.

20

The Prince and the Hermit

The high hedge hid him from the house now, and so under the impulse of a deadly fright he let out all his forces and sped toward a wood in the distance. He never looked back until he had almost gained the shelter of the forest; then he turned and descried two figures in the distance. That was sufficient; he did not wait to scan them critically, but hurried on, and never abated his pace till he was far within the twilight depths of the wood. Then he stopped, being persuaded that he was now tolerably safe. He listened intently, but the stillness was profound and solemn—awful, even, and depressing to the spirits. At wide intervals his straining ear did detect sounds, but they were so remote, and hollow, and mysterious that they seemed not to be real sounds, but only the moaning and complaining ghosts of departed ones. So the sounds were yet more dreary than the silence which they interrupted.

It was his purpose, in the beginning, to stay where he was the rest of the day; but a chill soon invaded his perspiring body, and he was at last obliged to resume movement in order to get warm. He struck straight through the forest, hoping to pierce to a road presently, but he was disappointed in this. He traveled on and on, but the farther he went, the denser the wood became apparently. The gloom began to thicken by and by, and the king realized that the night was coming on. It made him shudder to think of spending it in such an uncanny place; so he tried to hurry faster, but he only made the less speed, for he could not now see well enough to choose his steps judiciously; consequently he kept tripping over roots and tangling himself in vines and briers.

And how glad he was when at last he caught the glimmer of a light! He approached it warily, stopping often to look about him and listen. It came from an unglazed window

opening in a shabby little hut. He heard a voice now and
felt a disposition to run and hide; but he changed his mind
at once, for this voice was praying evidently. He glided to
the one window of the hut, raised himself on tiptoes, and
stole a glance within. The room was small; its floor was the
natural earth, beaten hard by use; in a corner was a bed of
rushes and a ragged blanket or two; near it was a pail, a
cup, a basin, and two or three pots and pans; there was a
short bench and a three-legged stool; on the hearth the remains of a fagot fire were smoldering; before a shrine, which
was lighted by a single candle, knelt an aged man; and on
an old wooden box at his side lay an open book and a human
skull. The man was of large, bony frame; his hair and whiskers were very long and snowy white; he was clothed in a
robe of sheepskins which reached from his neck to his heels.

"A holy hermit!" said the king to himself. "Now am I
indeed fortunate."

The hermit rose from his knees; the king knocked. A
deep voice responded, "Enter! But leave sin behind, for the
ground whereon thou shalt stand is holy!"

The king entered and paused. The hermit turned a pair
of gleaming, unrestful eyes upon him and said, "Who art
thou?"

"I am the king," came the answer, with placid simplicity.

"Welcome, king!" cried the hermit with enthusiasm.
Then, bustling about with feverish activity and constantly
saying "Welcome, welcome," he arranged his bench,
seated the king on it, by the hearth, threw some fagots on
the fire, and finally fell to pacing the floor with a nervous
stride.

"Welcome! Many have sought sanctuary here, but they
were not worthy, and were turned away. But a king who
casts his crown away, and despises the vain splendors of his
office, and clothes his body in rags to devote his life to
holiness and the mortification of the flesh—he is worthy, he
is welcome! Here shall he abide all his days till death
come." The king hastened to interrupt and explain, but the
hermit paid no attention to him, did not even hear him apparently, but went right on with his talk with a raised voice
and a growing energy. "And thou shalt be at peace here.
None shall find out thy refuge to disquiet thee with supplications to return to that empty and foolish life which God hath

moved thee to abandon. Thou shalt pray here; thou shalt study the Book; thou shalt meditate upon the follies and delusions of this world, and upon the sublimities of the world to come; thou shalt feed upon crusts and herbs, and scourge thy body with whips daily to the purifying of thy soul. Thou shalt wear a hair shirt next thy skin; thou shalt drink water only; and thou shalt be at peace, yes, wholly at peace, for whoso comes to seek thee shall go his way again, baffled; he shall not find thee, he shall not molest thee.''

The old man, still pacing back and forth, ceased to speak aloud and began to mutter. The king seized this opportunity to state his case, and he did it with an eloquence inspired by uneasiness and apprehension. But the hermit went on muttering and gave no heed. And still muttering, he approached the king and said impressively, ''Sh! I will tell you a secret!'' He bent down to impart it, but checked himself and assumed a listening attitude. After a moment or two he went on tiptoe to the window opening, put his head out and peered around in the gloaming, then came tiptoeing back again, put his face close down to the king's, and whispered, ''I am an archangel!''

The king started violently and said to himself, ''Would God I were with the outlaws again; for lo, now am I the prisoner of a madman!'' His apprehensions were heightened, and they showed plainly in his face.

In a low, excited voice the hermit continued, ''I see you feel my atmosphere! There's awe in your face! None may be in this atmosphere and not be thus affected, for it is the very atmosphere of heaven. I go thither and return in the twinkling of an eye. I was made an archangel on this very spot, it is five years ago, by angels sent from heaven to confer that awful dignity. Their presence filled this place with an intolerable brightness. And they knelt to me, king! Yes, they knelt to me! For I was greater than they. I have walked in the courts of heaven and held speech with the patriarchs. Touch my hand—be not afraid—touch it. There, now thou hast touched a hand which has been clasped by Abraham and Isaac and Jacob! For I have walked in the golden courts, I have seen the Deity face to face!'' He paused to give his speech effect; then his face suddenly changed, and he started to his feet again, saying with angry energy, ''Yes, I am an archangel, *a mere archangel!* I that might have been pope! It is verily true. I was told it from heaven in a dream twenty years ago; ah, yes, I was to be pope! And I *should* have been pope, for heaven had said it, but the king dissolved my religious house, and I, poor, obscure, unfriended monk, was cast homeless upon the world, robbed of my mighty destiny!'' Here he began to mumble again and beat his forehead in futile rage with his fist, now and then articulating a venomous curse, and now and then a pathetic, ''Wherefore I am nought but an archangel—I that should have been pope!''

So he went on for an hour, whilst the poor little king sat and suffered. Then all at once the old man's frenzy departed and he became all gentleness. His voice softened, he came down out of his clouds and fell to prattling along so simply and so humanly that he soon won the king's heart completely. The old devotee moved the boy nearer to the fire and made him comfortable, doctored his small bruises and abrasions with a deft and tender hand, and then set about preparing and cooking a supper, chatting pleasantly all the time and occasionally stroking the lad's cheek or patting his head in such a gently caressing way that in a little while all the fear and repulsion inspired by the archangel were changed to reverence and affection for the man.

This happy state of things continued while the two ate the supper; then, after a prayer before the shrine, the hermit put the boy to bed in a small adjoining room, tucking him in as snugly and lovingly as a mother might; and so, with a parting caress, left him and sat down by the fire and began to poke the brands about in an absent and aimless way. Presently he paused, then tapped his forehead several times with his fingers as if trying to recall some thought which had escaped from his mind. Apparently he was unsuccessful. Now he started quickly up and entered his guest's room and said, ''Thou art king?''

''Yes,'' was the response drowsily uttered.

''What king?''

''Of England.''

''Of England! Then Henry is gone!''

''Alack, it is so. I am his son.''

A black frown settled down upon the hermit's face, and he clenched his bony hands with a vindictive energy. He stood a few moments, breathing fast and swallowing repeatedly, then said in a husky voice, ''Dost know it was he that turned us out into the world houseless and homeless?''

There was no response. The old man bent down and scanned the boy's reposeful face and listened to his placid breathing. "He sleeps—sleeps soundly"; and the frown vanished away and gave place to an expression of evil satisfaction. A smile flitted across the dreaming boy's features. The hermit muttered, "So, his heart is happy," and he turned away. He went stealthily about the place, seeking here and there for something, now and then halting to listen, now and then jerking his head around and casting a quick glance toward the bed, and always muttering, always mumbling to himself. At last he found what he seemed to want—a rusty old butcher knife and a whetstone. Then he crept to his place by the fire, sat himself down, and began to whet the knife softly on the stone, still muttering, mumbling, ejaculating. The winds sighed around the lonely place, the mysterious voices of the night floated by out of the distances. The shining eyes of venturesome mice and rats peered out at the old man from cracks and coverts, but he went on with his work, rapt absorbed, and noted none of these things.

At long intervals he drew his thumb along the edge of his knife and nodded his head with satisfaction. "It grows sharper," he said; "yes, it grows sharper."

He took no note of the flight of time, but worked tranquilly on, entertaining himself with his thoughts, which broke out occasionally in articulate speech: "His father wrought us evil, he destroyed us—and is gone down into the eternal fires! Yes, down into the eternal fires! He escaped us, but it was God's will, yes, it was God's will, we must not repine. But he hath not escaped the fires! No, he hath not escaped the fires, the consuming, unpitying, remorseless fires—and *they* are everlasting!"

And so he wrought, and still wrought, mumbling—chuckling a low rasping chuckle at times, and at times breaking again into words: "It was his father that did it all. I am but an archangel; but for him, I should be pope!"

The king stirred. The hermit sprang noiselessly to the bedside and went down upon his knees, bending over the prostrate form with his knife uplifted. The boy stirred again; his eyes came open for an instant, but there was no speculation in them, they saw nothing; the next moment his tranquil breathing showed that his sleep was sound once more.

The hermit watched and listened for a time, keeping his

position and scarcely breathing; then he slowly lowered his
arm and presently crept away, saying, "It is long past midnight; it is not best that he should cry out, lest by accident
someone be passing."

He glided about his hovel, gathering a rag here, a thong
there, and another one yonder; then he returned, and by
careful and gentle handling he managed to tie the king's
ankles together without waking him. Next he essayed to tie
the wrists; he made several attempts to cross them, but the
boy always drew one hand or the other away just as the cord
was ready to be applied; but at last, when the archangel was
almost ready to despair, the boy crossed his hands himself,
and the next moment they were bound. Now a bandage was
passed under the sleeper's chin and brought up over his head
and tied fast; and so softly, so gradually, and so deftly were
the knots drawn together and compacted that the boy slept
peacefully through it all without stirring.

Hendon to the Rescue

The old man glided away, stooping, stealthy, catlike, and brought the low bench. He seated himself upon it, half his body in the dim and flickering light and the other half in shadow; and so, with his craving eyes bent upon the slumbering boy, he kept his patient vigil there, heedless of the drift of time, and softly whetted his knife and mumbled and chuckled; and in aspect and attitude he resembled nothing so much as a grisly, monstrous spider gloating over some hapless insect that lay bound and helpless in his web.

After a long while the old man, who was still gazing, yet not seeing, his mind having settled into a dreamy abstraction, observed on a sudden that the boy's eyes were open—wide open and staring, staring up in frozen horror at the knife! The smile of a gratified devil crept over the old man's face, and he said, without changing his attitude or his occupation, "Son of Henry the Eighth, hast thou prayed?"

The boy struggled helplessly in his bonds and at the same time forced a smothered sound through his closed jaws, which the hermit chose to interpret as an affirmative answer to his question.

"Then pray again. Pray the prayer for the dying!"

A shudder shook the boy's frame, and his face blenched. Then he struggled again to free himself, turning and twisting himself this way and that, tugging frantically, fiercely, desperately—but uselessly—to burst his fetters; and all the while, the old ogre smiled down upon him, and nodded his head, and placidly whetted his knife, mumbling from time to time. "The moments are precious; they are few and precious; pray the prayer for the dying!"

The boy uttered a despairing groan and ceased from his struggles, panting. The tears came then and trickled, one after the other, down his face; but this piteous sight wrought no softening effect upon the savage old man.

The dawn was coming now; the hermit observed it and spoke up sharply with a touch of nervous apprehension in his voice, "I may not indulge this ecstasy longer! The night is already gone. It seems but a moment, only a moment; would it had endured a year! Seed of the Church's spoiler, close thy perishing eyes, an' thou fearest to look upon—"

The rest was lost in inarticulate mutterings. The old man sunk upon his knees, his knife in his hand, and bent himself over the moaning boy.

Hark! There was a sound of voices near the cabin; the knife dropped from the hermit's hand; he cast a sheepskin over the boy and started up, trembling. The sounds increased, and presently the voices became rough and angry; then came blows, and cries for help; then a clatter of swift footsteps retreating. Immediately came a succession of thundering knocks upon the cabin door, followed by, "Hullo-o-o! Open! And dispatch, in the name of all the devils!"

Oh, this was the blessedest sound that had ever made music in the king's ears, for it was Miles Hendon's voice!

The hermit, grinding his teeth in impotent rage, moved swiftly out of the bedchamber, closing the door behind him; and straightway the king heard a talk to this effect proceeding from the "chapel":

"Homage and greeting, reverend sir! Where is the boy—*my* boy?"

"What boy, friend?"

"What boy! Lie me no lies, sir priest, play me no deceptions! I am not in the humor for it. Near to this place I caught the scoundrels who I judged did steal him from me, and I made them confess; they said he was at large again, and they had tracked him to your door. They showed me his very footprints. Now palter no more; for look you, holy sir, an' thou produce him not— Where is the boy?"

"Oh, good sir, peradventure you mean the ragged regal vagrant that tarried here the night. If such as you take interest in such as he, know then that I have sent him of an errand. He will be back anon."

"How soon? How soon? Come, waste not the time; cannot I overtake him? How soon will he be back?"

"Thou needst not stir; he will return quickly."

"So be it then. I will try to wait. But stop! *You* sent him of an errand? You! Verily this is a lie—he would not go. He would pull thy old beard, an' thou didst offer him such an insolence. Thou hast lied, friend; thou hast surely lied! He would not go for thee nor for any man.''

"For any *man,* no; haply not. But I am not a man.''

"*What!* Now o' God's name what art thou then?''

"It is a secret; mark thou reveal it not. I am an archangel!''

There was a tremendous ejaculation from Miles Hendon—not altogether unprofane—followed by, ''This doth well and truly account for his complaisance! Right well I knew he would budge nor hand nor foot in the menial service of any mortal; but lord, even a king must obey when an archangel gives the word o' command! Let me—sh! What noise was that?''

All this while the little king had been yonder, alternately quaking with terror and trembling with hope; and all the while too he had thrown all the strength he could into his anguished moanings, constantly expecting them to reach Hendon's ear but always realizing, with bitterness, that they failed, or at least made no impression. So this last remark of his servant came as comes a reviving breath from fresh fields to the dying; and he exerted himself once more, and with all his energy, just as the hermit was saying, ''Noise? I hear only the wind.''

"Mayhap it was. Yes, doubtless that was it. I have been hearing it faintly all the— There it is again! It is not the wind! What an odd sound! Come, we will hunt it out!''

Now the king's joy was nearly insupportable. His tired lungs did their utmost—and hopefully, too—but the sealed jaws and the muffling sheepskin sadly crippled the effort. Then the poor fellow's heart sank to hear the hermit say, ''Ah, it came from without—I think from the copse yonder. Come, I will lead the way.''

The king heard the two pass out, talking; heard their footsteps die quickly away; then he was alone with a boding, brooding, awful silence.

It seemed an age till he heard the steps and voices approaching again, and this time he heard an added sound—the trampling of hoofs apparently. Then he heard Hendon say, ''I will not wait longer. I *cannot* wait longer. He has lost his way in this thick wood. Which direction took he? Quick, point it out to me.''

"He— But wait; I will go with thee.''

"Good—good! Why, truly thou art better than thy looks. Marry I do not think there's not another archangel with so right a heart as thine. Wilt ride? Wilt take the wee donkey that's for my boy, or wilt thou fork thy holy legs over this ill-conditioned slave of a mule that I have provided for myself? And had been cheated in too, had he cost but the indifferent sum of a month's usury on a brass farthing let to a tinker out of work."

"No, ride thy mule and lead thine ass; I am surer on mine own feet and will walk."

"Then prithee mind the little beast for me while I take my life in my hands and make what success I may toward mounting the big one."

Then followed a confusion of kicks, cuffs, tramplings, and plungings, accompanied by a thunderous intermingling of volleyed curses, and finally a bitter apostrophe to the mule, which must have broken its spirit, for hostilities seemed to cease from that moment.

With unutterable misery the fettered little king heard the voices and footsteps fade away and die out. All hope forsook him now for the moment, and a dull despair settled down upon his heart. "My only friend is deceived and got rid of," he said; "the hermit will return and—" He finished with a gasp, and at once fell to struggling so frantically with his bonds again that he shook off the smothering sheepskin.

And now he heard the door open! The sound chilled him to the marrow; already he seemed to feel the knife at his throat. Horror made him close his eyes; horror made him open them again—and before him stood John Canty and Hugo!

He would have said, "Thank God!" if his jaws had been free.

A moment or two later his limbs were at liberty, and his captors, each gripping him by an arm, were hurrying him with all speed through the forest.

A Victim of Treachery

Once more "King Foo-foo the First" was roving with the tramps and outlaws, a butt for their coarse jests and dull-witted railleries, and sometimes the victim of small spite-fulnesses at the hands of Canty and Hugo when the Ruffler's back was turned. None but Canty and Hugo really disliked him. Some of the others liked him, and all admired his pluck and spirit. During two or three days, Hugo, in whose ward and charge the king was, did what he covertly could to make the boy uncomfortable; and at night, during the customary orgies, he amused the company by putting small indignities upon him—always as if by accident. Twice he stepped upon the king's toes—accidentally—and the king, as became his royalty, was contemptuously unconscious of it and indifferent to it; but the third time Hugo entertained himself in that way, the king felled him to the ground with a cudgel, to the prodigious delight of the tribe. Hugo, consumed with anger and shame, sprang up, seized a cudgel, and came at his small adversary in a fury. Instantly a ring was formed around the gladiators, and the betting and cheering began. But poor Hugo stood no chance whatever. His frantic and lubberly 'prenticework found but a poor market for itself when pitted against an arm which had been trained by the first masters of Europe in single-stick, quarter-staff, and every art and trick of swordsmanship. The little king stood, alert but at graceful ease, and caught and turned aside the thick rain of blows with a facility and precision which set the motley onlookers wild with admiration; and every now and then, when his practiced eye detected an opening, and a lightning-swift rap upon Hugo's head followed as a result, the storm of cheers and laughter that swept the place was something wonderful to hear. At the end of fifteen minutes, Hugo, all battered, bruised, and the target for a pitless bombardment of ridicule, slunk from

the field; and the unscathed hero of the fight was seized
and borne aloft upon the shoulders of the joyous rabble
to the place of honor beside the Ruffler, where with vast
ceremony he was crowned king of the Gamecocks, his
meaner title being at the same time solemnly canceled
and annulled, and a decree of banishment from the gang
pronounced against any who should thenceforth utter
it.

All attempts to make the king serviceable to the troop
had failed. He had stubbornly refused to act; moreover, he
was always trying to escape. He had been thrust into an
unwatched kitchen the first day of his return; he not only
came forth empty-handed, but tried to rouse the house-
mates. He was sent out with a tinker to help him at his
work; he would not work; moreover, he threatened the
tinker with his own soldering iron; and finally both Hugo
and the tinker found their hands full with the mere matter
of keeping him from getting away. He delivered the thun-
ders of his royalty upon the heads of all who hampered his
liberties or tried to force him to service. He was sent out,
in Hugo's charge, in company with a slatternly woman and
a diseased baby to beg; but the result was not encouraging:
he declined to plead for the mendicants or be a party to
their cause in any way.

Thus several days went by; and the miseries of this tramping life, and the weariness and sordidness and meanness
and vulgarity of it, became gradually and steadily so intolerable to the captive that he began at last to feel that his
release from the hermit's knife must prove only a temporary
respite from death at best.

But at night, in his dreams, these things were forgotten,
and he was on his throne, and master again. This, of
course, intensified the sufferings of the awakening, so the
mortifications of each succeeding morning of the few that
passed between his return to bondage and the combat with
Hugo grew bitterer and bitterer, and harder and harder to
bear.

The morning after that combat, Hugo got up with a heart
filled with vengeful purposes against the king. He had two
plans in particular. One was to inflict upon the lad what
would be, to his proud spirit and "imagined" royalty, a
peculiar humiliation; and if he failed to accomplish this,
his other plan was to put a crime of some kind upon the

king and then betray him into the implacable clutches of the law.

In pursuance of the first plan, he purposed to put a "clime" upon the king's leg, rightly judging that that would mortify him to the last and perfect degree; and as soon as the clime should operate, he meant to get Canty's help, and *force* the king to expose his leg in the highway and beg for alms. "Clime" was the cant term for a sore artificially created. To make a clime, the operator made a paste or poultice of unslaked lime, soap, and the rust of old iron, and spread it upon a piece of leather, which was then bound tightly upon the leg. This would presently fret off the skin and make the flesh raw and angry looking; blood was then rubbed upon the limb, which, being fully dried, took on a dark and repulsive color. Then a bandage of soiled rags was put on in a cleverly careless way which would allow the hideous ulcer to be seen and move the compassion of the passersby.*

Hugo got the help of the tinker whom the king had cowed with the soldering iron; they took the boy on a tinkering tramp, and as soon as they were out of sight of the camp they threw him down and the tinker held him while Hugo bound the poultice tight and fast upon his leg.

The king raged and stormed and promised to hang the two the moment the scepter was in his hand again, but they kept a firm grip upon him and enjoyed his impotent struggling and jeered at his threats. This continued until the poultice began to bite, and in no long time its work would have been perfected if there had been no interruption. But there was, for about this time the "slave" who had made the speech denouncing England's laws appeared on the scene and put an end to the enterprise and stripped off the poultice and bandage.

The king wanted to borrow his deliverer's cudgel and warm the jackets of the two rascals on the spot; but the man said no, it would bring trouble—leave the matter till night; the whole tribe being together then, the outside world would not venture to interfere or interrupt. He marched the party back to camp and reported the affair to the Ruffler, who listened, pondered, and then decided that the king should

*From *The English Rogue;* London, 1665.

not be again detailed to beg, since it was plain he was worthy of something higher and better, wherefore, on the spot he promoted him from the mendicant rank and appointed him to steal!

Hugo was overjoyed. He had already tried to make the king steal and failed, but there would be no more trouble of that sort now, for of course the king would not dream of defying a distinct command delivered directly from headquarters. So he planned a raid for that very afternoon, purposing to get the king in the law's grip in the course of it; and to do it, too, with such ingenious strategy that it should seem to be accidental and unintentional, for the king of the Gamecocks was popular now, and the gang might not deal overgently with an unpopular member who played so serious a treachery upon him as the delivering him over to the common enemy, the law.

Very well. All in good time Hugo strolled off to a neighboring village with his prey; and the two drifted slowly up and down one street after another, the one watching sharply for a sure chance to achieve his evil purpose, and the other watching as sharply for a chance to dart away and get free of his infamous captivity forever.

Both threw away some tolerably fair-looking opportunities; for both, in their secret hearts, were resolved to make absolutely sure work this time, and neither meant to allow his fevered desires to seduce him into any venture that had much uncertainty about it.

Hugo's chance came first. For at last a woman approached who carried a fat package of some sort in a basket. Hugo's eyes sparkled with sinful pleasure as he said to himself, "Breath o' my life an' I can but put *that* upon him, 'tis good-den and God keep thee, king of the Gamecocks!" He waited and watched, outwardly patient but inwardly consuming with excitement, till the woman had passed by and the time was ripe; then said in a low voice, "Tarry here till I come again," and darted stealthily after the prey.

The king's heart was filled with joy: he could make his escape now if Hugo's quest only carried him far enough away.

But he was to have no such luck. Hugo crept behind the woman, snatched the package, and came running back, wrapping it in an old piece of blanket which he carried on his arm. The hue and cry was raised in a moment by the woman, who knew her loss by the lightening of her burden, although she had not seen the pilfering done. Hugo thrust the bundle into the king's hands without halting, saying, "Now speed ye after me with the rest, and cry 'Stop, thief!' but mind ye lead them astray!"

The next moment Hugo turned a corner and darted down a crooked alley, and in another moment or two he lounged into view again, looking innocent and indifferent, and took up a position behind a post to watch results.

The insulted king threw the bundle on the ground, and the blanket fell away from it just as the woman arrived with an augmenting crowd at her heels; she seized the king's wrist with one hand, snatched up her bundle with the other, and began to pour out a tirade of abuse upon the boy while he struggled, without success, to free himself from her grip.

Hugo had seen enough—his enemy was captured and the law would get him now—so he slipped away, jubilant and chuckling, and wended campwards, framing a judicious version of the matter to give to the Ruffler's crew as he strode along.

The king continued to struggle in the woman's strong grasp, and now and then cried out in vexation, "Unhand me, thou foolish creature; it was not I that bereaved thee of thy paltry goods."

The crowd closed around, threatening the king and calling him names; a brawny blacksmith in leather apron and sleeves rolled to his elbows made a reach for him, saying he would trounce him well for a lesson; but just then a long sword flashed in the air and fell with convincing force upon the man's arm, flat side down, the fantastic owner of it remarking pleasantly at the same time, "Marry, good souls, let us proceed gently, not with ill blood and uncharitable words. This is a matter for the law's consideration, not private and unofficial handling. Loose thy hold from the boy, goodwife."

The blacksmith averaged the stalwart soldier with a glance, then went muttering away, rubbing his arm; the woman released the boy's wrist reluctantly; the crowd eyed the stranger unlovingly, but prudently closed their mouths.

The king sprang to his deliverer's side, with flushed cheeks and sparkling eyes, exclaiming, "Thou hast lagged sorely, but thou comest in good season now, Sir Miles; carve me this rabble to rags!"

The Prince a Prisoner

Hendon forced back a smile and bent down and whispered in the king's ear, "Softly, softly, my prince; wag thy tongue warily; nay, suffer it not to wag at all. Trust in me—all shall go well in the end." Then he added to himself: "*Sir* Miles! Bless me, I had totally forgot I was a knight! Lord how marvelous a thing it is, the grip his memory doth take upon his quaint and crazy fancies! An empty and foolish title is mine, and yet it is something to have deserved it, for I think it is more honor to be held worthy to be a specter-knight in his Kingdom of Dreams and Shadows, than to be held base enough to be an earl in some of the *real* kingdoms of this world."

The crowd fell apart to admit a constable, who approached and was about to lay his hand upon the king's shoulder when Hendon said, "Gently, good friend, withhold your hand; he shall go peaceably; I am responsible for that. Lead on, we will follow."

The officer led, with the woman and her bundle; Miles and the king followed after, with the crowd at their heels. The king was inclined to rebel, but Hendon said to him in a low voice, "Reflect, sire; your laws are the wholesome breath of your own royalty; shall their source resist them, yet require the branches to respect them? Apparently one of these laws has been broken; when the king is on his throne again, can it ever grieve him to remember that when he was seemingly a private person he loyally sunk the king in the citizen and submitted to its authority?"

"Thou art right; say no more; thou shalt see that whatsoever the king of England requires a subject to suffer under the law, he will himself suffer while he holdeth the station of a subject."

When the woman was called upon to testify before the justice of the peace, she swore that the small prisoner at the bar was the person who had committed the theft; there was none able to show the contrary, so the king stood convicted. The bundle was now unrolled, and when the contents proved to be a plump little dressed pig, the judge looked troubled, whilst Hendon turned pale, and his body was thrilled with an electric shiver of dismay; but the king remained unmoved, protected by his ignorance. The judge meditated during an ominous pause, then turned to the woman with the question, "What dost thou hold this property to be worth?"

The woman courtesied and replied, "Three shillings and eightpence, your worship; I could not abate a penny and set forth the value honestly."

The justice glanced around uncomfortably upon the crowd, then nodded to the constable and said, "Clear the court and close the doors."

It was done. None remained but the two officials, the accused, the accuser, and Miles Hendon. This latter was rigid and colorless, and on his forehead big drops of cold sweat gathered, broke and blended together, and trickled down his face. The judge turned to the woman again and said in a compassionate voice, " 'Tis a poor ignorant lad, and mayhap was driven hard by hunger, for these be grievous times for the unfortunate; mark you, he hath not an evil face, but when hunger driveth— Good woman! Dost know that when one steals a thing above the value of thirteen pence ha'penny the law saith he shall *hang* for it!"

The little king started, wide-eyed with consternation, but controlled himself and held his peace; but not so the woman. She sprang to her feet, shaking with fright, and cried out, "Oh, good lack, what have I done! God-a-mercy, I would not hang the poor thing for the whole world! Ah, save me from this, your worship; what shall I do, what *can* I do?"

The justice maintained his judicial composure and simply said, "Doubtless it is allowable to revise the value, since it is not yet writ upon the record."

"Then in God's name call the pig eightpence, and heaven bless the day that freed my conscience of this awesome thing!"

Miles Hendon forgot all decorum in his delight, and surprised the king and wounded his dignity by throwing his arms around him and hugging him. The woman made her grateful adieus and started away with her pig; and when the constable opened the door for her, he followed her out into the narrow hall. The justice proceeded to write in his record book. Hendon, always alert, thought he would like to know why the officer followed the woman out; so he slipped softly into the dusky hall and listened. He heard a conversation to this effect:

"It is a fat pig and promises good eating; I will buy it of thee; here is the eightpence."

"Eightpence, indeed! Thou'lt do no such thing. It cost me three shillings and eightpence, good honest coin of the last reign, that old Harry that's just dead ne'er touched nor tampered with. A fig for thy eightpence!"

"Stands the wind in that quarter? Thou wast under oath, and so swore falsely when thou saidst the value was but eightpence. Come straightway back with me before his worship and answer for the crime! And then the lad will hang."

"There, there, dear heart, say no more, I am content. Give me the eightpence, and hold thy peace about the matter."

The woman went off crying; Hendon slipped back into the courtroom, and the constable presently followed, after hiding his prize in some convenient place. The justice wrote a while longer, then read the king a wise and kindly lecture and sentenced him to a short imprisonment in the common jail, to be followed by a public flogging. The astounded king opened his mouth and was probably going to order the good judge to be beheaded on the spot, but he caught a warning sign from Hendon and succeeded in closing his mouth again before he lost anything out of it. Hendon took him by the hand now, made reverence to the justice, and the two departed in the wake of the constable toward the jail. The moment the street was reached, the inflamed monarch halted, snatched away his hand, and exclaimed, "Idiot, dost imagine I will enter a common jail *alive?*"

Hendon bent down and said somewhat sharply, "*Will* you trust in me? Peace! And forbear to worsen our chances with dangerous speech. What God wills, will happen; thou canst not hurry it, thou canst not alter it; therefore wait, and be patient; 'twill be time enow to rail or rejoice when what is to happen has happened."

The Escape

The short winter day was nearly ended. The streets were deserted save for a few random stragglers, and these hurried straight along, with the intent look of people who were only anxious to accomplish their errands as quickly as possible and then snugly house themselves from the rising wind and the gathering twilight. They looked neither to the right nor to the left; they paid no attention to our party; they did not even seem to see them. Edward the Sixth wondered if the spectacle of a king on his way to jail had ever encountered such marvelous indifference before. By and by the constable arrived at a deserted market square and proceeded to cross it. When he had reached the middle of it, Hendon laid his hand upon his arm and said in a low voice, "Bide a moment, good sir; there is none in hearing, and I would say a word to thee."

"My duty forbids it, sir; prithee hinder me not; the night comes on."

"Stay, nevertheless, for the matter concerns thee nearly. Turn thy back a moment and seem not to see: *let this poor lad escape.*"

"This to me, sir! I arrest thee in——"

"Nay, be not too hasty. See thou be careful and commit no foolish error"—then he shut his voice down to a whisper and said in the man's ear—"the pig thou hast purchased for eightpence may cost thee thy neck, man!"

The poor constable, taken by surprise, was speechless at first, then found his tongue and fell to blustering and threatening; but Hendon was tranquil and waited with patience till his breath was spent; then said, "I have a liking to thee, friend, and would not willingly see thee come to harm. Observe, I heard it all—every word. I will prove it to thee." Then he repeated the conversation which the officer and the woman had had together in the hall, word for word, and ended with, "There, have I set it forth correctly? Should not I be able to set it forth correctly before the judge, if occasion required?"

The man was dumb with fear and distress for a moment; then he rallied and said with forced lightness, " 'Tis making a mighty matter indeed out of a jest; I but plagued the woman for mine amusement."

"Kept you the woman's pig for amusement?"

The man answered sharply, "Nought else, good sir. I tell thee 'twas but a jest."

"I do begin to believe thee," said Hendon with a perplexing mixture of mockery and half conviction in his tone; "but tarry thou here a moment whilst I run and ask his worship, for nathless, he being a man experienced in law, in jests, in——"

He was moving away, still talking; the constable hesitated, fidgeted, spat out an oath or two, then cried out, "Hold, hold, good sir; prithee wait a little—the judge! Why, man, he hath no more sympathy with a jest than hath a dead corpse! Come, and we will speak further. Ods body! I seem to be in evil case, and all for an innocent and thoughtless pleasantry. I am a man of family; and my wife and little ones— List to reason, good your worship; what wouldst thou of me?"

"Only that thou be blind and dumb and paralytic whilst one may count a hundred thousand, counting slowly," said Hendon with the expression of a man who asks but a reasonable favor, and that a very little one.

"It is my destruction!" said the constable despairingly. "Ah, be reasonable, good sir; only look at this matter on all its sides, and see how mere a jest it is—how manifestly and how plainly it is so. And even if one granted it were not a jest, it is a fault so small that e'en the grimmest penalty it could call forth would be but a rebuke and warning from the judge's lips."

Hendon replied with a solemnity which chilled the air about him, "This jest of thine hath a name in law; wot you what it is?"

"I knew it not! Peradventure I have been unwise. I never dreamed it had a name; as, sweet heaven, I thought it was original."

"Yes, it hath a name. In the law this crime is called *Non compos mentis lex talionis sic transit gloria mundi.*"

"Ah, my God!"

"And the penalty is death!"

"God be merciful to me, a sinner!"

"By advantage taken of one in fault, in dire peril, and at thy mercy, thou hast seized goods above thirteen pence ha'penny, paying but a trifle for the same; and this, in the eye of the law, is constructive barratry, misprision of treason, malfeasance in office, *ad hominem expurgatis in statu quo*—and the penalty is death by the halter, without ransom, commutation, or benefit of clergy."

"Bear me up, bear me up, sweet sir, my legs do fail me! Be thou merciful; spare me this doom, and I will turn my back and see nought that shall happen."

"Good! Now thou'rt wise and reasonable. And thou'lt restore the pig?"

"I will, I will indeed, nor ever touch another, though heaven send it and an archangel fetch it. Go—I am blind for thy sake—I see nothing. I will say thou didst break in and wrest the prisoner from my hands by force. It is but a crazy, ancient door; I will batter it down myself betwixt midnight and the morning."

"Do it, good soul; no harm will come of it; the judge hath a loving charity for this poor lad and will shed no tears and break no jailer's bones for his escape."

Hendon Hall

As soon as Hendon and the king were out of sight of the constable, his Majesty was instructed to hurry to a certain place outside the town and wait there whilst Hendon should go to the inn and settle his account. Half an hour later the two friends were blithely jogging eastward on Hendon's sorry steeds. The king was warm and comfortable now, for he had cast his rags and clothed himself in the secondhand suit which Hendon had bought on London Bridge.

Hendon wished to guard against overfatiguing the boy; he judged that hard journeys, irregular meals, and illiberal measures of sleep would be bad for his crazed mind, whilst rest, regularity, and moderate exercise would be pretty sure to hasten its cure; he longed to see the stricken intellect made well again and its diseased visions driven out of the tormented little head; therefore he resolved to move by easy stages toward the home whence he had so long been banished, instead of obeying the impulse of his impatience and hurrying along night and day.

When he and the king had journeyed about ten miles, they reached a considerable village and halted there for the night at a good inn. The former relations were resumed; Hendon stood behind the king's chair while he dined, and waited upon him; undressed him when he was ready for bed; then took the floor for his own quarters and slept athwart the door rolled up in a blanket.

The next day, and the day after, they jogged lazily along talking over the adventures they had met since their separation, and mightily enjoying each other's narratives. Hendon detailed all his wide wanderings in search of the king and described how the archangel had led him a fool's journey all over the forest and taken him back to the hut finally when he found he could not get rid of him. Then, he said, the old man went into the bedchamber and came staggering back looking brokenhearted and saying he had expected to find that the boy had returned and lain down in there to rest, but it was not so. Hendon had waited at the hut all day; hope of the king's return died out then, and he departed upon the quest again.

"And old Sanctum Sanctorum *was* truly sorry your Highness came not back," said Hendon; "I saw it in his face."

"Marry I will never doubt *that!*" said the king; and then told his own story, after which Hendon was sorry he had not destroyed the archangel.

During the last day of the trip Hendon's spirits were soaring. His tongue ran constantly. He talked about his old father and his brother Arthur, and told of many things which illustrated their high and generous characters; he went into loving frenzies over his Edith, and was so gladhearted that he was even able to say some gentle and brotherly things about Hugh. He dwelt a deal on the coming meeting at Hendon Hall; what a surprise it would be to everybody, and what an outburst of thanksgiving and delight there would be.

It was a fair region, dotted with cottages and orchards, and the road led through broad pasturelands whose receding expanses, marked with gentle elevations and depressions, suggested the swelling and subsiding undulations of the sea. In the afternoon the returning prodigal made constant deflections from his course to see if by ascending some hillock he might not pierce the distance and catch a glimpse of his home. At last he was successful and cried out excitedly, "There is the village, my prince, and there is the Hall close by! You may see the towers from here; and that wood there— that is my father's park. Ah, *now* thou'lt know what state and grandeur be! A house with seventy rooms—think of that!—and seven and twenty servants! A brave lodging for such as we, is it not so? Come, let us speed; my impatience will not brook further delay."

All possible hurry was made; still, it was after three o' clock before the village was reached. The travelers scampered through it, Hendon's tongue going all the time. "Here is the church—covered with the same ivy, none gone, none added." "Yonder is the inn, the old Red Lion; and yonder is the marketplace." "Here is the Maypole, and here the pump; nothing is altered—nothing but the people, at any rate; ten years make a change in people; some of these I seem to know, but none know me." So his chat ran on. The end of the village was soon reached; then the travelers struck into a crooked, narrow road, walled in with tall hedges, and hurried briskly along it for a half mile, then passed into a vast flower garden through an imposing gateway whose huge stone pillars bore sculptured armorial devices. A noble mansion was before them.

"Welcome to Hendon Hall, my king!" exclaimed Miles. "Ah, 'tis a great day! My father and my brother, and the lady Edith will be so mad with joy that they will have eyes and tongue for none but me in the first transports of the meeting, and so thou'lt seem but coldly welcomed; but mind it not; 'twill soon seem otherwise, for when I say thou art my ward and tell them how costly is my love for thee, thou'lt see them take thee to their breasts for Miles Hendon's sake and make their house and hearts thy home forever after!"

The next moment Hendon sprang to the ground before the great door, helped the king down, then took him by the hand and rushed within. A few steps brought him to a spacious apartment; he entered, seated the king with more hurry than ceremony, then ran toward a young man who sat at a writing table in front of a generous fire of logs.

"Embrace me, Hugh," he cried, "and say thou'rt glad I am come again! And call our father, for home is not home till I shall touch his hand, and see his face, and hear his voice once more!"

But Hugh only drew back, after betraying a momentary surprise, and bent a grave stare upon the intruder—a stare which indicated somewhat of offended dignity at first, then changed, in response to some inward thought or purpose, to an expression of marveling curiosity mixed with a real or assumed compassion. Presently he said in a mild voice, "Thy wits seem touched, poor stranger; doubtless thou hast suffered privations and rude buffetings at the world's hands; thy looks and dress betoken it. Whom dost thou take me to be?"

"Take thee? Prithee for whom else than whom thou art? I take thee to be Hugh Hendon," said Miles sharply.

The other continued in the same soft tone, "And whom dost thou imagine thyself to be?"

"Imagination hath nought to do with it! Dost thou pretend thou knowest me not for thy brother Miles Hendon?"

An expression of pleased surprise flitted across Hugh's face, and he exclaimed, "What! Thou art not jesting? Can the dead come to life? God be praised if it be so! Our poor lost boy restored to our arms after all these cruel years! Ah, it seems too good to be true, it *is* too good to be true; I charge thee, have pity, do not trifle with me! Quick, come to the light—let me scan thee well!"

He seized Miles by the arm, dragged him to the window, and began to devour him from head to foot with his eyes, turning him this way and that and stepping briskly around him and about him to prove him from all points of view, whilst the returned prodigal, all aglow with gladness, smiled, laughed, and kept nodding his head and saying, "Go on, brother, go on, and fear not; thou'lt find nor limb nor feature that cannot bide the test. Scour and scan me to thy content, my good old Hugh. I am indeed thy old Miles, thy same old Miles, thy lost brother, is't not so? Ah, 'tis a great day—I *said* 'twas a great day! Give me thy hand, give me thy cheek; lord, I am like to die of very joy!"

He was about to throw himself upon his brother, but Hugh put up his hand in dissent, then dropped his chin mournfully upon his breast, saying with emotion, "Ah, God of his mercy give me strength to bear this grievous disappointment!"

Miles, amazed, could not speak for a moment; then he found his tongue and cried out, "*What* disappointment? Am I not thy brother?"

Hugh shook his head sadly and said, "I pray heaven it may prove so, and that other eyes may find the resemblances that are hid from mine. Alack, I fear me the letter spoke but too truly."

"What letter?"

"One that came from over sea, some six or seven years ago. It said my brother died in battle."

"It was a lie! Call thy father; he will know me."

"One may not call the dead."

"Dead?" Miles's voice was subdued, and his lips trembled. "My father dead! Oh, this is heavy news. Half my new joy is withered now. Prithee let me see my brother

Arthur; he will know me; he will know me and console me.''

"He also is dead.''

"God be merciful to me, a stricken man! Gone, both gone—the worthy taken and the worthless spared, in me! Ah! I crave your mercy! Do not say the lady Edith——''

"Is dead? No, she lives.''

"Then, God be praised, my joy is whole again! Speed thee, brother, let her come to me! An' *she* say I am not myself, but she will not; no, no, *she* will know me; I were a fool to doubt it. Bring her, bring the old servants; they too will know me.''

"All are gone but five—Peter, Halsey, David, Bernard, and Margaret.''

So saying, Hugh left the room. Miles stood musing a while, then began to walk the floor, muttering. "The five arch villains have survived the two and twenty leal and honest—'tis an odd thing.''

He continued walking back and forth, muttering to himself; he had forgotten the king entirely. By and by his Majesty said gravely, and with a touch of genuine compassion, though the words themselves were capable of being interpreted ironically, "Mind not thy mischance, good man; there be others in the world whose identity is denied and whose claims are derided. Thou hast company.''

"Ah, my king,'' cried Hendon, coloring slightly, "do not thou condemn me; wait, and thou shalt see. I am no impostor; she will say it; you shall hear it from the sweetest lips in England. I an impostor? Why, I know this old hall, these pictures of my ancestors, and all things that are about us as a child knoweth its own nursery. Here was I born and bred, my lord; I speak the truth; I would not deceive thee; and should none else believe, I pray thee do not *thou* doubt me; I could not bear it.''

"I do not doubt thee,'' said the king with a childlike simplicity and faith.

"I thank thee out of my heart!'' exclaimed Hendon with a fervency which showed that he was touched. The king added, with the same gentle simplicity, "Dost thou doubt *me?*''

A guilty confusion seized upon Hendon, and he was grateful that the door opened to admit Hugh at that moment and saved him the necessity of replying.

A beautiful lady, richly clothed, followed Hugh, and after her came several liveried servants. The lady walked slowly, with her head bowed and her eyes fixed upon the floor. The face was unspeakably sad. Miles Hendon sprang forward, crying out, "Oh, my Edith, my darling"—

But Hugh waved him back gravely and said to the lady, "Look upon him. Do you know him?"

At the sound of Miles's voice the woman had started slightly and her cheeks had flushed; she was trembling now. She stood still during an impressive pause of several moments, then slowly lifted up her head and looked into Hendon's eyes with a stony and frightened gaze; the blood sank out of her face, drop by drop, till nothing remained but the gray pallor of death; then she said, in a voice as dead as the face, "I know him not!" and turned, with a moan and a stifled sob, and tottered out of the room.

Miles Hendon sank into a chair and covered his face with his hands. After a pause, his brother said to the servants, "You have observed him. Do you know him?"

They shook their heads; then the master said, "The servants know you not, sir. I fear there is some mistake. You have seen that my wife knew you not."

"Thy *wife!*" In an instant Hugh was pinned to the wall with an iron grip about his throat. "Oh, thou fox-hearted slave, I see it all! Thou'st writ the lying letter thyself, and my stolen bride and goods are its fruit. There, now get thee gone, lest I shame mine honorable soldiership with the slaying of so pitiful a manikin!"

Hugh, red-faced and almost suffocated, reeled to the nearest chair and commanded the servants to seize and bind the murderous stranger. They hesitated, and one of them said, "He is armed, Sir Hugh, and we are weaponless."

"Armed? What of it, and ye so many? Upon him, I say!"

But Miles warned them to be careful what they did, and added, "Ye know me of old—I have not changed; come on, an' it like you."

This reminder did not hearten the servants much; they held back.

"Then go, ye paltry cowards, and arm yourselves and guard the doors, whilst I send one to fetch the watch," said Hugh. He turned at the threshold and said to Miles, "You'll find it to your advantage to offend not with useless endeavors at escape.''

''Escape? Spare thyself discomfort, an' that is all that troubles thee. For Miles Hendon is master of Hendon Hall and all its belongings. He will remain; doubt it not.''

26

Disowned

The king sat musing a few moments, then looked up and said, " 'Tis strange—most strange. I cannot account for it."

"No, it is not strange, my liege. I know him, and this conduct is but natural. He was a rascal from his birth."

"Oh, I spake not of *him,* Sir Miles."

"Not of him? Then of what? What is it that is strange?"

"That the king is not missed."

"How? Which? I doubt I do not understand."

"Indeed? Doth it not strike you as being passing strange that the land is not filled with couriers and proclamations describing my person and making search for me? Is it no matter for commotion and distress that the head of the state is gone, that I am vanished away and lost?"

"Most true, my king, I had forgot." Then Hendon sighed and muttered to himself, "Poor ruined mind—still busy with its pathetic dream."

"But I have a plan that shall right us both. I will write a paper in three tongues—Latin, Greek and English—and thou shalt haste away with it to London in the morning. Give it to none but my uncle the lord Hertford; when he shall see it, he will know and say I wrote it. Then he will send for me."

"Might it not be best, my prince, that we wait here until I prove myself and make my rights secure to my domains? I should be so much the better able then to——"

The king interrupted him imperiously, "Peace! What are thy paltry domains, thy trivial interests, contrasted with matters which concern the weal of a nation and the integrity of a throne!" Then he added in a gentle voice, as if he were sorry for his severity, "Obey, and have no fear; I will right thee, I will make thee whole—yes, more than whole. I shall remember, and requite."

So saying, he took the pen and set himself to work. Hendon contemplated him lovingly awhile, then said to himself, ''An' it were dark, I should think it *was* a king that spoke; there's no denying it, when the humor's upon him he doth thunder and lighten like your true king; now where got he that trick? See him scribble and scratch away contentedly at his meaningless pothooks, fancying them to be Latin and Greek; and except my wit shall serve me with a lucky device for diverting him from his purpose, I shall be forced to pretend to post away tomorrow on this wild errand he hath invented for me.''

The next moment Sir Miles's thoughts had gone back to the recent episode. So absorbed was he in his musings that when the king presently handed him the paper which he had been writing, he received it and pocketed it without being conscious of the act. ''How marvelous strange she acted,'' he muttered. ''I think she knew me, and I think she did *not* know me. These opinions do conflict, I perceive it plainly; I cannot reconcile them; neither can I by argument dismiss either of the two or even persuade one to outweigh the other. The matter standeth simply thus: she *must* have known my face, my figure, my voice, for how could it be otherwise? Yet she *said* she knew me not, and that is proof perfect, for she cannot lie. But stop—I think I begin to see. Peradventure he hath influenced her—commanded her—compelled her to lie. That is the solution! The riddle is unriddled. She seemed dead with fear; yes, she was under his compulsion. I will seek her; I will find her; now that he is away, she will speak her true mind. She will remember the old times when we were little playfellows together, and this will soften her heart, and she will no more betray me, but will confess to me. There is no treacherous blood in her; no, she was always honest and true. She has loved me in those old days; this is my security, for whom one has loved one cannot betray.''

He stepped eagerly toward the door; at that moment it opened, and the lady Edith entered. She was very pale, but she walked with a firm step, and her carriage was full of grace and gentle dignity. Her face was sad as before.

Miles sprang forward with a happy confidence to meet her, but she checked him with a hardy perceptible gesture, and he stopped where he was. She seated herself and asked him to do likewise. Thus simply did she take the sense of old comradeship out of him and transform him into stranger and a guest. The surprise of it, the bewildering unexpectedness of it, made him begin to question, for a moment, if he *was* the person he was pretending to be after all.

The lady Edith said, "Sir, I have come to warn you. The mad cannot be persuaded out of their delusions, perchance; but doubtless they may be persuaded to avoid perils. I think this dream of yours hath the seeming of honest truth to you, and therefore is not criminal; but do not tarry here with it, for here it is dangerous." She looked steadily into Miles's face a moment, then added impressively, "It is the more dangerous for you that you *are* much like what our lost lad must have grown to be if he had lived."

"Heavens, madam, but I *am* he!"

"I truly think you think it, sir. I question not your honesty in that; I but warn you, that is all. My husband is master in this region; his power hath hardly any limit; the people prosper or starve as he wills. If you resembled not the man whom you profess to be, my husband might bid you pleasure yourself with your dream in peace; but trust me, I know him well, I know what he will do; he will say to all that you are but a mad impostor, and straightway all will echo him." She bent upon Miles that same steady look once more and added, "If you *were* Miles Hendon, and he knew it and all the region knew it—consider what I am saying, weigh it well—you would stand in the same peril, your punishment would be no less sure; he would deny you and denounce you, and none would be bold enough to give you countenance."

"Most truly I believe it," said Miles bitterly. "The power that can command one lifelong friend to betray and disown another be obeyed, may well look to be obeyed in quarters where bread and life are on the stake and no cobweb ties of loyalty and honor are concerned."

A faint tinge appeared for a moment in the lady's cheek, and she dropped her eyes to the floor; but her voice betrayed no emotion which she proceeded, "I have warned you, I must still warn you, to go hence. This man will destroy you, else. He is a tyrant who knows no pity. I, who am his fettered slave, know this. Poor Miles, and Arthur, and my dear guardian, Sir Richard, are free of him and at rest; better that you were with them than that you bide here in the clutches of this miscreant. Your pretensions are a menace to his title and possessions; you have assaulted him in his own house; you are ruined if you stay. Go—do not hesitate. If you lack money, take this purse, I beg of you, and bribe the servants to let you pass. Oh, be warned, poor soul, and escape while you may.''

Miles declined the purse with a gesture and rose up and stood before her.

''Grant me one thing,'' he said. ''Let your eyes rest upon mine so that I may see if they be steady. There, now answer me. Am I Miles Hendon?''

''No. I know you not.''

''Swear it!''

The answer was low but distinct, ''I swear.''

''Oh, this passes belief!''

''Fly! Why will you waste the precious time? Fly, and save yourself.''

At that moment the officers burst into the room, and a violent struggle began; but Hendon was soon overpowered and dragged away. The king was taken also, and both were bound and led to prison.

In Prison

The cells were all crowded, so the two friends were chained in a large room where persons charged with trifling offenses were commonly kept. They had company, for there were some twenty manacled and fettered prisoners here, of both sexes and of varying ages—an obscene and noisy gang. The king chafed bitterly over the stupendous indignity thus put upon his royalty, but Hendon was moody and taciturn. He was pretty thoroughly bewildered. He had come home a jubilant prodigal expecting to find everybody wild with joy over his return, and instead had got the cold shoulder and a jail. The promise and the fulfillment differed so widely that the effect was stunning; he could not decide whether it was most tragic or most grotesque. He felt much as a man might who had danced blithely out to enjoy a rainbow and got struck by lightning.

But gradually his confused and tormenting thoughts settled down into some sort of order, and then his mind centered itself upon Edith. He turned her conduct over and examined it in all lights, but he could not make anything satisfactory out of it. Did she know him? Or didn't she know him? It was a perplexing puzzle and occupied him a long time, but he ended finally with the conviction that she did know him and had repudiated him for interested reasons. He wanted to load her name with curses now, but this name had so long been sacred to him that he found he could not bring his tongue to profane it.

Wrapped in prison blankets of a soiled and tattered condition, Hendon and the king passed a troubled night. For a bribe the jailer had furnished liquor to some of the prisoners; singing of ribald songs, fighting, shouting, and carousing was the natural consequence. At last, a while after midnight, a man attacked a woman and nearly killed her by beating her over the head with his manacles before the jailer could come to the rescue. The jailer restored peace by giving the man a sound clubbing about the head and shoulders; then the carousing ceased, and after that all had an opportunity to sleep who did not mind the annoyance of the moanings and groanings of the two wounded people.

During the ensuing week, the days and nights were of a monotonous sameness as to events; men whose faces Hendon remembered more or less distinctly came by day to gaze at the "impostor" and repudiate and insult him; and by night the carousing and brawling went on with symmetrical regularity.

However, there was a change of incident at last. The jailer brought in an old man and said to him, "The villain is in this room; cast thy old eyes about to see if thou canst say which is he."

Hendon glanced up and experienced a pleasant sensation for the first time since he had been in the jail. He said to himself, "This is Blake Andrews, a servant all his life in my father's family—a good honest soul, with a right heart in his breast. That is, formerly. But none are true now; all are liars. This man will know me—and will deny me too, like the rest."

The old man gazed around the room, glanced at each face in turn, and finally said, "I see none here but paltry knaves, scum o' the streets. Which is he?"

The jailer laughed.

"Here," he said; "scan this big animal, and grant me an opinion."

The old man approached and looked Hendon over long and earnestly, then shook his head and said, "Marry, *this* is no Hendon—nor ever was!"

"Right! Thy old eyes are sound yet. An' I were Sir Hugh, I would take the shabby carl and—"

The jailer finished by lifting himself atiptoe with an imaginary halter, at the same time making a gurgling noise in his throat suggestive of suffocation. The old man said vindictively, "Let him bless God an' he fare no worse. An' *I* had the handling o' the villain, he should roast, or I am no true man!"

The jailer laughed a pleasant hyena laugh and said, "Give him a piece of thy mind, old man; they all do it. Thou'lt find it good diversion."

Then he sauntered toward his anteroom and disappeared.

The old man dropped upon his knees and whispered, "God be thanked, thou'rt come again, my master! I believed thou wert dead these seven years, and lo, here thou art alive! I knew thee the moment I saw thee; and main hard work it was to keep a stony countenance and seem to see none here but tuppenny knaves and rubbish o' the streets. I am old and poor, Sir Miles; but say the word and I will go forth and proclaim the truth, though I be strangled for it."

"No," said Hendon; "thou shalt not. It would ruin thee, and yet help but little in my cause. But I thank thee, for thou hast given me back somewhat of my lost faith in my kind."

The old servant became very valuable to Hendon and the king, for he dropped in several times a day to "abuse" the former and always smuggled in a few delicacies to help out the prison bill of fare; he also furnished the current news. Hendon reserved the dainties for the king; without them his Majesty might not have survived, for he was not able to eat the coarse and wretched food provided by the jailer. Andrews was obliged to confine himself to brief visits in order to avoid suspicion, but he managed to impart a fair degree of information each time—information delivered in a low voice for Hendon's benefit, and interlarded with insulting epithets delivered in a louder voice for the benefit of other hearers.

So little by little the story of the family came out. Arthur had been dead six years. This loss, with the absence of news from Hendon, impaired the father's health; he believed he was going to die, and he wished to see Hugh and Edith settled in life before he passed away; but Edith begged hard for delay, hoping for Miles's return; then the letter came which brought the news of Miles's death; the shock prostrated Sir Richard; he believed his end was very near, and he and Hugh insisted upon the marriage; Edith begged for and obtained a month's respite; then another and finally a third; the marriage then took place by the deathbed of Sir Richard. It had not proved a happy one. It was whispered about the country that shortly after the nuptials the bride found among her husband's papers several rough and incomplete drafts of the fatal letter and had accused him of precipitating the marriage, and Sir Richard's death too, by a wicked forgery. Tales of cruelty to the lady Edith and the servants were to be heard on all hands; and since the father's death Sir Hugh had thrown off all soft disguises and become a pitiless master toward all who in any way depended upon him and his domains for bread.

There was a bit of Andrews' gossip which the king listened to with a lively interest, "There is rumor that the king is mad. But in charity forbear to say *I* mentioned it, for 'tis death to speak of it, they say."

His Majesty glared at the old man and said, "The king is *not* mad, good man, and thou'lt find it to thy advantage to busy thyself with matters that nearer concern thee than this seditious prattle."

"What doth the lad mean?" said Andrews, surprised at this brisk assault from an unexpected quarter. Hendon gave a sign, and he did not pursue his question, but went on with his budget, "The late king is to be buried at Windsor in a day or two—the sixteenth of the month—and the new king will be crowned at Westminster the twentieth."

"Methinks they must needs find him first," muttered his Majesty; then added confidently, "but they will look to that—and also shall I."

"In the name of—"

But the old man got no further: a warning sign from Hendon checked his remark. He resumed the thread of his gossip, "Sir Hugh goeth to the coronation, and with grand hopes. He confidently looketh to come back a peer, for he is high in favor with the Lord Protector."

"What Lord Protector?" asked his Majesty.

"His grace the Duke of Somerset."

"What Duke of Somerset?"

"Marry, there is but one—Seymour, Earl of Hertford."

The king asked sharply, "Since when is *he* a duke, and Lord Protector?"

"Since the last day of January."

"And prithee who made him so?"

"Himself and the Great Council, with help of the king."

His Majesty started violently. "The *king!*" he cried. "*What* king, good sir?"

"What king, indeed! (God-a-mercy, what aileth the boy?) Sith we have but one, 'tis not difficult to answer—his most sacred Majesty King Edward the Sixth, whom God preserve! Yea, and a dear and gracious little urchin is he too; and whether he be mad or no—and they say he mendeth daily—his praises are on all men's lips; and all bless him, likewise, and offer prayers that he may be spared to reign long in England, for he began humanely, with saving the old Duke of Norfolk's life, and now is he bent on destroying the cruelest of the laws that harry and oppress the people.''

This news struck his Majesty dumb with amazement and plunged him into so deep dismal a reverie that he heard no more of the old man's gossip. He wondered if the "little urchin'' was the beggar boy whom he left dressed in his own garments in the palace. It did not seem possible that this could be, for surely his manners and speech would betray him if he pretended to be the Prince of Wales; then he would be driven out, and search made for the true prince. Could it be that the court had set up some sprig of the nobility in his place? No, for his uncle would not allow that; he was all-powerful and could and would crush such a movement, of course. The boy's musings profited him nothing; the more he tried to unriddle the mystery, the more perplexed he became, the more his head ached, and the worse he slept. His impatience to get to London grew hourly, and his captivity became almost unendurable.

Hendon's arts all failed with the king—he could not be comforted; but a couple of women who were chained near him succeeded better. Under their gentle ministrations he found peace and learned a degree of patience. He was very grateful and came to love them dearly and to delight in the sweet and soothing influence of their presence. He asked them why they were in prison, and when they said they were Baptists, he smiled and inquired, "Is that a crime to be shut up for, in a prison? Now I grieve, for I shall lose ye—they will not keep ye long for such a little thing.''

They did not answer, and something in their faces made him uneasy. He said eagerly, "You do not speak; be good to me and tell me—there will be no other punishment? Prithee tell me there is no fear of that.''

They tried to change the topic, but his fears were aroused, and he pursued it, "Will they scourge thee? No, no, they would not be so cruel! Say they would not. Come, they *will* not, will they?''

The women betrayed confusion and distress, but there was no avoiding an answer, so one of them said in a voice choked with emotion, "Oh, thou'lt break our hearts, thou gentle spirit! God will help us to bear our——''

"It is a confession!'' the king broke in. "Then they *will*

scourge thee, the stonyhearted wretches! But oh, thou must not weep; I cannot bear it. Keep up thy courage; I shall come to my own in time to save thee from this bitter thing, and I will do it!''

When the king awoke in the morning, the women were gone.

''They are saved!'' he said, joyfully; then added despondently, ''but woe is me, for they were my comforters.''

Each of them had left a shred of ribbon pinned to his clothing in token of remembrance. He said he would keep these things always and that soon he would seek out these dear good friends of his and take them under his protection.

Just then the jailer came in with some subordinates and commanded that the prisoners be conducted to the jailyard. The king was overjoyed: it would be a blessed thing to see the blue sky and breathe the fresh air once more. He fretted and chafed at the slowness of the officers, but his turn came at last and he was released from his staple and ordered to follow the other prisoners, with Hendon.

The court, or quadrangle, was stone-paved and open to the sky. The prisoners entered it through a massive archway of masonry, and were placed in file, standing with their backs against the wall. A rope was stretched in front of them, and they were also guarded by their officers. It was a chill and lowering morning, and light snow which had fallen during the night whitened the great empty space and added to the general dismalness of its aspect. Now and then a wintry wind shivered through the place and sent the snow eddying hither and thither.

In the center of the court stood two women, chained to posts. A glance showed the king that these were his good friends. He shuddered and said to himself, ''Alack, they are not gone free, as I had thought. To think that such as these should know the lash! In England! Aye, there's the shame of it—not in Heathenesse, but Christian England! They will be scourged; and I, whom they have comforted and kindly entreated, must look on and see the great wrong done; it is strange, so strange, that I, the very source of power in this broad realm, am helpless to protect them. But let these miscreants look well to themselves, for there is a day coming when I will require of them a heavy reckoning for this work. For every blow they strike now they shall feel a hundred then.''

A great gate swung open and a crowd of citizens poured in. They flocked around the two women and hid them from the king's view. A clergyman entered and passed through the crowd, and he also was hidden. The king now heard talking back and forth as if questions were being asked and answered, but he could not make out what was said. Next there was a deal of bustle and preparation, and much passing and repassing of officials through that part of the crowd that stood on the further side of the women; and whilst this proceeded a deep hush gradually fell upon the people.

Now, by command, the masses parted and fell aside, and the king saw a spectacle that froze the marrow in his bones. Fagots had been piled about the two women, and a kneeling man was lighting them!

The women bowed their heads and covered their faces with their hands; the yellow flames began to climb upward among the snapping and crackling fagots, and wreaths of blue smoke to stream away on the wind; the clergyman lifted his hands and began a prayer; just then two young girls came flying through the great gate uttering piercing screams and threw themselves upon the women at the stake. Instantly they were torn away by officers, and one of them was kept in a tight grip, but the other broke loose, saying she would die with her mother; and before she could be stopped she had flung her arms about her mother's neck again. She was torn away once more, and with her gown on fire. Two of three men held her, and the burning portion of her gown was snatched off and thrown flaming aside, she struggling all the while to free herself, and saying she would be alone in the world now, and begging to be allowed to die with her mother. Both the girls screamed continually and fought for freedom, but suddenly this tumult was drowned under a volley of heart-piercing shrieks of mortal agony; the king glanced from the frantic girls to the stake, then turned away and leaned his ashen face against the wall, and looked no more. He said, "That which I have seen in that one little moment will never go out from my memory, but will abide there; and I shall see it all the days, and dream of it all the nights, till I die. Would God I had been blind!"

Hendon was watching the king. He said to himself with satisfaction, "His disorder mendeth, he hath changed, and groweth gentler. If he had followed his wont, he would have stormed at these varlets, and said he was king, and com-

manded that the women be turned loose unscathed. Soon
his delusion will pass away and be forgotten, and his poor
mind will be whole again. God speed the day!''

That same day several prisoners were brought in to remain overnight, who were being conveyed under guard to
various places in the kingdom to undergo punishment for
crimes committed. The king conversed with these—he had
made it a point from the beginning to instruct himself for
the kingly office by questioning prisoners whenever the opportunity offered—and the tale of their woes wrung his
heart. One of them was a poor half-witted woman who had
stolen a yard or two of cloth from a weaver; she was to be
hanged for it. Another was a man accused of stealing a
horse; he said the proof had failed, and he had imagined
that he was safe from the halter; but no, he was hardly free
before he was arraigned for killing a deer in the king's park;
this was proved against him, and now he was on his way to
the gallows. There was a tradesman's apprentice whose case
particularly distressed the king; this youth said he found a
hawk one evening that had escaped from its owner, and he
took it home with him, imagining himself entitled to it; but
the court convicted him of stealing it and sentenced him to
death.

The king was furious over these inhumanities and wanted
Hendon to break jail and fly with him to Westminster so that
he could mount his throne and hold out his scepter in mercy
over these unfortunate people and save their lives. "Poor
child," sighed Hendon, "these woeful tales have brought
his malady upon him again; alack, but for this evil hap, he
would have been well in a little time."

Among these prisoners was an old lawyer—a man with a
strong face and a dauntless mien. Three years past he had
written a pamphlet against the Lord Chancellor, accusing
him of injustice, and had been punished for it by the loss
of his ears in the pillory and degradation from the bar, and
in addition had been fined £3,000 and sentenced to imprisonment for life. Lately he had repeated his offense; and in
consequence was now under sentence to lose *what remained
of his ears*, pay a fine of £5,000, be branded on both cheeks,
and remain in prison for life.

"These be honorable scars," he said, and turned back
his gray hair and showed the mutilated stubs of what had
once been his ears.

The king's eye burned with passion. He said, "None believe in me; neither wilt thou. But no matter; within the compass of a month thou shalt be free; and more, the laws that have dishonored thee and shamed the English name shall be swept from the statute books. The world is made wrong; kings should go to school to their own laws at times, and so learn mercy."*

*See Notes to Chapter 27 at end of volume.

The Sacrifice

Meantime Miles was growing sufficiently tired of confinement and inaction. But now his trial came on, to his great gratification, and he thought he could welcome any sentence provided a further imprisonment should not be a part of it. But he was mistaken about that. He was in a fine fury when he found himself described as a "sturdy vagabond" and sentenced to sit two hours in the pillory for bearing that character and for assaulting the master of Hendon Hall. His pretensions as to brothership with his prosecutor, and rightful heirship to the Hendon honors and estates, were left contemptuously unnoticed as being not even worth examination.

He raged and threatened on his way to punishment, but it did no good; he was snatched roughly along by the officers and got an occasional cuff besides for his unreverent conduct.

The king could not pierce through the rabble that swarmed behind, so he was obliged to follow in the rear, remote from his good friend and servant. The king had been nearly condemned to the stocks himself for being in such bad company, but had been let off with a lecture and a warning in consideration of his youth. When the crowd at last halted, he flitted feverishly from point to point around its outer rim hunting a place to get through, and at last, after a deal of difficulty and delay, succeeded. There sat his poor henchman in the degrading stocks, the sport and butt of a dirty mob—he the body servant of the king of England! Edward had heard the sentence pronounced, but he had not realized the half that it meant. His anger began to rise as the sense of this new indignity which had been put upon him sank home; it jumped to summer heat the next moment, when he saw an egg sail through the air and crush itself against Hendon's cheek, and heard the crowd roar its enjoyment of the episode. He sprang across the open circle and confronted the officer in charge, crying, "For shame! This is my servant; set him free! I am the——"

"Oh, peace!" exclaimed Hendon in a panic. "Thou'lt destroy thyself. Mind him not, officer, he is mad."

"Give thyself no trouble as to the matter of minding him, good man; I have small mind to mind him; but as to teaching him somewhat, to that I am well inclined." He turned to a subordinate and said, "Give the little fool a taste or two of the lash, to mend his manners."

"Half a dozen will better serve his turn," suggested Sir Hugh, who had ridden up a moment before to take a passing glance at the proceedings.

The king was seized. He did not even struggle, so paralyzed was he with the mere thought of the monstrous outrage that was proposed to be inflicted upon his sacred person. History was already defiled with the record of the scourging of an English king with whips; it was an intolerable reflection that he must furnish a duplicate of that shameful page. He was in the toils; there was no help for him: he must either take this punishment or beg for its remission. Hard conditions; he would take the stripes—a king might do that, but a king could not beg.

But meantime Miles Hendon was resolving the difficulty. "Let the child go," said he; "ye heartless dogs, do ye not see how young and frail he is? Let him go; I will take his lashes."

"Marry, a good thought, and thanks for it," said Sir Hugh, his face lighting with a sardonic satisfaction. "Let the little beggar go, and give this fellow a dozen in his place—an honest dozen, well laid on." The king was in the act of entering a fierce protest, but Sir Hugh silenced him with the potent remark, "Yes, speak up, do, and free thy mind; only, mark ye, that for each word you utter he shall get six strokes the more."

Hendon was removed from the stocks and his back laid bare, and whilst the lash was applied the poor little king turned away his face and allowed unroyal tears to channel his cheeks unchecked. "Ah, brave good heart," he said to himself, "this loyal deed shall never perish out of my memory. I will not forget it; and neither shall *they!*" he added with passion. Whilst he mused, his appreciation of Hendon's magnanimous conduct grew to greater and still greater dimensions in his mind, and so also did his gratefulness for it. Presently he said to himself, "Who saves his prince from wounds and possible death—and this he did for me—performs high service; but it is little—it is nothing, oh, less than nothing!—when 'tis weighed against the act of him who saves his prince from shame!"

Hendon made no outcry under the scourge, but bore the heavy blows with soldierly fortitude. This, together with his redeeming the boy by taking his stripes for him, compelled the respect of even that forlorn and degraded mob that was gathered there; and its gibes and hootings died away, and no sound remained but the sound of the falling blows. The stillness that pervaded the place when Hendon found himself once more in the stocks was in strong contrast with the insulting clamor which had prevailed there so little a while before. The king came softly to Hendon's side and whispered in his ear, "Kings cannot ennoble thee, thou good, great soul, for One who is higher than kings hath done that for thee; but a king can confirm thy nobility to men." He picked up the scourge from the ground, touched Hendon's bleeding shoulders lightly with it, and whispered, "Edward of England dubs thee earl!"

Hendon was touched. The water welled to his eyes, yet at the same time the grisly humor of the situation and circumstances so undermined his gravity that it was all he could do to keep some sight of his inward mirth from showing outside. To be suddenly hoisted, naked and gory, from the common stocks to the Alpine altitude and splendor of an earldom seemed to him the last possibility in the line of the grotesque. He said to himself, "Now am I finely tinseled indeed! The specter knight of the Kingdom of Dreams and Shadows is become a specter earl! A dizzy flight for a callow wing! An' this go on, I shall presently be hung like a very maypole with fantastic gauds and make-believe honors. But I shall value them, all valueless as they are, for the love that doth bestow them. Better these poor mock dignities of mine, that come unasked from a clean hand and a right spirit, than real ones bought by servility from grudging and interested power."

The dreaded Sir Hugh wheeled his horse about, and as he spurred away, the living wall divided silently to let him pass, and as silently closed together again. And so remained; nobody went so far as to venture a remark in favor of the prisoner or in compliment to him, but no matter, the absence of abuse was a sufficient homage in itself. A latecomer who was not posted as to the present circumstances and who delivered a sneer at the "impostor" and was in the act of following it with a dead cat was promptly knocked down and kicked out, without any words, and then the deep quiet resumed sway once more.

29

To London

When Hendon's term of service in the stocks was finished,
he was released and ordered to quit the region and come
back no more. His sword was restored to him, and also his
mule and his donkey. He mounted and rode off, followed
by the king, the crowd opening with quiet respectfulness to
let them pass, and then dispersing when they were gone.

Hendon was soon absorbed in thought. There were questions of high import to be answered. What should he do?
Whither should he go? Powerful help must be found somewhere or he must relinquish his inheritance and remain under the imputation of being an impostor besides. Where
could he hope to find this powerful help? Where, indeed! It
was a knotty question. By and by a thought occurred to him
which pointed to a possibility—the slenderest of slender
possibilities, certainly, but still worth considering, for lack
of any other that promised anything at all. He remembered
what old Andrews had said about the young king's goodness
and his generous championship of the wronged and unfortunate. Why not go and try to get speech of him and beg
for justice? Ah, yes, but could so fantastic a pauper get
admission to the august presence of a monarch? Never mind;
let that matter take care of itself; it was a bridge that would
not need to be crossed till he should come to it. He was an
old campaigner, and used to inventing shifts and ex-
pedients; no doubt he would be able to find a way. Yes, he
would strike for the capital. Maybe his father's old friend
Sir Humphrey Marlow would help him—"good old Sir
Humphrey, head lieutenant of the late king's kitchen, or sta-
bles, or something"—Miles could not remember just what
or which. Now that he had something to turn his energies
to, a distinctly defined object to accomplish, the fog of humiliation and depression which had settled down upon his
spirits lifted and blew away, and he raised his head and

looked about him. He was surprised to see how far he had
come; the village was away behind him. The king was jogging along in his wake with his head bowed, for he too was
deep in plans and thinkings. A sorrowful misgiving clouded
Hendon's newborn cheerfulness: would the boy be willing
to go again to a city where, during all his brief life, he had
never known anything but ill usage and pinching want? But
the question must be asked; it could not be avoided; so
Hendon reined up and called out, "I had forgotten to inquire whither we are bound. Thy commands, my liege!"

"To London!"

Hendon moved on again, mightily contented with the answer, but astounded at it too.

The whole journey was made without an adventure of
importance. But it ended with one. About ten o'clock on
the night of the nineteenth of February, they stepped upon
London Bridge in the midst of a writhing, struggling jam of
howling and hurrahing people whose beer-jolly faces stood
out strongly in the glare from manifold torches; and at that
instant the decaying head of some former duke or other
grandee tumbled down between them, striking Hendon on
the elbow and then bounding off among the hurrying confusion of feet. So evanescent and unstable are men's works
in this world! The late good king is but three weeks dead
and three days in his grave, and already the adornments
which he took such pains to select from prominent people
for his noble bridge are falling. A citizen stumbled over that
head and drove his own head into the back of somebody in
front of him, who turned and knocked down the first person
that came handy, and was promptly laid out himself by that
person's friend. It was the right ripe time for a free fight,
for the festivities of the morrow—Coronation Day—were already beginning; everybody was full of strong drink and
patriotism; within five minutes the free fight was occupying
a good deal of ground; within ten or twelve it covered an
acre or so and was become a riot. By this time Hendon and
the king were hopelessly separated from each other and lost
in the rush and turmoil of the roaring masses of humanity.
And so we leave them.

Tom's Progress

Whilst the true king wandered about the land poorly clad, poorly fed, cuffed and derided by tramps one while, herding with thieves and murderers in a jail another, and called idiot and impostor by all impartially, the mock king, Tom Canty, enjoyed a quite different experience.

When we saw him last, royalty was just beginning to have a bright side for him. This bright side went on brightening more and more every day; in a very little while it was become almost all sunshine and delightfulness. He lost his fears; his misgivings faded out and died; his embarrassments departed and gave place to an easy and confident bearing. He worked the whipping boy mine to ever-increasing profit.

He ordered my lady Elizabeth and my lady Jane Grey into his presence when he wanted to play or talk, and dismissed them when he was done with them, with the air of one familiarly accustomed to such performances. It no longer confused him to have these lofty personages kiss his hand at parting.

He came to enjoy being conducted to bed in state at night and dressed with intricate and solemn ceremony in the morning. It came to be a proud pleasure to march to dinner attended by a glittering procession of officers of state and gentlemen-at-arms; insomuch, indeed, that he doubled his guard of gentlemen-at-arms and made them a hundred. He liked to hear the bugles sounding down the long corridors and the distant voices responding, "Way for the king!"

He even learned to enjoy sitting in throned state in council and seeming to be something more than the Lord Protector's mouthpiece. He liked to receive great ambassadors and their gorgeous trains and listen to the affectionate messages they brought from illustrious monarchs who called him "brother." O happy Tom Canty, late of Offal Court!

He enjoyed his splendid clothes and ordered more; he found his four hundred servants too few for his proper grandeur and trebled them. The adulation of salaaming courtiers came to be sweet music to his ears. He remained kind and gentle and a sturdy and determined champion of all that were oppressed, and he made tireless war upon unjust laws; yet upon occasion, being offended, he could turn upon an earl, or even a duke, and give him a look that would make him tremble. Once, when his royal ''sister'' the grimly holy lady Mary set herself to reason with him against the wisdom of his course in pardoning so many people who would otherwise be jailed, or hanged, or burned, and reminded him that their august late father's prisons had sometimes contained as high as sixty thousand convicts at one time and that during his admirable reign he had delivered seventy-two thousand thieves and robbers over to death by the executioner.* the boy was filled with generous indignation and commanded her to go to her closet, and beseech God to take away the stone that was in her breast and give her a human heart.

Did Tom Canty never feel troubled about the poor little rightful prince, who had treated him so kindly and flown out with such hot zeal to avenge him upon the insolent sentinel at the palace gate? Yes; his first royal days and nights were pretty well sprinkled with painful thoughts about the lost prince, and with sincere longings for his return, and happy restoration to his native rights and splendors. But as time wore on, and the prince did not come, Tom's mind became more and more occupied with his new and enchanting experiences, and by little and little the vanished monarch faded almost out of his thoughts; and finally, when he did intrude upon them at intervals, he was become an unwelcome specter, for he made Tom feel guilty and ashamed.

Tom's poor mother and sisters traveled the same road out of his mind. At first he pined for them, sorrowed for them, longed to see them, but later the thought of their coming some day in their rags and dirt, and betraying him with their kisses, and pulling him down from his lofty place, and dragging him back to penury and degradation and the slums made him shudder. At last they ceased to trouble his thoughts almost wholly. And he was content, even glad; for

*Hume's *England*.

whenever their mournful and accusing faces did rise before him now, they made him feel more despicable than the worms that crawl.

At midnight of the nineteenth of February Tom Canty was sinking to sleep in his rich bed in the palace, guarded by his loyal vassals and surrounded by the pomps of royalty, a happy boy, for tomorrow was the day appointed for his solemn crowning as king of England. At that same hour Edward, the true king, hungry and thirsty, soiled and draggled, worn with travel, and clothed in rags and shreds—his share of the results of the riot—was wedged in among a crowd of people who were watching with deep interest hurrying gangs of workmen who streamed in and out of Westminster Abbey, busy as ants: they were making the last preparation for the royal coronation.

The Recognition Procession

When Tom Canty awoke the next morning, the air was heavy with a thunderous murmur; all the distances were charged with it. It was music to him, for it meant that the English world was out in its strength to give loyal welcome to the great day.

Presently Tom found himself once more the chief figure in a wonderful floating pageant on the Thames, for by ancient custom the "recognition procession" through London must start from the Tower, and he was bound thither.

When he arrived there, the sides of the venerable fortress seemed suddenly rent in a thousand places, and from every rent leaped a red tongue of flame and a white gush of smoke; a deafening explosion followed, which drowned the shoutings of the multitude and made the ground tremble; the flame jets, the smoke, and the explosions were repeated over and over again with marvelous celerity, so that in a few moments the old Tower disappeared in the vast fog of its own smoke, all but the very top of the tall pile called the White Tower: this, with its banners, stood out above the dense bank of vapor as a mountain peak projects above a cloud rack.

Tom Canty, splendidly arrayed, mounted a prancing war steed, whose rich trappings almost reached to the ground; his "uncle" the Lord Protector Somerset, similarly mounted, took place in his rear; the king's guard formed in single ranks on either side, clad in burnished armor; after the Protector followed a seemingly interminable procession of resplendent nobles attended by their vassals; after these came the Lord Mayor and the aldermanic body, in crimson-velvet robes and with their gold chains across their breasts; and after these the officers and members of all the guilds of London, in rich raiment and bearing the showy banners of the several corporations. Also in the procession, as a special guard of honor through the city, was the Ancient and Honorable Artillery Company, an organization already three hundred years old at that time, and the only military body in England possessing the privilege (which it still possesses in our day) of holding itself independent of the commands of Parliament. It was a brilliant spectacle, and was hailed with acclamations all along the line as it took its stately way through the packed multitudes of citizens. The chronicler says, "The king, as he entered the city, was received by the people with prayers, welcomings, cries, and tender words, and all signs which argue an earnest love of subjects toward their sovereign; and the king, by holding up his glad countenance to such as stood afar off, and most tender language to those that stood nigh his Grace, showed himself no less thankful to receive the people's goodwill than they to offer it. To all that wished him well, he gave thanks. To such as bade 'God save his Grace,' he said in return, 'God save you all!' and added that he thanked them with all his heart. Wonderfully transported were the people with the loving answers and gestures of their king."

In Fenchurch Street a "fair child, in costly apparel," stood on a stage to welcome his Majesty to the city. The last verse of his greeting was in these words:

> Welcome, O king, as much as hearts can think;
> Welcome again, as much as tongue can tell;
> Welcome to joyous tongues, and hearts that will not shrink:
> God thee preserve, we pray, and wish thee ever well.

The people burst forth in a glad shout, repeating with one voice what the child had said. Tom Canty gazed abroad over the surging sea of eager faces, and his heart swelled with exultation and he felt that the one thing worth living for in this world was to be a king, and a nation's idol. Presently he caught sight, at a distance, of a couple of his ragged Offal Court comrades—one of them the Lord High Admiral in his late mimic court, the other the First Lord of the Bedchamber in the same pretentious fiction; and his pride swelled higher than ever. Oh, if they could only recognize him now! What unspeakable glory it would be if they could recognize him and realize that the derided mock king of the slums and back alleys was become a real king, with illustrious dukes and princes for his humble menials and the

English world at his feet! But he had to deny himself and
choke down his desire, for such a recognition might cost
more than it would come to; so he turned away his head
and left the two soiled lads to go on with their shoutings
and glad adulations, unsuspicious of whom it was they were
lavishing them upon.

Every now and then rose the cry, "A largess! A largess!"
and Tom responded by scattering a handful of bright new
coins abroad for the multitude to scramble for.

The chronicler says, "At the upper end of Gracechurch
Street, before the sign of the Eagle, the city had erected a
gorgeous arch, beneath which was a stage which stretched
from one side of the street to the other. This was a historical
pageant, representing the king's immediate progenitors.
There sat Elizabeth of York in the midst of an immense
white rose whose petals formed elaborate furbelows around
her; by her side was Henry VII, issuing out of a vast red
rose, disposed in the same manner; the hands of the royal
pair were locked together, and the wedding ring ostenta-
tiously displayed. From the red and white roses proceeded
a stem which reached up to a second stage, occupied by
Henry VIII, issuing from a red-and-white rose, with the
effigy of the new king's mother, Jane Seymour, represented
by his side. One branch sprang from this pair, which
mounted to a third stage, where sat the effigy of Edward VI
himself, enthroned in royal majesty; and the whole pageant
was framed with wreaths of roses, red and white."

This quaint and gaudy spectacle so wrought upon the re-
joicing people that their acclamations utterly smothered the
small voice of the child whose business it was to explain the
thing in eulogistic rhymes. But Tom Canty was not sorry,
for this loyal uproar was sweeter music to him than any
poetry, no matter what its quality might be. Whithersoever
Tom turned his happy young face, the people recognized
the exactness of his effigy's likeness to himself, the flesh
and blood counterpart, and new whirlwinds of applause
burst forth.

The great pageant moved on, and still on, under one tri-
umphal arch after another, and past a bewildering succession of spectacular and symbolic tableaux, each of which
typified and exalted some virtue, or talent, or merit of the
little king's. "Throughout the whole of Cheapside, from
every penthouse and window, hung banners and streamers;

and the richest carpets, stuffs, and cloth of gold tapestried the streets—specimens of the great wealth of the stores within; and the splendor of this thoroughfare was equaled in the other streets, and in some even surpassed.''

"And all these wonders and these marvels are to welcome me—me!" murmured Tom Canty.

The mock king's cheeks were flushed with excitement, his eyes were flashing, his senses swam in a delirium of pleasure. At this point, just as he was raising his hand to fling another rich largess, he caught sight of a pale, astounded face which was strained forward out of the second rank of the crowd, its intense eyes riveted upon him. A sickening consternation struck through him; he recognized his mother! And up flew his hand, palm outward, before his eyes—that old involuntary gesture born of a forgotten episode and perpetuated by habit. In an instant more she had torn her way out of the press, and past the guards, and was at his side. She embraced his leg, she covered it with kisses, and cried, "O my child, my darling!" lifting toward him a face that was transfigured with joy and love. The same instant an officer of the king's guard snatched her away with a curse and sent her reeling back whence she came with a vigorous impulse from his strong arm. The words "I do not know you, woman!" were falling from Tom Canty's lips when this piteous thing occurred, but it smote him to the heart to see her treated so; and as she turned for a last glimpse of him, whilst the crowd was swallowing her from his sight, she seemed so wounded, so brokenhearted, that a shame fell upon him which consumed his pride to ashes and withered his stolen royalty. His grandeurs were stricken valueless; they seemed to fall away from him like rotten rags.

The procession moved on, and still on, through ever-augmenting splendors and ever-augmenting tempests of welcome, but to Tom Canty they were as if they had not been. He neither saw nor heard. Royalty had lost its grace and sweetness; its pomps were become a reproach. Remorse was eating his heart out. He said, "Would God I were free of my captivity!"

He had unconsciously dropped back into the phraseology of the first days of his compulsory greatness.

The shining pageant still went winding like a radiant and interminable serpent down the crooked lanes of the quaint

old city, and through the huzzahing hosts; but still the king
rode with bowed head and vacant eyes, seeing only his
mother's face and that wounded look in it.

"Largess, largess!" The cry fell upon an unheeding ear.

"Long live Edward of England!" It seemed as if the earth
shook with the explosion, but there was no response from
the king. He heard it only as one hears the thunder of the
surf when it is blown to the ear out of a great distance, for
it was smothered under another sound which was still
nearer, in his own breast, in his accusing conscience—a
voice which kept repeating those shameful words, "I do not
know you, woman!"

The words smote upon the king's soul as the strokes of a
funeral bell smite upon the soul of a surviving friend when
they remind him of secret treacheries suffered at his hands
by him that is gone.

New glories were unfolded at every turning; new wonders, new marvels, sprung into view; the pent clamors of
waiting batteries were released; new raptures poured from
the throats of the waiting multitudes; but the king gave no
sign, and the accusing voice that went moaning through his
comfortless breast was all the sound he heard.

By and by the gladness in the faces of the populace
changed a little and became touched with a something like
solicitude or anxiety; an abatement in the volume of applause was observable too. The Lord Protector was quick
to notice these things; he was as quick to detect the cause.
He spurred to the king's side, bent low in his saddle, uncovered, and said, "My liege, it is an ill time for dreaming.
The people observe thy downcast head, thy clouded mien,
and they take it for an omen. Be advised; unveil the sun of
royalty and let it shine upon these boding vapors and dis-
perse them. Lift up thy face and smile upon the people."

So saying, the duke scattered a handful of coins to right
and left, then retired to his place. The mock king did me-
chanically as he had been bidden. His smile had no heart
in it, but few eyes were near enough or sharp enough to
detect that. The noddings of his plumed head as he saluted
his subjects were full of grace and graciousness; the largess
which he delivered from his hand was royally liberal, so the
people's anxiety vanished and the acclamations burst forth
again in as mighty a volume as before.

Still once more, a little before the progress was ended,

the duke was obliged to ride forward and make remonstrance. He whispered, "O dread sovereign! Shake off these fatal humors; the eyes of the world are upon thee." Then he added with sharp annoyance, "Perdition catch that crazy pauper!'Twas she that hath disturbed your Highness."

The gorgeous figure turned a lusterless eye upon the duke and said in a dead voice, "She was my mother!"

"My God!" groaned the Protector as he reigned his horse backward to his post. "The omen was pregnant with prophecy. He is gone mad again!"

Coronation Day

Let us go backward a few hours and place ourselves in Westminster Abbey at four o'clock in the morning of this memorable Coronation Day. We are not without company, for although it is still night, we find the torchlighted galleries already filling up with people who are well content to sit still and wait seven or eight hours till the time shall come for them to see what they may not hope to see twice in their lives—the coronation of a king. Yes, London and Westminster have been astir ever since the warning guns boomed at three o'clock, and already crowds of untitled rich folk who have bought the privilege of trying to find sitting room in the galleries are flocking in at the entrances reserved for their sort.

The hours drag along tediously enough. All stir has ceased for some time, for every gallery has long ago been packed. We may sit now and look and think at our leisure. We have glimpses, here and there and yonder, through the dim cathedral twilight, of portions of many galleries and balconies wedged full with people, the other portions of these galleries and balconies being cut off from sight by intervening pillars and architectural projections. We have in view the whole of the great north transept—empty and waiting for England's privileged ones. We see also the ample area or platform, carpeted with rich stuffs, whereon the throne stands. The throne occupies the center of the platform, and is raised above it upon an elevation of four steps. Within the seat of the throne is enclosed a rough, flat rock—the stone of Scone—which many generations of Scottish kings sat on to be crowned, and so it in time became holy enough to answer a like purpose for English monarchs. Both the throne and its footstool are covered with cloth of gold.

Stillness reigns, the torches blink dully, the time drags heavily. But at last the lagging daylight asserts itself, the torches are extinguished, and a mellow radiance suffuses the great spaces. All features of the noble building are distinct now, but soft and dreamy, for the sun is lightly veiled with clouds.

At seven o'clock the first break in the drowsy monotony occurs, for on the stroke of this hour the first peeress enters the transept, clothed like Solomon for splendor, and is conducted to her appointed place by an official clad in satins and velvets, whilst a duplicate of him gathers up the lady's long train, follows after, and when the lady is seated, arranges the train across her lap for her. He then places her footstool according to her desire, after which he puts her coronet where it will be convenient to her hand when the time for the simultaneous coroneting of the nobles shall arrive.

By this time the peeresses are flowing in in a glittering stream, and the satin-clad officials are flitting and glinting everywhere, seating them and making them comfortable. The scene is animated enough now. There is stir and life, and shifting color everywhere. After a time, quiet reigns again, for the peeresses are all come and are all in their places—a solid acre, or such a matter, of human flowers, resplendent in variegated colors and frosted like a Milky Way with diamonds. There are all ages here: brown, wrinkled, white-haired dowagers who are able to go back, and still back, down the stream of time and recall the crowning of Richard III and the troublous days of that old forgotten age; and there are handsome middle-aged dames; and lovely and gracious young matrons; and gentle and beautiful young girls with beaming eyes and fresh complexions who may possibly put on their jeweled coronets awkwardly when the great time comes, for the matter will be new to them and their excitement will be a sore hindrance. Still, this may not happen, for the hair of all these ladies has been arranged with a special view to the swift and successful lodging of the crown in its place when the signal comes.

We have seen that this massed array of peeresses is sown thick with diamonds, and we also see that it is a marvelous spectacle, but now we are about to be astonished in earnest. About nine the clouds suddenly break away and a shaft of sunshine cleaves the mellow atmosphere and drifts slowly along the ranks of ladies, and every rank it touches flames into a dazzling splendor of many-colored fires, and we tin-

gle to our fingertips with the electric thrill that is shot
through us by the surprise and the beauty of the spectacle!
Presently a special envoy from some distant corner of the
Orient, marching with the general body of foreign ambassadors, crosses this bar of sunshine, and we catch our breath,
the glory that streams and flashes and palpitates about him
is so overpowering, for he is crusted from head to heel with
gems, and his slightest movement showers a dancing radiance all around him.

Let us change the tense for convenience. The time drifted
along—one hour—two hours—two hours and a half; then the
deep booming of artillery told that the king and his grand
procession had arrived at last, so the waiting multitude re-
joiced. All knew that a further delay must follow, for the
king must be prepared and robed for the solemn ceremony;
but this delay would be pleasantly occupied by the assem-
bling of the peers of the realm in their stately robes. These
were conducted ceremoniously to their seats and their coronets placed conveniently at hand; and meanwhile the multitude in the galleries were alive with interest, for most of
them were beholding for the first time dukes, earls, and
barons, whose names had been historical for five hundred
years. When all were finally seated, the spectacle from the
galleries and all coigns of vantage was complete—a gorgeous one to look upon and to remember.

Now the robed and mitered great heads of the church and
their attendants filed in upon the platform and took their
appointed places; these were followed by the Lord Protector
and other great officials, and these again by a steel-clad
detachment of the guard.

There was a waiting pause; then, at a signal, a triumphant
peal of music burst forth, and Tom Canty, clothed in a long
robe of cloth of gold, appeared at a door and stepped upon
the platform. The entire multitude rose, and the ceremony
of the Recognition ensued.

Then a noble anthem swept the Abbey with its rich waves
of sound; and thus heralded and welcomed, Tom Canty was
conducted to the throne. The ancient ceremonies went on
with impressive solemnity, whilst the audience gazed; and
as they drew nearer and nearer to completion, Tom Canty
grew pale, and still paler, and a deep and steadily deepening
woe and despondency settled down upon his spirits and upon
his remorseful heart.

At last the final act was at hand. The Archbishop of Canterbury lifted up the crown of England from its cushion and held it out over the trembling mock king's head. In the same instant a rainbow radiance flashed along the spacious transept, for with one impulse every individual in the great concourse of nobles lifted a coronet and poised it over his or her head—and paused in that attitude.

A deep hush pervaded the Abbey. At this impressive moment a startling apparition intruded upon the scene—an apparition observed by none in the absorbed multitude until it suddenly appeared, moving up the great central aisle. It was a boy, bareheaded, ill-shod, and clothed in coarse plebeian garments that were falling to rags. He raised his hand with a solemnity which ill comported with his soiled and sorry aspect and delivered this note of warning, "I forbid you to set the crown of England upon that forfeited head. *I* am the king!"

In an instant several indignant hands were laid upon the boy; but in the same instant Tom Canty, in his regal vestments, made a swift step forward and cried out in a ringing voice, "Loose him and forbear! He *is* the king!"

A sort of panic of astonishment swept the assemblage, and they partly rose in their places and stared in a bewildered way at one another and at the chief figures in this scene, like persons who wondered whether they were awake and in their senses or asleep and dreaming. The Lord Protector was as amazed as the rest, but quickly recovered himself and exclaimed in a voice of authority, "Mind not his Majesty, his malady is upon him again; seize the vagabond!"

He would have been obeyed, but the mock king stamped his foot and cried out, "On your peril! Touch him not; he is the king!"

The hands were withheld; a paralysis fell upon the house; no one moved, no one spoke; indeed no one knew how to act or what to say in so strange and surprising an emergency. While all minds were struggling to right themselves, the boy still moved steadily forward, with high port and confident mien; he had never halted from the beginning; and while the tangled minds still floundered helplessly, he stepped upon the platform, and the mock king ran with a glad face to meet him and fell on his knees before him and said, "Oh, my lord the king, let poor Tom Canty be first to swear fealty to thee and say, 'Put on thy crown and enter into thine own again!' "

The Lord Protector's eye fell sternly upon the newcomer's face, but straightway the sternness vanished away and gave place to an expression of wondering surprise. This thing happened also to the other great officers. They glanced at each other and retreated a step by a common and unconscious impulse. The thought in each mind was the same: "What a strange resemblance!"

The Lord Protector reflected a moment or two in perplexity; then he said with grave respectfulness, "By your favor, sir, I desire to ask certain questions which——"

"I will answer them, my lord."

The duke asked him many questions about the court, the late king, the prince, the princesses; the boy answered them correctly and without hesitating. He described the rooms of state in the palace, the late king's apartments, and those of the Prince of Wales.

It was strange, it was wonderful; yes, it was unaccountable—so all said that heard it. The tide was beginning to turn, and Tom Canty's hopes to run high, when the Lord Protector shook his head and said, "It is true it is most wonderful, but it is no more than our lord the king likewise can do." This remark and this reference to himself as still the king saddened Tom Canty, and he felt his hopes crumbling from under him. "These are not *proofs*," added the Protector.

The tide was turning very fast now, very fast indeed, but in the wrong direction; it was leaving poor Tom Canty stranded on the throne and sweeping the other out to sea. The Lord Protector communed with himself—shook his head—the thought forced itself upon him, "It is perilous to the state and to us all to entertain so fateful a riddle as this; it could divide the nation and undermine the throne." He turned and said, "Sir Thomas, arrest this— No, hold!" His face lighted, and he confronted the ragged candidate with this question, "Where lieth the Great Seal? Answer me this truly, and the riddle is unriddled, for only he that was Prince of Wales *can* so answer! On so trivial a thing hang a throne and a dynasty!"

It was a lucky thought, a happy thought. That it was so considered by the great officials was manifested by the silent applause that shot from eye to eye around their circle in the

form of bright, approving glances. Yes, none but the true
prince could dissolve the stubborn mystery of the vanished
Great Seal; this forlorn little impostor had been taught his
lesson well, but here his teachings must fail, for his teacher
himself could not answer *that* question—ah, very good, very
good indeed; now we shall be rid of this troublesome and
perilous business in short order! And so they nodded invis-
ibly, and smiled inwardly with satisfaction, and looked to
see this foolish lad stricken with a palsy of guilty confusion.
How surprised they were, then, to see nothing of the sort
happen—how they marveled to hear him answer up
promptly, in a confident and untroubled voice, and say,
"There is nought in this riddle that is difficult." Then,
without so much as a by-your-leave to anybody, he turned
and gave this command, with the easy manner of one accustomed to doing such things: "My lord St. John, go you
to my private cabinet in the palace—for none knoweth the
place better than you—and, close down to the floor, in the
left corner remotest from the door that opens from the
antechamber, you shall find in the wall a brazen nailhead;
press upon it and a little jewel closet will fly open which
not even you do know of—no, nor any soul else in all the
world but me and the trusty artisan that did contrive it for
me. The first thing that falleth under your eye will be the
Great Seal; fetch it hither."

All the company wondered at this speech, and wondered
still more to see the little mendicant pick out this peer without hesitancy or apparent fear of mistake, and call him by
name with such a placidly convincing air of having known
him all his life. The peer was almost surprised into obeying.
He even made a movement as if to go, but quickly recovered
his tranquil attitude and confessed his blunder with a blush.
Tom Canty turned upon him and said sharply, "Why dost
thou hesitate? Hast not heard the king's command? Go!"

The lord St. John made a deep obeisance—and it was
observed that it was a significantly cautious and noncom-
mittal one, it not being delivered at either of the kings, but
at the neutral ground about halfway between the two—and
took his leave.

Now began a movement of the gorgeous particles of that
official group which was slow, scarcely perceptible, and yet
steady and persistent—a movement such as is observed in a
kaleidoscope that is turned slowly, whereby the components

of one splendid cluster fall away and join themselves to another; a movement which little by little, in the present case, dissolved the glittering crowd that stood about Tom Canty and clustered it together again in the neighborhood of the newcomer. Tom Canty stood almost alone. Now ensued a brief season of deep suspense and waiting, during which even the few fainthearts still remaining near Tom Canty gradually scraped together courage enough to glide, one by one, over to the majority. So at last Tom Canty, in his royal robes and jewels, stood wholly alone and isolated from the world, a conspicuous figure occupying an eloquent vacancy.

Now the lord St. John was seen returning., As he advanced up the mid-aisle the interest was so intense that the low murmur of conversation in the great assemblage died out and was succeeded by a profound hush, a breathless stillness, through which his footfalls pulsed with a dull and distant sound. Every eye was fastened upon him as he moved along. He reached the platform, paused a moment, then moved toward Tom Canty with a deep obeisance and said, "Sire, the Seal is not there!"

A mob does not melt away from the presence of a plague patient with more haste than the band of pallid and terrified courtiers melted away from the presence of the shabby little claimant of the crown. In a moment he stood all alone, without friend or supporter, a target upon which was concentrated a bitter fire of scornful and angry looks.

The Lord Protector called out fiercely, "Cast the beggar into the street and scourge him through the town; the paltry knave is worth no more consideration!"

Officers of the guard sprang forward to obey, but Tom Canty waved them off and said, "Back! Whoso touches him perils his life!"

The Lord Protector was perplexed in the last degree. He said to the lord St. John, "Searched you well? But it boots not to ask that. It doth seem passing strange. Little things, trifles, slip out of one's ken, and one does not think it matter for surprise; but how a so bulky thing as the Seal of England can vanish away and no man be able to get track of it again— a massy golden disk—"

Tom Canty, with beaming eyes, sprang forward and shouted, "Hold, that is enough. Was it round? And thick? And had it letters and devices graved upon it? Yes? Oh, *now* I know what this Great Seal is that there's been such worry and pother about! An' ye had described it to me, ye could have had it three weeks ago. Right well I know where it lies, but it was not I that put it there—first.''

"Who, then, my liege?'' asked the Lord Protector.

"He that stands there—the rightful king of England. And he shall tell you himself where it lies; then you will believe he knew it of his own knowledge. Bethink thee, my king— spur thy memory—it was the last, the very *last* thing thou didst that day before thou didst rush forth from the palace, clothed in my rags, to punish the soldier that insulted me.''

A silence ensued, undisturbed by a movement or a whisper, and all eyes were fixed upon the newcomer, who stood, with bent head and corrugated brow, groping in his memory among a thronging multitude of valueless recollections for one single little elusive fact, which, found, would seat him upon a throne—unfound, would leave him as he was, for good and all, a pauper and an outcast. Moment after moment passed—the moments built themselves into minutes— still the boy struggled silently on, and gave no sign. But at last he heaved a sigh, shook his head slowly, and said with a trembling lip and in a despondent voice, "I call the scene back—all of it—but the Seal hath no place in it.'' He paused, then looked up and said with gentle dignity, "My lords and gentlemen, if ye will rob your rightful sovereign of his own for lack of this evidence which he is not able to furnish, I may not stay ye, being powerless. But——''

"Oh, folly. Oh, madness, my king!'' cried Tom Canty in a panic. "Wait! Think! Do not give up! The cause is not lost! Nor *shall* be, neither! List to what I say—follow every word; I am going to bring that morning back again, every hap just as it happened. We talked; I told you of my sisters, Nan and Bet—ah, yes, you remember that; and about mine old grandam, and the rough games of the lads of Offal Court—yes, you remember these things also; very well, follow me still; you shall recall everything. You gave me food and drink, and did with princely courtesy send away the servant so that my low breeding might not shame me before them—ah, yes, this also you remember.''

As Tom checked off his details, and the other boy nodded his head in recognition of them, the great audience and the officials stared in puzzled wonderment; the tale sounded like true history, yet how could this impossible conjunction between a prince and a beggar boy have come about? Never was a company of people so perplexed, so interested, and so stupefied before.

"For a jest, my prince, we did exchange garments. Then we stood before a mirror; and so alike were we that both said it seemed as if there had been no change made—yes, you remember that. Then you noticed that the soldier had hurt my hand. Look! Here it is; I cannot yet even write with it, the fingers are so stiff. At this your Highness sprang up, vowing vengeance upon that soldier, and ran toward the door; you passed a table; that thing you call the Seal lay on that table; you snatched it up and looked eagerly about, as if for a place to hide it; your eye caught sight of——"

"There, 'tis sufficient! And the dear God be thanked!" exclaimed the ragged claimant in a mighty excitement. "Go, my good St. John; in an armpiece of the Milanese armor that hangs on the wall thou'lt find the Seal!"

"Right, my king! Right!" cried Tom Canty. "*Now* the scepter of England is thine own; and it were better for him that would dispute it that he had been born dumb! Go, my lord St. John; give thy feet wings!"

The whole assemblage was on its feet now and well nigh out of its mind with uneasiness, apprehension, and consuming excitement. On the floor and on the platform a deafening buzz of frantic conversation burst forth, and for some time nobody knew anything or heard anything or was interested in anything but what his neighbor was shouting into his ear or he was shouting into his neighbor's ear. Time—nobody knew how much of it—swept by unheeded and unnoted. At last a sudden hush fell upon the house, and in the same moment St. John appeared upon the platform and held the Great Seal aloft in his hand. Then such a shout went up!

"Long live the true king!"

For five minutes the air quaked with shouts and the crash of musical instruments, and was white with a storm of waving handkerchiefs; and through it all a ragged lad, the most conspicuous figure in England, stood flushed and happy and proud in the center of the spacious platform with the great vassals of the kingdom kneeling around him.

Then all rose, and Tom Canty cried out, "Now, O my king, take these regal garments back and give poor Tom, thy servant, his shreds and remnants again."

The Lord Protector spoke up, "Let the small varlet be stripped and flung into the Tower."

But the new king, the true king, said, "I will not have it so. But for him I had not got my crown again; none shall lay a hand upon him to harm him. And as for thee, my good uncle, my Lord Protector, this conduct of thine is not grateful toward this poor lad, for I hear he hath made thee a duke"—the Protector blushed—"yet he was not a king; wherefore, what is thy fine title worth now? Tomorrow you shall sue to me, *through him,* for its confirmation, else no duke, but a simple earl, shalt thou remain."

Under this rebuke his grace the Duke of Somerset retired a little from the front for the moment. The king turned to Tom and said kindly, "My poor boy, how was it that you could remember where I hid the Seal when I could not remember it myself?"

"Ah, my king, that was easy, since I used it divers days."

"Used it, yet could not explain where it was?"

"I did not know it was *that* they wanted. They did not describe it, your Majesty."

"Then how used you it?"

The red blood began to steal up into Tom's cheeks, and he dropped his eyes and was silent.

"Speak up, good lad, and fear nothing," said the king. "How used you the Great Seal of England?"

Tom stammered a moment in a pathetic confusion, then got it out, "To crack nuts with!"

Poor child, the avalanche of laughter that greeted this nearly swept him off his feet. But if a doubt remained in any mind that Tom Canty was not the king of England and familiar with the august appurtenances of royalty, this reply disposed of it utterly.

Meantime the sumptuous robe of state had been removed from Tom's shoulders to the king's, whose rags were effectually hidden from sight under it. Then the coronation ceremonies were resumed; the true king was anointed and the crown set upon his head, whilst cannon thundered the news to the city, and all London seemed to rock with applause.

Edward as King

Miles Hendon was picturesque enough before he got into the riot on London Bridge; he was more so when he got out of it. He had but little money when he got in, none at all when he got out. The pickpockets had stripped him of his last farthing.

But no matter, so he found his boy. Being a soldier, he did not go at his task in a random way, but set to work first of all to arrange his campaign.

What would the boy naturally do? Where would he naturally go? Well, argued Miles, he would naturally go to his former haunts, for that is the instinct of unsound minds when homeless and forsaken, as well as of sound ones. Whereabouts were his former haunts? His rags, taken together with the low villain who seemed to know him and who even claimed to be his father, indicated that his home was in one or another of the poorest and meanest districts of London. Would the search for him be difficult or long? No, it was likely to be easy and brief. He would not hunt for the boy, he would hunt for a crowd; in the center of a big crowd or a little one, sooner or later, he should find his poor little friend, sure; and the mangy mob would be entertaining itself with pestering and aggravating the boy, who would be proclaiming himself king, as usual. Then Miles Hendon would cripple some of those people, and carry off his little ward, and comfort and cheer him with loving words, and the two would never be separated any more.

So Miles started on his quest. Hour after hour he tramped through back alleys and squalid streets seeking groups and crowds, and finding no end of them, but never any sign of the boy. This greatly surprised him but did not discourage him. To his notion there was nothing the matter with his plan of campaign; the only miscalculation about it was that the campaign was becoming a lengthy one, whereas he had expected it to be short.

When daylight arrived at last, he had made many a mile and canvassed many a crowd, but the only result was that he was tolerably tired, rather hungry, and very sleepy. He wanted some breakfast, but there was no way to get it. To beg for it did not occur to him; as to pawning his sword, he would as soon have thought of parting with his honor; he could spare some of his clothes—yes, but one could as easily find a customer for a disease as for such clothes.

At noon he was still tramping—among the rabble which followed after the royal procession now, for he argued that this regal display would attract his little lunatic powerfully. He followed the pageant through all its devious windings about London and all the way to Westminster and the Abbey. He drifted here and there amongst the multitudes that were massed in the vicinity for a weary long time, baffled and perplexed, and finally wandered off thinking and trying to contrive some way to better his plan of campaign. By and by, when he came to himself out of his musings, he discovered that the town was far behind him and that the day was growing old. He was near the river and in the country; it was a region of fine rural seats—not the sort of district to welcome clothes like his.

It was not at all cold, so he stretched himself on the ground in the lee of a hedge to rest and think. Drowsiness presently began to settle upon his senses; the faint and far-off boom of cannon was wafted to his ear, and he said to himself, "The new king is crowned," and straightway fell asleep. He had not slept or rested before for more than thirty hours. He did not wake again until near the middle of the next morning.

He got up lame, stiff, and half famished, washed himself in the river, stayed his stomach with a pint or two of water, and trudged off toward Westminster grumbling at himself for having wasted so much time. Hunger helped him to a new plan now; he would try to get speech with old Sir Humphrey Marlow and borrow a few marks, and—but that was enough of a plan for the present; it would be time enough to enlarge it when this first stage should be accomplished.

Toward eleven o'clock he approached the palace; and although a host of showy people were about him, moving in the same direction, he was not inconspicuous—his costume took care of that. He watched these people's faces narrowly, hoping to find a charitable one whose possessor might be willing to carry his name to the old lieutenant; as to trying to get into the palace himself, that was simply out of the question.

Presently our whipping boy passed him, then wheeled about and scanned his figure well, saying to himself, "An' that is not the very vagabond his Majesty is in such a worry about, then am I an ass—though belike I was that before. He answereth the description to a rag; that God should make two such would be to cheapen miracles by wasteful repetition. I would I could contrive an excuse to speak with him."

Miles Hendon saved him the trouble, for he turned about then as a man generally will when somebody mesmerizes him by gazing hard at him from behind; and observing a strong interest in the boy's eyes, he stepped toward him and said, "You have just come out from the palace: do you belong there?"

"Yes, your worship."

"Know you Sir Humphrey Marlow?"

The boy started and said to himself, "Lord! Mine old departed father!" Then he answered aloud, "Right well, your worship."

"Good; is he within?"

"Yes," said the boy; and added to himself, "Within his grave."

"Might I crave your favor to carry my name to him and say I beg to say a word in his ear?"

"I will dispatch the business right willingly, fair sir."

"Then say Miles Hendon, son of Sir Richard, is here without; I shall be greatly bounden to you, my good lad."

The boy looked disappointed; "The king did not name him so," he said to himself, "but it mattereth not; this his twin brother and can give his Majesty news of t'her Sir-Odds-and-Ends, I warrant." So he said to Miles, "Step in there a moment, good sir, and wait till I bring you word."

Hendon retired to the palace indicated; it was a recess sunk in the place wall, with a stone bench in it—a shelter for sentinels a in bad weather. He had hardly seated himself when some halberdiers in charge of an officer passed by. The officer saw him, halted his men, and commanded Hendon to come forth. He obeyed, and was promptly arrested as a suspicious character prowling within the precincts of

the palace. Things began to look ugly. Poor Miles was going
to explain, but the officer roughly silenced him and ordered
his men to disarm him and search him.

"God of his mercy grant that they find somewhat," said
poor Miles; "I have searched enow and failed, yet is my
need greater than theirs."

Nothing was found but a document. The officer tore it
open, and Hendon smiled when he recognized the "pothooks" made by his lost little friend that black day at Hendon Hall. The officer's face grew dark as he read the English
paragraph, and Miles blenched to the opposite color as he
listened.

"Another new claimant of the crown!" cried the officer.
"Verily they breed like rabbits today. Seize the rascal, men,
and see ye keep him fast whilst I convey this precious paper
within and send it to the king."

He hurried away, leaving the prisoner in the grip of the
halberdiers.

"Now is my evil luck ended at last," muttered Hendon,
"for I shall dangle at a rope's end for a certainty, by reason
of that bit of writing. And what will become of my poor
lad! Ah, only the good God knoweth."

By and by he saw the officer coming again in a great
hurry, so he plucked his courage together, purposing to meet
his trouble as became a man. The officer ordered the men
to loose the prisoner and return his sword to him, then
bowed respectfully and said, "Please you sir, to follow
me."

Hendon followed, saying to himself, "An' I were not
traveling to death and judgment, and so must needs econ-
omize in sin, I would throttle this knave for his mock courtesy."

The two traversed a populous court and arrived at the
grand entrance of the palace, where the officer, with another
bow, delivered Hendon into the hands of a gorgeous official,
who received him with profound respect and led him forward through a great hall lined on both sides with rows of
splendid flunkies (who made reverential obeisance as the
two passed along, but fell into death throes of silent laughter
at our stately scarecrow the moment his back was turned)
and up a broad staircase, among flocks of fine folk, and
finally conducted him into a vast room, clove a passage for
him through the assembled nobility of England, then made

a bow, reminded him to take his hat off, and left him standing in the middle of the room, a mark for all eyes, for plenty of indignant frowns, and for a sufficiency of amused and derisive smiles.

Miles Hendon was entirely bewildered. There sat the young king under a canopy of state five steps away, with his head bent down and aside, speaking with a sort of human bird of paradise—a duke, maybe; Hendon observed to himself that it was hard enough to be sentenced to death in the full vigor of life without having this peculiarly public humiliation added. He wished the king would hurry about it; some of the gaudy people nearby were becoming offensive. At this moment the king raised his head slightly and Hendon caught a good view of his face. The sight nearly took his breath away! He stood gazing at the fair young face like one transfixed, then presently ejaculated, "Lo, the lord of the Kingdom of Dreams and Shadows on his throne!"

He muttered some broken sentences, still gazing and marveling, then turned his eyes around and about, scanning the gorgeous throng and the splendid saloon, murmuring, "But these are *real*—verily these are *real*—surely it is not a dream."

He stared at the king again and thought, "*Is* it a dream? Or *is* he the veritable sovereign of England, and not the friendless poor Tom o' Bedlam I took him for? Who shall solve me this riddle?"

A sudden idea flashed in his eye, and he strode to the wall, gathered up a chair, brought it back, planted it on the floor, and sat down in it!

A buzz of indignation broke out, a rough hand was laid upon him, and a voice exclaimed, "Up, thou mannerless clown! Wouldst sit in the presence of the king?"

The disturbance attracted his Majesty's attention, who stretched forth his hand and cried out, "Touch him not; it is his right!"

The throng fell back, stupefied. The king went on, "Learn ye all, ladies, lords and gentlemen, that this is my trusty and well-beloved servant Miles Hendon, who interposed his good sword and saved his prince from bodily harm and possible death; and for this he is a knight, by the king's voice. Also learn that for a higher service, in that he saved his sovereign stripes and shame, taking these upon himself, he is a peer of England, Earl of Kent, and shall have gold and lands meet for the dignity. More—the privilege which he hath just exercised is his by royal grant, for we have ordained that the chiefs of his line shall have and hold the right to sit in the presence of the Majesty of England henceforth, age after age, so long as the crown shall endure. Molest him not.''

Two persons who, through delay, had only arrived from the country during this morning and had now been in this room only five minutes stood listening to these words and looking at the king, then at the scarecrow, then at the king again, in a sort of torpid bewilderment. These were Sir Hugh and the lady Edith. But the new earl did not see them. He was still staring at the monarch in a dazed way and muttering, ''Oh, body o' me! *This* my pauper! This my lunatic! This is he whom *I* would show what grandeur was in my house of seventy rooms and seven and twenty servants! This is he who had never known aught but rags for raiment, kicks for comfort, and offal for diet! This is he whom *I* adopted and would make respectable! Would God I had a bag to hide my head in!''

Then his manners suddenly came back to him, and he dropped upon his knees, with his hands between the king's and swore allegiance and did homage for his lands and titles. Then he rose and stood respectfully aside, a mark still for all eyes—and much envy too.

Now the king discovered Sir Hugh and spoke out with wrathful voice and kindling eye, ''Strip this robber of his false show and stolen estates and put him under lock and key till I have need of him.''

The late Sir Hugh was led away.

There was a stir at the other end of the room now; the assemblage fell apart, and Tom Canty, quaintly but richly clothed, marched down between these living walls, preceded by an usher. He knelt before the king, who said, ''I have learned the story of these past few weeks and am well pleased with thee. Thou hast governed the realm with right royal gentleness and mercy. Thou hast found thy mother and thy sisters again? Good; they shall be cared for, and thy father shall hang if thou desire it and the law consent. Know, all ye that hear my voice, that from this day they that abide in the shelter of Christ's Hospital and share the king's bounty shall have their minds and hearts fed, as well as their baser parts; and this boy shall dwell there, and hold the chief place in its honorable body of governors during life. And for that he hath been a king, it is meet that other than common observance shall be his due; wherefore, note this his dress of state, for by it he shall be known, and none shall copy it; and wheresoever he shall come, it shall remind the people that he hath been royal in his time, and none shall deny him his due of reverence or fail to give him salutation. He hath the throne's protection, he hath the Crown's support, he shall be known and called by the honorable title of the King's Ward.''

The proud and happy Tom Canty rose and kissed the king's hand, and was conducted from the presence. He did not waste any time, but flew to his mother to tell her and Nan and Bet all about it and get them to help him enjoy the great news.*

*See Notes to Chapter 33 at end of volume.

Conclusion

Justice and Retribution

When the mysteries were all cleared up, it came out by confession of Hugh Hendon that his wife had repudiated Miles by his command that day at Hendon Hall—a command assisted and supported by the perfectly trustworthy promise that if she did not deny that he was Miles Hendon and stand firmly to it, he would have her life; whereupon she said take it, she did not value it—and she would not repudiate Miles; then the husband said he would spare her life but have Miles assassinated! This was a different matter, so she gave her word and kept it.

Hugh was not prosecuted for his threats or for stealing his brother's estates and title because the wife and brother would not testify against him, and the former would not have been allowed to do it even if she had wanted to. Hugh deserted his wife and went over to the Continent, where he presently died; and by and by the Earl of Kent married his relict. There were grand times and rejoicings at Hendon village when the couple paid their first visit to the Hall.

Tom Canty's father was never heard of again.

The king sought out the farmer who had been branded and sold as a slave, and reclaimed him from his evil life with the Ruffler's gang, and put him in the way of a comfortable livelihood.

He also took that old lawyer out of prison and remitted his fine. He provided good homes for the daughters of the two Baptist women whom he saw burned at the stake, and roundly punished the official who laid the undeserved stripes upon Miles Hendon's back.

He saved from the gallows the boy who had captured the stray falcon, and also the woman who had stolen a remnant of cloth from a weaver; but he was too late to save the man who had been convicted of killing a deer in the royal forest.

He showed favor to the justice who had pitied him when

he was supposed to have stolen a pig, and he had the gratification of seeing him grow in the public esteem and become a great and honored man.

As long as the king lived he was fond of telling the story
of his adventures, all through, from the hour the sentinel
cuffed him away from the palace gate till the final midnight
when he deftly mixed himself into a gang of hurrying workmen and so slipped into the Abbey and climbed up and hid
himself in the Confessor's tomb, and then slept so long next
day that he came within one of missing the coronation altogether. He said that the frequent rehearsing of the precious lesson kept him strong in his purpose to make its
teachings yield benefits to his people; and so, whilst his life
was spared he should continue to tell the story, and thus
keep its sorrowful spectacles fresh in his memory and the
springs of pity replenished in his heart.

Miles Hendon and Tom Canty were favorites of the king
all through his brief reign, and his sincere mourners when
he died. The good Earl of Kent had too much sense to abuse
his peculiar privilege, but he exercised it twice after the
instance we have seen of it before he was called from the
world—once at the accession of Queen Mary, and once at
the accession of Queen Elizabeth. A descendant of his exercised it at the accession of James I. Before this one's son
chose to use the privilege, near a quarter of a century had
elapsed, and the "privilege of the Kents" had faded out of
most people's memories; so when the Kent of that day appeared before Charles I and his court and sat down in the
sovereign's presence to assert and perpetuate the right of his
house, there was a fine stir indeed! But the matter was soon
explained, and the right confirmed. The last earl of the line
fell in the wars of the commonwealth fighting for the king,
and the odd privilege ended with him.

Tom Canty lived to be a very old man, a handsome, white-
haired old fellow of grave and benignant aspect. As long as
he lasted he was honored; and he was also reverenced, for
his striking and peculiar costume kept the people reminded
that "in his time he had been royal"; so whenever he appeared the crowd fell apart, making way for him and whispering, one to another, "Doff thy hat, it is the King's
Ward!" And so they saluted and got his kindly smile in
return, and they valued it too, for his was an honorable
history.

Yes, King Edward VI lived only a few years, poor boy, but he lived them worthily. More than once when some great dignitary, some gilded vassal of the crown, made argument against his leniency and urged that some law which he was bent upon amending was gentle enough for its purpose and wrought no suffering or oppression which anyone need mightily mind, the young king turned the mournful eloquence of his great compassionate eyes upon him and answered, "What dost *thou* know of suffering and oppression? I and my people know, but not thou."

The reign of Edward VI was a singularly merciful one for those harsh times. Now that we are taking leave of him, let us try to keep this in our minds, to his credit.

Notes

Note 1—Page 27

Christ's Hospital Costume

IT is most reasonable to regard the dress as copied from the costume of the citizens of London of that period, when long blue coats were the common habit of apprentices and servingmen, and yellow stockings were generally worn; the coat fits closely to the body but has loose sleeves, and beneath is worn a sleeveless yellow undercoat; around the waist is a red leathern girdle; a clerical band around the neck; and a small flat black cap about the size of a saucer completes the costume.—Timbs's *Curiosities of London*

Note 2—Page 29

IT appears that Christ's Hospital was not originally founded as a *school;* its object was to rescue children from the streets, to shelter, feed, clothe them, etc.—Timbs's *Curiosities of London*

Note 3—Page 36

The Duke of Norfolk's Condemnation Commanded

THE king was now approaching fast towards his end, and fearing lest Norfolk should escape him, he sent a message to the Commons, by which he desired them to hasten the bill, on pretence that Norfolk enjoyed the dignity of earl marshal, and it was necessary to appoint another, who might officiate at the ensuing ceremony of installing his son, Prince of Wales.—Hume, vol. iii., p. 307

Note 4—Page 46

IT was not till the end of this reign [Henry VIII] that any salads, carrots, turnips, or other edible roots were produced in England. The little of these vegetables that was used was formerly imported from Holland and Flanders. Queen Catherine, when she wanted a salad, was obliged to dispatch a messenger thither on purpose.— Hume's *History of England,* vol. iii, p. 314

Note 5—Page 51

Attainder of Norfolk

THE house of peers, without examining the prisoner, without trial or evidence, passed a bill of attainder against him and sent it down to the Commons. . . . The obsequious Commons obeyed his [the king's] directions; and the king, having affixed the royal assent to the bill by commissioners, issued orders for the execution of Norfolk on the morning of the twenty-ninth of January [the next day].—Hume's *England,* vol. iii, p. 306

Note 6—Page 61

The Loving Cup

THE loving cup, and the peculiar ceremonies observed in drinking from it, are older than English history. It is thought that both are Danish importations. As far back as knowledge goes, the loving cup has always been drunk at English banquets. Tradition explains the ceremonies in this way: in the rude ancient times it was deemed a wise precaution to have both hands of both drinkers employed, lest while the pledger pledged his love and fidelity to the pledgee, the pledgee take that opportunity to slip a dirk into him!

Note 7—Page 66

The Duke of Norfolk's Narrow Escape

HAD Henry VIII survived a few hours longer, his order for the duke's execution would have been carried into effect. "But news being carried to the Tower that the king himself had expired that night, the lieutenant deferred obeying the warrant; and it was not thought advisable by the council to begin a new reign by the death of the greatest nobleman in the kingdom, who had been condemned by a sentence so unjust and tyrannical.''—Hume's *England*, vol. iii, p. 307

Note 8—Page 90

The Whipping Boy

JAMES I and Charles II had whipping boys, when they were little fellows, to take their punishment for them when they fell short in their lessons; so I have ventured to furnish my small prince with one, for my own purposes.

Notes to Chapter 15—Page 102

Character of Hertford

THE young king discovered an extreme attachment to his uncle, who was, in the main, a man of moderation and probity.—Hume's *England*, vol. iii, p. 324

But if he [the Protector] gave offense by assuming too much state, he deserves great praise on account of the laws passed this session, by which the rigor of former statutes was much mitigated and some security given to the freedom of the constitution. All laws were repealed which extended the crime of treason beyond the statute of the twenty-fifth of Edward III; all laws enacted during the late reign extending the crime of felony; all the former laws against Lollardy, or heresy, together with the statute of the Six Articles. None were to be accused for words, but within a month after they were spoken. By these repeals several of the most rigorous laws that ever had passed in England were annulled; and some dawn, both of civil and religious liberty, began to appear to the people. A repeal also passed of that law, the destruction of all laws, by which the king's proclamation was made of equal force with a statute.—*Ibid.*, vol. iii, p. 339

Boiling to Death

IN the reign of Henry VIII poisoners were by act of Parliament condemned to be boiled to death. This act was repealed in the following reign.

In Germany, even in the seventeenth century, this horri-

ble punishment was inflicted on coiners and counterfeiters. Taylor, the Water Poet, describes an execution he witnessed in Hamburg in 1616. The judgment pronounced against a coiner of false money was that he should "be boiled to death in oil; not thrown into the vessel at once, but with a pulley or rope to be hanged under the armpits and then let down into the oil by degrees; first the feet, and next the legs, and so to boil his flesh from his bones alive."
—Dr. J. Hammond Trumbull's *Blue Laws, True and False*, p. 13

The Famous Stocking Case

A WOMAN and her daughter nine years old were hanged in Huntingdon for selling their souls to the devil and raising a storm by pulling off their stockings!—*Ibid.*, p. 20

Note 10—Page 112

Enslaving

So young a king and so ignorant a peasant were likely to make mistakes, and this is an instance in point. This peasant was suffering from this law by *anticipation;* the king was venting his indignation against a law which was not yet in existence, for this hideous statute was to have birth in this little king's own reign. However, we know from the humanity of his character that it could never have been suggested by him.

Notes to Chapter 23—Page 145

Death for Trifling Larcenies

WHEN Connecticut and New haven were framing their first codes, larceny above the value of twelvepence was a capital crime in England, as it had been since the time of Henry I.—Dr. J. Hammond Trumbull's *Blue Laws, True and False*, p. 17

The curious old book called *The English Rogue* makes the limit thirteen pence ha'penny, death being the portion of any who steal a thing "above the value of thirteen pence ha'penny."

Notes to Chapter 27—Page 168

FROM many descriptions of larceny, the law expressly took away the benefit of clergy; to steal a horse, or a hawk, or woolen cloth from the weaver was a hanging matter. So it was, to kill a deer from the king's forest or to export sheep from the kingdom—Dr. J. Hammond Trumbull's *Blue Laws, True and False,* p. 13

William Prynne, a learned barrister, was sentenced [long after Edward the Sixth's time] to lose both his ears in the pillory, to degradation from the bar, a fine of £3,000, and imprisonment for life. Three years afterwards he gave new offense to Laud by publishing a pamphlet against the hierarchy. He was again prosecuted and sentenced to lose what remained of his ears, to pay a fine of £5,000, to be branded on both his cheeks with the letters S.L. (for Seditious Libeler), and to remain in prison for life. The severity of this sentence was equaled by the savage rigor of its execution.—*Ibid.,* p. 12

Notes to Chapter 33—Page 200

Christ's Hospital, or Blue Coat School, "the Noblest Institution in the World"

THE ground on which the priory of the Grey Friars stood was conferred by Henry the Eighth on the Corporation of London [who caused the institution there of a home for poor boys and girls]. Subsequently Edward the Sixth caused the old priory to be properly repaired, and founded within it that noble establishment called the Blue Coat School, or Christ's Hospital, for the education and maintenance of orphans and the children of indigent persons. . . . Edward would not let him [Bishop Ridley] depart till the letter was written [to the Lord Mayor], and then charged him to deliver it himself, and sign his special request and commandment that no time might be lost in proposing what was convenient, and apprising him of the proceedings. The work was zealously undertaken, Ridley himself engaging in it; and the result was the founding of Christ's Hospital for the Education of Poor Children. [The king endowed several other charities at the same time.] "Lord God," said he, "I yield thee most hearty thanks that thou hast given me life thus long to finish this work to the glory of thy name!" That innocent and most exemplary life was drawing rapidly to its close, and in a few days he rendered up his spirit to his Creator, praying God to defend the realm from papistry. —J. Heneage Jesse's *London, Its Celebrated Characters and Places*

In the Great Hall hangs a large picture of King Edward VI seated on his throne in a scarlet and ermined robe, holding the scepter in his left hand and presenting with the other the charter to the kneeling Lord Mayor. By his side stands the Chancellor, holding the seals, and next to him are other officers of state. Bishop Ridley kneels before him with uplifted hands as if supplicating a blessing on the event; whilst the aldermen, etc., with the Lord Mayor, kneel on both sides, occupying the middle ground of the picture; and lastly, in front are a double row of boys on one side and girls on the other, from the master and matron down to the boy and girl who have stepped forward from their respective rows and kneel with raised hands before the king.—Timbs's *Curiosities of London,* p. 98

Christ's Hospital, by ancient custom, possesses the privilege of addressing the sovereign on the occasion of his or her coming into the city to partake of the hospitality of the Corporation of London.—*Ibid.*

The Dining Hall, with its lobby and organ gallery, occupies the entire story, which is 187 feet long, 51 feet wide, and 47 feet high; it is lit by nine large windows, filled with stained glass on the south side; and is, next to Westminster Hall, the noblest room in the metropolis. Here the boys, now about eight hundred in number, dine; and here are held the "Suppings in Public," to which visitors are admitted by tickets, issued by the treasurer and by the governors of Christ's Hospital. The tables are laid with cheese in wooden bowls; beer in wooden piggins, poured from leathern jacks; and bread brought in large baskets. The official company enter; the Lord Mayor, or President, takes his seat in a state chair, made of oak from St. Catherine's Church, by the Tower; a hymn is sung, accompanied by the organ; a "Grecian," or head boy, reads the prayers from the pulpit, silence being enforced by three drops of a wooden hammer. After prayer the supper commences, and the visitors walk between the tables. At its close, the "trade boys" take up the baskets, bowls, jacks, piggins, and candlesticks and pass in procession, the bowing to the governors being curiously

formal. This spectacle was witnessed by Queen Victoria and
Prince Albert in 1845.

Among the more eminent Blue Coat Boys are Joshua
Barnes, editor of Anacreon and Euripides; Jeremiah Mark-
land, the eminent critic, particularly in Greek literature;
Camden, the antiquary; Bishop Stillingfleet; Samuel Rich-
ardson, the novelist; Thomas Mitchell, the translator of Ar-
istophanes; Thomas Barnes, many years editor of the
London *Times;* Coleridge, Charles Lamb, and Leigh Hunt.

No boy is admitted before he is seven years old or after
he is nine; and no boy can remain in the school after he is
fifteen, king's boys and "Grecians" alone excepted. There
are about five hundred governors, at the head of whom are
the sovereign and the Prince of Wales. The qualification for
a governor is payment of £500.—*Ibid.*

GENERAL NOTE

ONE hears much about the "hideous blue laws of Connecticut," and is accustomed to shudder piously when they
are mentioned. There are people in America—and even in England!—who imagine that they were a very monument of ma-
lignity, pitilessness, and inhumanity, whereas in reality they
were about the first *sweeping departure from judicial atroc-
ity* which the "civilized" world had seen. This humane and
kindly Blue-Law code, of two hundred and forty years ago,
stands all by itself, with ages of bloody law on the further
side of it, and a century and three quarters of bloody English law on this side of it.

There has never been a time—under the blue laws or any
other—when above *fourteen* crimes were punishable by
death in Connecticut. But in England, within the memory
of men who are still hale in body and mind, *two hundred
and twenty-three* crimes were punishable by death!* These
facts are worth knowing—and worth thinking about, too.

*See Dr. J. Hammond Trumbull's *Blue Laws, True and False,* p. 11

Afterword

In the summer of 1876 Mark Twain began work on a sequel to *The Adventures of Tom Sawyer.* He intended to call the new book *The Adventures of Huckleberry Finn,* and he was confident that it would prove to be just as easy to write as its predecessor had. The first sixteen chapters were spun off in no time at all; and then suddenly, words failed him. Although he was tempted for a while to burn the abortive manuscript forthwith, he eventually decided to lay it aside in the hope that his inspiration would return. Seven years would pass, however, before he would be able to complete his recalcitrant masterpiece, and in this Biblical period of barrenness he turned to other writing tasks. *A Tramp Abroad* appeared in 1880, *The Prince and the Pauper* in 1882, and *Life on the Mississippi* in 1883. The first was a European travel book in the comic mode made famous by *The Innocents Abroad* (1869); the third approached Twain's favorite subject, the Mississippi River, from an autobiographical rather than a fictional point of view; both, in sum, were very characteristic works. But *The Prince and the Pauper* was even more expressive of its author's genius. Indeed, nothing he ever wrote, not even *Huckleberry Finn,* introduces us to more of the themes that preoccupied—and finally obsessed—Mark Twain's imagination than does the story of Tom Canty and Edward Tudor.

First of all, there is the coincidence on which the entire narrative turns: the waif from Offal Court and the Prince of Wales look remarkably alike. All his writing life Mark Twain was fascinated by the twinhood theme, for the condition of twinhood made it possible (or literarily plausible, at any rate) for two people to switch identities, and the thought of becoming someone else, of living another person's life, had a persistent appeal for ex-steamboat pilot Samuel Clemens, who became world-famous as Mark Twain. In *The Prince and the Pauper,* written in the happiest period of Twain's life, the switching of identities leads to perils but is also productive of great happiness. The switch frees both boys from the supervision of tyrannical fathers (a recurrent fantasy in Mark Twain's fiction that undoubtedly reflects his own tortured relationship with John Marshall Clemens), widens their intellectual horizons, sharpens their moral sense, makes them better human beings in every way. But in Mark Twain's later years, the years of his wife's descent into permanent invalidism and of the death of Susie Clemens (one of the two daughters to whom he had buoyantly dedicated *The Prince and the Pauper* and the favorite of all his children), the years of his disastrous financial involvement with the Paige typesetting machine, of his ensuing bankruptcy, and of his utter disenchantment with the squalid materialism of American life—a disenchantment made all the more profound by his guilty knowledge that he too had succumbed to the allure of the "bitch-goddess, SUCCESS"—he began to conceive of identity-switching as a horror, a trap, a moral dead end from which there is no escape. In this mood he conjured up the story *Pudd'nhead Wilson* (1894), which told of how a Negro and white baby had been switched in their cradles and grew up inside one another's skins, so to speak, with disastrous consequences all around. In the later nineties his tortured imagination summoned up vision after vision of children with boys' temperaments caught in girls' bodies, of men trapped inside animals' bodies, of countless pitiful creatures struggling in vain to free themselves from personalities they abominated. The open-ended universe that had permitted Huck Finn, none the worse for wear, to slide in and out of the identities of Sarah Mary Williams, George Jackson, and an English valet, and that had allowed Tom Canty and Edward Tudor to exchange roles for a brief but educatienal season, had shut down with a vengeance.

Thus the basic idea for the story of *The Prince and the Pauper* anticipates many of the works of Mark Twain's later period. The novel also looks back to some of his earlier achievements, especially *The Adventures of Tom Sawyer.* For in *The Prince and the Pauper* we also have a hero whose name is Tom, whose imagination has been nurtured on romantic books, and whose conduct has been fundamentally altered by his reading:

By and by Tom's reading and dreaming about princely life wrought such a strong effect upon him that he began to *act* the prince, unconsciously. His speech and manners became curiously ceremonious and courtly, to the vast admiration and amusement of his intimates.

The *mise-en-scène* is sixteenth-century England, but the situation is none the less strongly reminiscent of boyish amusements in that enchanted world of St. Petersburg on the Mississippi, the world of Tom Sawyer's gang wherein all boys were knights. The sole difference between Tom Canty and Tom Sawyer in this regard is that Tom Canty is given the opportunity to turn fantasy into reality. Tom Sawyer has to work his imagination full time to sustain the illusion that Cardiff Hill represents the battlements of a medieval castle, or whatever, and that Joe Harper is actually a paid-up member of the Round Table, but Tom Canty is carried out of the "mimic kingdom" he has established in the midst of awful Offal Court and set down in the center of the pomp and splendor of a genuine court. Tom Sawyer, the envy of all St. Petersburg boys, would surely have envied his sixteeth-century counterpart.

Once the hero's romantic dream becomes reality, however, Mark Twain immediately proceeds to disparage its glamour. Tom Canty, as it turns out, is not only an English Tom Sawyer; he also has a strong streak of Huck Finn in him. Reflecting Mark Twain's curious amalgam of romanticism and antiromanticism, Tom Canty is at once excited by his new surroundings and disillusioned by them. Like Huck at the Widow Douglas', Tom finds respectability tedious, protocol a bore, and fancy clothes a wearisome restraint. Like Hank Morgan, that grown-up version of Huck Finn who is the hero of *A Connecticut Yankee in King Arthur's Court* (1889), Tom cannot help puncturing royal stuffiness with knife thrusts of vernacular common sense:

Another secretary began to read a preamble concerning the expenses of the late king's household, which had amounted to £28,000 during the preceding six months—a sum so vast that it made Tom Canty gasp. . . . Tom spoke out, with lively apprehension, "We be going to the dogs, 'tis plain. 'Tis meet and necessary that we take a smaller house and set the servants at large. . . ."

Again like Hank Morgan—and this leads us to the heart of Twain's antiromanticism—Tom discovers that the panoply of court life is a false front concealing a hideously unjust social order based on systematic exploitation and legalized murder. In many ways, of course, *The Prince and the Pauper* can be considered a children's book; it was first conceived as an entertainment for Twain's own daughters, and it has gone on delighting children ever since. But what lifts the book out of the category of a mere entertainment for unformed minds is the deadly seriousness of its social satire. As a democratic American, passionately proud of his country's achievement, Twain could not abide the fact that many of his countrymen—including his fellow novelist Henry James—seemed to prefer the institutions of English life, and he was determined to expose those institutions for what they really were. (What Twain did not understand was that Anglophile Americans were not necessarily blind to the social injustices of Old World society; if Twain had only troubled to read James's *The Princess Casamassima*, published in the same decade as *The Prince and the Pauper* and *A Connecticut Yankee*, he might have recognized some of the same indictments of hierarchical England as he himself was leveling.)

England was not the only object of Twain's antiromantic scorn; his satire was double-edged, cutting both sides of the Atlantic. Twain had been born and brought up in a slave state, and for a brief period he had served as an officer in a Confederate militia company at the outset of the Civil War. By the time, however, of his marriage to a Northern girl and his taking up residence in Hartford, Connecticut, he had long since become what his closest friend, William Dean Howells, called "a de-Southernized Southerner," *i.e.*, he had become convinced that the institution of slavery was the most hideous evil in American history and that the South had been dreadfully wrong in defending it. In seeking to explain to himself how it was that the South had fallen into such error, Twain came to the conclusion that the romantic illusions of the antebellum society were at fault. In Twain's succinct phrase, Walter Scott "had caused the Civil War," by which he meant that Scott's novels had been the collective source book from which the South had derived its mad belief in the code duello and the whole apparatus of pseudofeudalism by which it had beguiled itself into believing that

Negroes in bondage were faithful retainers, blissfully content with their lot, and that their white exploiters were the soul of benevolence. In the 1880's, a decade that saw the return of the Bourbons to power in the Southern states, Mark Twain used his storytelling talent to warn against the recrudescence of discredited dreams.

Tom Canty, the underdog who becomes an upperdog, furnishes one perspective on the injustices of antidemocratic life; Edward Tudor, the prince who is plunged into the maelstrom of the London slums and the impoverished countryside, furnishes another. In telling this part of his story, Mark Twain drew more heavily than usual on his favorite literary model. As it has to many American writers, from Hugh Henry Brackenridge to William Dean Howells to William Faulkner, Cervantes' immortal *Don Quixote* appealed to Mark Twain more profoundly than any other prose work in literature, and its effect on his own literary creations can be seen in *Huckleberry Finn, A Connecticut Yankee,* many of his short stories, and most clearly of all in the adventures of the prince-turned-pauper. Unlike Cervantes' knight, the little prince is not really mad, but everyone thinks he is, including his faithful, Sancho Panza-like companion, Miles Hendon. The result is irony, for his repeated commands that justice be enacted are universally regarded as the very signature of his insanity, whereas in fact those commands spring from an increasing *loss* of illusion about the nature of reality rather than the reverse. Like Huck Finn's progress down the Mississippi, the little prince's adventures are an education in human viciousness and depravity. Through the awestruck eyes of an alienated youth we see pictures of the English underworld that are as uncompromisingly realistic as Hogarth's paintings and that have a special, nightmarish quality all their own:

A grim and unsightly picture met his eye. A bright fire was burning in the middle of the floor at the other end of the barn; and around it, and lit weirdly up by the red glare, lolled and sprawled the motliest company of tattered gutter scum and ruffians, of both sexes, he had ever read or dreamed of. There were huge, stalwart men, brown with exposure, long-haired, and clothed in fantastic rags; there were middle-sized youths of truculent countenance, and similarly clad; there were blind mendicants with patched or bandaged eyes, crippled ones with wooden legs and crutches; there was a villainous-looking peddler with his pack, a knife-grinder, a tinker, and a barber-surgeon with the implements of their trades; some of the females were hardly grown girls, some were at prime, some were old and wrinkled hags, and all were loud, brazen, foul-mouthed; and all soiled and slatternly; there were three sore-faced babies; there were a couple of starveling curs, with strings about their necks, whose office was to lead the blind.

The agonizing question is, can these miserable people be saved? Throughout his career Mark Twain entertained the dream of a savior who would come to redeem an imperfect world, and he projected this dream into his fiction again and again. Pudd'nhead Wilson dedicates his life to social justice; Hank Morgan becomes the "Boss" of Arthurian England and endeavors to give the people a "new deal"; the heroine of *Personal Recollections of Joan of Arc* (1896) charges an entire nation with the vitality of her vision; Huck Finn becomes the liberator of Nigger Jim. In *The Prince and the Pauper* both Tom Canty and Edward Tudor enact the role of savior, the former more effectively because for the bulk of the novel he has the power; but in the end the little prince also comes triumphantly into his own. In one of those "circus scenes" that Mark Twain so delighted in, the little prince drifts raggedly up the aisle of Westminster Abbey and stops the coronation ceremony—for all the world like Tom Sawyer showing up at his own funeral—in order to claim his kingship and to enunciate his program. The ending of *The Prince and the Pauper* is very happy indeed.

Yet beneath the soul-satisfying rush of events at the novel's conclusion there runs an undercurrent of pessimism. The reign of Edward Tudor is doomed, we are told, to be short-lived; the savior will not occupy the throne of England for very long. This morbid fact complemented Mark Twain's increasingly bitter feelings about his own role in post-Civil War American society. Like his favorite historical character, Joan of Arc, Twain too wished to call a nation to greatness; he too had a vision of life's possibilities that he wished to share with his countrymen. But in the United States of the Gilded Age, the national heroes were millionaires, and literary artists were entertainers, nothing more; their opinions on social questions were taken with a grain of salt. Consigned to the role of America's court jester, Mark Twain found grinning more and more unbearable, and he wove his savage frustrations into the fabric of many of his works. Thus in *The Prince and the Pauper* it is significant that all the important characters clamor to be recognized for who they really are, and for most of the novel their clamor is ignored. Miles Hendon, Edward Tudor, and Tom Canty all have their true identities denied them; all are disowned, and society laughs at their claims. In the end everything is made right—Miles, Tom, and Edward all come into their rightful inheritance. But their victory is narrowly won, and the happy state of the author's mind that was reflected in that victory proved to be even more temporary than Edward Tudor's reign. Two years afterward, in *Huckleberry Finn,* the voices of alienation and disinheritance are heard once more, and grow louder ever after, until in the end the mocking laughter of *The Mysterious Stranger* (1916) echoes through an empty universe.

KENNETH S. LYNN

Selected Bibliography

Works by Mark Twain

The Celebrated Jumping Frog of Calaveras County, 1865 Story (Signet Classic 0451–524586)

The Innocents Abroad, 1869 Travel (Signet Classic 0451–525027)

Roughing It, 1872 Travel (Signet Classic 0451–524071)

The Gilded Age (with Charles Dudley Warner), 1873 Novel

The Adventures of Tom Sawyer, 1876 Novel (Signet Classic 0451–523555)

The Facts Concerning the Recent Carnival of Crime of Connecticut, 1876 Story (Signet Classic 0451–524586)

A Tramp Abroad, 1880 Travel

The Prince and the Pauper, 1882 Novel (Signet Classic 0451–521935)

The Stolen White Elephant, 1882 Story (Signet Classic 0451–524586)

Life on the Mississippi, 1883 Travel (Signet Classic 0451–521722)

The Adventures of Huckleberry Finn, 1884 Novel (Signet Classic 0451–523733)

A Connecticut Yankee in King Arthur's Court, 1889 Novel (Signet Classic 0451–524756)

Luck, 1891 Story (Signet Classic 0451–524586)

The American Claimant, 1892 Novel

The 1,000,000 Bank Note, 1893 Story (Signet Classic 0451–524586)

The Tragedy of Pudd'nhead Wilson and the Comedy of Those Extraordinary Twins, 1894 Novel (Signet Classic 0451–523741)

Personal Recollections of Joan of Arc, 1896 Novel

Tom Sawyer Abroad, Tom Sawyer, Detective, and Other Stories, 1896 Novels and Stories (Signet Classic 0451–519612)

How to Tell a Story and Other Essays, 1897 Essays

The Man that Corrupted Hadleyburg, 1899 Story (Signet Classic 0451–524586)

The Five Boons of Life, 1902 Story (Signet Classic 0451–524586)

Was It Heaven? Or Hell?, 1902 Story (Signet Classic 0451–524586)

The Mysterious Stranger, 1916 Short Novel (Signet Classic 0451–524586)

BIOGRAPHY AND CRITICISM

Anderson, Frederic, ed. with Kenneth M. Sanderson. *Mark Twain: The Critical Heritage*. New York: Barnes and Noble, 1971.

Andrews, Kenneth R. *Nook Farm: Mark Twain's Hartford Circle*. Cambridge: Harvard Univ. Press, 1950.

Bellamy, Gladys Carmen. *Mark Twain as Literary Artist*. Norman: Univ. of Oklahoma Press, 1950.

Branch, Edgar M. *The Literary Apprenticeship of Mark Twain: With Selections from his Apprentice Writing*. Urbana: Univ. of Illinois Press, 1950.

Cox, James M. *Mark Twain: The Fate of Humor*. Princeton: Princeton Univ. Press, 1966.

DeVoto, Bernard. *Mark Twain at Work*. Cambridge: Harvard Univ. Press, 1942.

——. *Mark Twain's America*. Boston: Little, Brown, 1932.

Fench, Bryant M. *Mark Twain and "The Gilded Age."* Dallas: Southern Methodist Univ. Press, 1965.

Ferguson, DeLancey. *Mark Twain: Man and Legend*. Indianapolis: Bobbs-Merrill, 1943.

Gibson, William M. *The Art of Mark Twain*. New York: Oxford Univ. Press, 1976.

Hill, Hamlin. *Mark Twain: God's Fool*. New York: Harper and Row, 1973.

Howells, William Dean. *My Mark Twain: Reminiscences and Criticisms*. Ed. Marilyn Austin Baldwin. Baton Rouge: Louisiana State Univ. Press, 1967.

Kaplan, Justin. *Mark Twain and His World*. New York: Simon and Schuster, 1974.

——. *Mr. Clemens and Mark Twain*. New York: Simon and Schuster, 1966.

Leary, Lewis, ed. *A Casebook on Mark Twain's Wound*. New York: Thomas Y. Crowell, 1962.

——.*Southern Excursions: Essays on Mark Twain and Others.* Baton Rouge: Louisiana State Univ. Press, 1971.

Lynn, Kenneth S. *Mark Twain and Southwestern Humor.* Boston: Little, Brown, 1960.

MacDonald, Dwight. "Mark Twain." *The New Yorker,* 9 April 1960, pp. 160–96. Rpt. in *Against the American Grain.* New York: Random House, 1962, pp. 79–123.

Paine, Albert Bigelow. *Mark Twain: A Biography.* 3. vols. New York: Harper and Brothers, 1912.

Schmitter, Dean Morgan, ed. *Mark Twain.* New York: McGraw-Hill, 1974.

Smith, Henry Nash, ed. *Mark Twain: A Collection of Critical Essays.* Englewood Cliffs, N.J.: Prentice-Hall, 1968.

——.*Mark Twain: The Development of a Writer.* Cambridge: Harvard Univ. Press, 1962.

Spengemann, William C. *Mark Twain and the Backwoods Angel: The Matter of Innocence in the Works of Samuel L. Clemens.* Kent, Ohio: Kent State Univ. Press, 1966.

Stone, Albert E. *The Innocent Eye: Childhood in Mark Twain's Imagination.* New Haven: Yale Univ. Press, 1961.

Wagenknecht, Edward. *Mark Twain: The Man and his Work.* 3rd ed. Norman: Univ. of Oklahoma Press, 1967.

Wector, Dixon. *Sam Clemens of Hannibal.* Boston: Houghton Mifflin, 1952.

A Note on the Text

The Signet Classic text of *The Prince and the Pauper* is reprinted from the first edition, which was published in 1882 by James R. Osgood and Company, Boston. Spelling and punctuation have been brought into conformity with current American usage.

STIRRING CLASSICS

☐ **WUTHERING HEIGHTS by Emily Bronte. With a New Introduction by Susan Fromberg Schaeffer.** Here is the story of a savage, tormented foundling, Heathcliff, who falls wildly in love with Catherine Earnshaw, and of the violence and misery that result from their thwarted longing for each other. Filled with the raw beauty of the moors and an uncanny understanding of the terrible truths about men and women. (523385—$4.95)

☐ **MY ÁNTONIA by Willa Cather. With an Introduction by Sharon O'Brien.** A moving story of a pioneer woman. Willa Cather's lush descriptions of the rolling Nebraska grasslands interweave with the warmly human tale of a woman coming of age in the early days of the century to become an epic tale and a chronicle of America's past. One of those rare, highly-prized works of great literature. (525795—$4.95)

☐ **CHRIST IN CONCRETE by Pietro di Donato.** Vibrant with the rich ethnicity of the city neighborhood, sonorous with a prose that recalls the speaker's Italian origins, and impassioned in its outrage at prejudice and exploitation, this genuine American classic is a powerful social document and a rare, deeply moving human story about the immigrant experience. Throbbing with reality, harsh, beautiful, and uncompromising! (525752—$5.95)

☐ **THE SCARLET PIMPERNEL by Baroness Orczy.** With daring and élan an English nobleman assumes disguises and rescues members of the French aristocracy during the French Revolution. (523156—$4.95)

Prices slightly higher in Canada.

Buy them at your local bookstore or use this convenient coupon for ordering.

PENGUIN USA
P.O. Box 999 — Dept. #17109
Bergenfield, New Jersey 07621

Please send me the books I have checked above.
I am enclosing $_____ (please add $2.00 to cover postage and handling). Send check or money order (no cash or C.O.D.'s) or charge by Mastercard or VISA (with a $15.00 minimum). Prices and numbers are subject to change without notice.

Card #_____ Exp. Date _____
Signature_____
Name_____
Address_____
City _____ State _____ Zip Code _____

For faster service when ordering by credit card call **1-800-253-6476**

Allow a minimum of 4-6 weeks for delivery. This offer is subject to change without notice.